The Wherryman'

A Collection of Histori

By Kitty-Lydia Dye

Other Titles by Kitty-Lydia Dye

Romance novels

The Bride Who Rode in With the Storm – *Satin Romance*

Ichabod Crane and Headless Horseman Mysteries

The Mystery of the Headless Husband
The Howl of the Hessian Hound

Short Story Collections

The Wedding Mask and Other Tales: A Collection of Phantom of the Opera Short Stories
A Christmas Carriage Ride and Other Stories

Cover art by Marcia Dye

https://kittylydiadye.blogspot.com/
www.facebook.com/mdyeart

This is a selection of historical short stories and a serial which were originally published in *The People's Friend* magazine. Full details about dates and issue numbers can be found on the blog under the Published Works page. Also included are photographs taken by the author and a glossary for dialect, traditions and folklore.

Enjoy your trip to the past!

The Wherryman's Daughter

Spring

Summer

Autumn

Winter

Bitter Herbs and Sweet Pills

1845

When I saw the carboy in the shop window, I knew it had finally arrived. We were turning our backs on the old ways, leaving our memories and methods to dry like herbs... and then crumble and be forgotten. My livelihood was at stake.

"Rowena, you've gone ever so cold." Grandmother squeezed my hand. "Whatever is the matter?"

Of course, she could not see. I wished I couldn't as well, but shutting my eyes would not halt the rest of the world.

"They are opening a new shop," I told her.

People were drifting over. Children pressed their noses to the glass, watching avidly as bright liquids sloshed into the bottle.

A young man stood in the display, most likely the apprentice. He was a wiry thing, with hair like pampas grass. His eyebrows were furrowed as he focused on the small mouth of the bottle. It'd make more sense to use a funnel, but he seemed out to prove something.

The contents swirled around, throbbing, as if it might squelch up the side and climb out. Another bottle was placed and more liquids mixed. I quietly described to Grandmother what was happening, until there were three bottles, three colours for the humours: red for blood, yellow bile, blue phlegm.

We'd never needed a thing like this before. Our people had relied on the old ways. We still could. It was better, safer, rather than swallowing all sorts of pills –

Then the shop door opened. A woman and dark-haired man strode out, with trays of tiny vials all sorts of glimmering colours arranged like tempting sweets.

The woman was in her forties, back rigid and waist pinned tight by a corset. The dress she wore was so dark and severe that it made her face starkly pale, her cheekbones high and nose sharp.

She made me think of a rook. Her grey eyes, like chips of stone, slowly, disdainfully looked me over.

I wondered what she thought as she took in my pale curls, tangled with twigs that had caught on me in my foraging, my freckle splattered cheeks and sun-baked complexion, the rough dress that had a darning needle as a faithful companion, and my mud caked men's boots.

Yet she smiled widely.

"Welcome to the grand opening of Cooper and Swann Pharmacy," she announced, with a light fluting voice that was too forced to be a proper hoity toity accent. "No longer will you have to rely on ineffective, foul tasting herbal remedies. We have the latest medical innovations from London! Just for today, we will be giving out free samples of our most popular tonics. *Jenny's Pick Me Up* will loosen tight chests and give a good night's sleep. A must for every housewife's cabinet."

I couldn't help but mutter under my breath, "She sounds like a hawker trying to shift bathwater as medicine."

Grandmother chuckled. "Do not sound so petty, my dear. You're in your twenties, not a child."

The dark-haired man approached. He gave me an easy smile and handed me a bottle, then went to the next person.

I popped the cork and wafted it under my nose. Oranges and cloves. I tried the barest of sips. Laudanum – I almost spat it back out.

As I watched the people try theirs, they grimaced but looked pleased. Tastes were changing. They wanted something clinical; it made them think it was working.

My stomach churned, but I knew no pill could cure that. With a pharmacy opening in our small town, there would be no need for herbalists such as myself.

****

I had only one customer that morning. The rest of the day I was left alone with my worries.

My great grandmother had come here with a young child and no-one to support her. She had used her knowledge of local herbs to make a living caring for the townspeople's ills. Each woman passed the talent down. I had hoped to pass it on to my daughters, if I ever had the joy of bearing any.

The old traditions were eroding away. I was scared this new age of steam and machinery would have no place for me.

Mother and Father perished in a riding accident when I was a girl. Grandmother raised me. Now it was my turn to care for her.

However, I could not stand working in a mill, the cotton burrowing into my lungs. I didn't want to be another cog in the machine.

I had to be free, wandering the fields. Feel the sun place its hand on my cheek, the rain pepper kisses on my face and the wind tickle my hair. It was in my blood.

I needed an advantage over the pharmacy. It was dishonest, but if I knew what they used in their medicine I could brew something even better. I bet they had done just as much back in London.

I shouldn't feel as guilty as I did.

****

I waited for my chance. Days must have passed, but from the gossip I found out the people in the pharmacy were Jenny Cooper, a widow, her brother Joshua Swann and the apprentice Davey. And, every fortnight, a horse and cart came with fresh supplies.

I watched as Joshua unpacked. His dark hair was copper coloured at the edges and curled like corkscrews, bouncing slightly as he hefted the boxes. Even with such effort, his pale cheeks never went red. It was as though he'd been locked away in a sunless place. Every few moments, he paused to cough into his hand.

He must have noticed a prickle on the back of his neck, for he glanced up and caught me. I thought he might scowl, like his sister would. However, his eyes scrunched up and he smiled. I felt my face go hot, slowly my lips rose to match his.

Glass crunched.

Frustrated, Jenny snapped from inside, "He's dropped another jar of earthworms. Joshua, bring the brush!"

Our gazes broke. Joshua went into the laboratory, a hut at the back, and I snuck into the pharmacy.

Containers of all sorts were lined up on the shelves. I lifted the lid of one. My nose scrunched up at the metal *Everlasting Pills* rattling within. I wasn't certain how these would work, but I wouldn't fancy swallowing one. Peppermint tea was much gentler on the stomach.

I examined several bottles, noting the ingredients. Quite a few herbs, what I myself used, although most were drowned in opium or laudanum. Concoctions for purges, bruises, sleeplessness and headaches. All at reasonable prices.

My shoulders slumped. I couldn't compete against this. The shop could simply hand over a pill in an instant, whereas I needed time to pick the herbs and brew the specific potion.

I tried another box that was bigger than the others. I stuck my hand inside.

Something jabbed me. Tepid slime coated my fingers. I fell, barely supported by the counter.

A leech clung to the back of my hand. It went stiff as it slurped on my blood, like a black thorn. When I grasped the tail, it dug in even harder. I shrieked.

The shop bell rang.

"Well, well," a woman called, "what do we have here?"

Jenny stood over me, a curious sneer twisting her lips.

"Looks like these are better than a guard dog." Her accent had dropped ever so slightly.

"I wasn't doing anything wrong," I stammered.

Before she could respond, the door opened again. Joshua came in and rushed to my side.

"Davey must have left another leech loose. Don't worry, I'll get it off."

"Why do you even have such nasty creatures?"

It was Jenny who answered, "It's a much cleaner way to blood let a patient."

Joshua tickled the underside of the leech's belly. It fell into his open hand and was locked back in the box. A trickle of blood dripped from where I had been bitten, and it would not stop. Joshua applied a bandage, gently stroking my wrist.

Jenny held out her hand, pulling me up. I wobbled, still faint from the shock. She helped me to the door.

"Perhaps," she murmured, low enough so her brother could not hear, "you have learnt not to meddle in what you don't know?"

****

It took several days before the leech bite closed. No matter what salves I used, the only healer was patience.

The constant itching at least stopped me from thinking about the pharmacy, more specifically Joshua. Then the bandages came away clean and I knew I had to thank him.

It was embarrassing, especially as I had been caught spying. Hopefully only Jenny had guessed.

Inside the pharmacy, Joshua stood at the counter, pouring powders on a set of scales. Even though it was so busy, nothing broke his concentration. I made to approach.

"Don't you go distracting him," Jenny warned from where she had been stacking the shelves.

"Why not?"

"Each of our concoctions are carefully measured out. Although I'm certain you fling things into your pot willy-nilly or rely on how the moon is feeling."

I hated how patronising her tone was, how inferior she made me feel.

"At least my herbs won't kill someone," I retorted.

"You'd be surprised at how many we use. Unless, you've already seen?"

She opened one of the boxes, marked feverfew, and frowned.

"Run out? There's plenty outside," I suggested, then smiled, "if you can recognise it."

Jenny sniffed. "Goodness knows what creatures have been doing against it. Wait here."

I scowled. Bossy, toffee nosed madam!

There was no point glaring at Jenny's back, so I examined today's display. Bottles of tonic water throbbed with bubbles that looked like frogspawn.

One moment the bottle was fine, then I blinked and there was a smashing sound. Glass shards lay before my feet, water dripping off the shelf.

Everyone's eyes fell upon me.

"I – I wasn't anywhere near it. I –"

Another bottle exploded. I cried out, leaping back. Two more shattered and just as suddenly everything was peaceful. I didn't know what happened. It was like fire popping.

Jenny rushed over with a broom, sweeping up the mess. I was close enough to hear the unladylike curses she hissed under her breath.

"Everything is fine," she said brightly to the other customers. "The aerated gas can be a little temperamental."

A man laughed. "Looks more like witchcraft to me!"

****

After what had happened, I left the pharmacy, traipsing through the woods to collect herbs and mushrooms. Not that I was certain I would have any use for them.

I could marry, but the very thought made me frown. Plenty of women wedded for a comfortable life. Grandmother always wistfully sighed over the distant echo of wedding bells.

Silly as it was, I was holding out for love. I had not wanted to force it, hoping everything would fall into place, flourishing just as elderflower did when left alone. Yet the pharmacy, and everything it stood for, was unravelling all my plans.

"Rowena?"

"Joshua!"

I brushed off the bracken clinging to my hair and stood. He still had his easy smile, the one that calmed me.

I found I could not snap as I asked, "What do you want with me?"

"I actually came out to pick feverfew."

"Does your sister know?" A better question was: "Do you even know what feverfew looks like?"

"I wanted it to be a surprise. She's too stressed about making the place a success." His cheeks went pink or, at least, some colour appeared in his wan face. "I've seen illustrations in books. I'll be fine."

I returned to picking milk thistle. Peace fell as the noises of the woodland surrounded us. Rooks soared overhead, jackdaws close behind.

Joshua tilted his head, breathing in deeply. I watched him curiously.

"Are you well?"

"I'm just… in awe of this place, I suppose. It's so vast and empty."

Winds gently plucked at the heads of flowers drooping in sleep, the fragmentary leaves on the bushes shivered, and the brittle arms of the trees arched, groaning as they stretched.

I smelt the oncoming rain, a damp mixture of flowers, moss and earth. An almost cloudy smell. There was still daylight, but the trees were so dense further in they created their own darkness.

"It's not as quiet at night," I told him. "Owls shrieking in the hunt, foxes yowling, like spirit cries. As a girl, I used to have nightmares about these woods."

"Compared to London it is. The din and crowd were unrelenting – as if the city was a storm and everyone tiny little boats. You slept, but it was from falling over in exhaustion," he sighed, then choked.

He toppled, clutching his throat. I hurried to his side.

"My chest," he wheezed. "City smoke got to my lungs years ago. I'll be fine."

As I anxiously rubbed his back, he did not improve. Each dragged in breath was shorter. The coughing rattled. From my pocket I took out a pouch of lavender.

"Breathe that in, it'll ease things."

We clung together as we staggered to the pharmacy.

****

When Jenny saw us all her snobbery and pretensions ran off her face, leaving only fear. She held the shop door open.

"Quickly, get him to the cabinet," she ordered, posh accent completely gone.

The cabinet was in the corner. I pulled aside the curtain and set Joshua down on the chair.

Jenny grabbed a kettle with a long spout. She put this over the fireplace and once it was bubbling tucked it in with him. Slowly, steam poured out. The coughing started to subside, but he was still struggling to breathe.

"He needs eucalyptus," I told her.

"There's oil behind the counter."

I added it to the kettle, and soon the room was filled with mint and honey scents. Joshua leaned back, chest steadily rising and falling. Through the small window, he tried to smile reassuringly at us.

Jenny pulled up a stool next to the cabinet. I awkwardly hovered nearby.

"I should go," I mumbled. "Please, when he's better, let me know so I don't worry."

"If you hadn't been with him…" Jenny hooked her foot around another stool and pulled it next to her. "He'll want to thank you as well, once he's recovered."

We sat there, quiet and tense. Jenny jiggled her foot. I couldn't stand being still.

"How long has he been like this?" I asked.

"In the city, Joshua worked as a chimney sweep when he was a child. For hours he was trapped in the darkness, hardly able to breathe… it near killed him."

"Who are you really?"

"I suppose you know I'm not some highborn lady, but I am Cooper and a widow. I was a maid when I married Sammy. He was a sailor and away for so long I never bothered telling my mistress."

"So, you lied to her?"

"It's a silly rule, only having unmarried maids. She found out in the end and chucked me out without pay. I thought Sammy would be coming back, but his ship sank the day before it reached port." She turned her head aside. "Then I got a package from a friend of Sammy's, in case something ever happened to him. Money and brandy were in there, probably proceeds from smuggling. I bought a pharmacopeia, medicines, and brought Joshua here."

"Who's Davey, then? Your son?"

Jenny snorted. "He was cook's boy, always being shouted at and slapped by that brute. Davey saw us leaving and begged to come along." She chuckled gently. "He's clumsy and barely listens. Sometimes I wonder why I brought him, but I don't regret it."

I could see in her eyes that she wanted to beg me not to tell. She wouldn't say it; she was too stubborn.

I knew their secret. If I told it, then I doubted they would remain here for long. They would have to return to the city. I could keep selling my herbs.

As I looked at her weary face, I knew I could do no such thing. Just as I worried for my grandmother, Jenny cared for her brother. We were the same.

Somehow, we would have to find some way to work together.

****

"The crows are swooping," I called. "Best we get home."

Joshua stood, clutching a handful of spiky, yellow petaled St John's Wort. He tucked them into the basket with the borage, then looped his arm with mine. His hand went to his mouth, but he didn't cough.

"I… I keep on expecting to fall into another fit," he murmured. "But it's never coming back."

He still wheezed a bit. The smoky taint of the city would never leave him, yet he was getting better. I was thankful for it every day.

We walked into town, passing advertisements for soap, mustard and Cooper, Swann and Fairlace Pharmacy. The shop bell jingled as we entered.

"Welcome back, my dears," Grandmother called from behind the counter, grinding ingredients with her pestle and mortar.

Davey was next to her, measuring powders on the scales.

"Any accidents today?" I asked.

He laughed. "None!"

Jenny came in from the back.

"I've almost completed the latest batch of tonic water. Joshua, can you do the rest? Mrs Seals wanted some Worcestershire sauce measured up and cooked by tonight."

"I'll help," I said, kissing Joshua's cheek and following Jenny into the kitchen.

As I took off my cloak and rolled up my sleeves, I glanced back at the new carboy in the window. We had all poured in a little something – Jenny was red, Joshua blue, Davey had even added a drop of Oil of Earthworm, while Grandmother and I had added our own herbal blends.

The mixture was a pinkish colour, with strands of lavender floating. It was certainly unique. We had plenty of people come in asking about it, then Jenny gave them the hard sell.

We were an odd mix yet, somehow, we had blended well enough.

Carried by the Wind

1880

Every morning at four o'clock, I heard the trundling wheels of Arthur's handcart along the street. Yawning and wiping the sleep from my eyes, I crawled out of bed to peek out of my window so I could catch a glimpse of him.

There he was, more punctual than the cockerel. Arthur was only a few years older than I was, yet he already owned the fish shop next to my aunt's sweet emporium.

Aunt was always full of praise for him, saying that hard work and determination had been what got him there. *Hard work, determination and good looks*, I thought with a smile.

Arthur passed by my window, pushing a cart heaving with today's catch from the fish traders. As the rising sun crept over the stacks of houses in the yard, the light caught on the fish scales. They sparkled with so many shades of blue that it seemed as if Arthur carried the sea with him.

The sudden glitter made him turn aside his head and cover his eyes with a broad, sun stroked arm. When he looked again, he saw me still in my nightdress!

Embarrassed, I wrapped my bed sheet around my head to hide my shame at being caught. He winked and cheekily waved, face as bright and warm as the morning. My fingers uselessly fluttered, attempting to wave back, to try and appear carefree even though my heart was drumming up a storm. Red speckled my cheeks.

Arthur opened his mouth, perhaps to call something out. My nerve went. I pulled shut the curtains and hurried downstairs, where the family were already up and squabbling over breakfast.

****

Today was washday. I took my bucket out to the pump in the

courtyard, joining the line of girls. I murmured a few good mornings as I waited, but I hardly knew them as I had moved here from Wheatacre. I squirmed shyly as they gossiped about things and people I knew nothing about.

Jessie O'Brien, a woman my aunt had warned me to avoid, swaggered into the yard with her bucket balanced on her hip. She surveyed us all patiently standing and then strode to the front. Another girl was shoved out of the way just as she had her hand on the pump.

"I was here first, Jess!" the girl snapped, prodding her in the back.

Jessie spun around, her hoop earrings swinging and tangling in her dark curls. She grabbed her by the collar. The girl tugged at Jessie's hair. They fell to the side as a scuffle ensued.

The others' eyes were bright with excitement. Some were even making bets on who would win. I couldn't just stand there and watch, as if it was an amusement. Jessie had the upper hand. She was twice her size.

I hastily filled my bucket. With a grunt, I threw the water over the scrapping pair. The cold shock made them break apart. Jessie slunk away, her exotic, cat-like eyes narrowed. I swallowed, worried about what she might do.

As I had chased Jessie away, the other girls clapped me on the back and let me go first. I heaved my bucket to the copper tub in the house. I had already lit the wood underneath, and soon the water began to bubble and pop.

In went the shirts, skirts and unmentionables. I dragged them around with the wooden paddle. Sweat poured down me. The heat from the tub made me breathless and dizzy. Then, with a board and a pat of lye soap, I harshly scrubbed them clean.

Now to put them on the line. Jessie had returned to the yard. I ignored her scowl. The wool was damp and heavy as I twisted and wrung everything. My already raw hands ached.

There was the faint tickle of smoke, but I did not pay it any mind. It was probably uncle puffing away on his pipe, as Aunt wasn't outside.

Halfway through pegging out the clothes, I noticed something strange. There were smuts staining them, ruining Aunt's best linen.

The smoke had grown stronger, almost choking. It wasn't coming from uncle's pipe. I followed the thick, dark trail to the small shack in the corner.

I tried to shout, but the pegs were clenched in my mouth. I spat them into my hand.

"Arthur!"

I banged on the door. When it opened, a blast of salt, cooking fish and the sea rushed out. Charcoal smears coated Arthur's face. All I could see was his smirking mouth and crinkled up eyes as he tried not to laugh at my outrage.

Over his shoulder, I saw overflowing racks of bloaters and kippers. Brine dripped from their tails. Underneath them was the wood he burnt to smoke them and my washing.

"Look!" I pointed at the line. "You promised you'd stop using the smokehouse on our washday. I'll have to clean them all over again."

Jessie called teasingly, "We shan't have clean nightdresses for tonight, Mr Rumsby."

"Miss O'Brien!" I hissed, flushing with humiliation.

What was she trying to suggest? My father would have put me over his knee for such talk.

She went on, loud and raucous, "Miss Prim and Proper, with her little country mouse ways, looking down her nose at us yard girls!"

Arthur wiped his face with the bottom of his apron. "Sorry, ladies."

My mind was still on my poor sore hands and wasted washing. "Sorry isn't enough. I spent all of last night sorting and soaking them."

"Well, then, will this work as an apology? There's a fair being set up on Yarmouth pier. Why don't you come with me, just the two of us?"

Everything about me was a mess. My hair was lank and flesh blotchy from the steam. My dress was stained and the cuffs encrusted with soap scum. This was not how I had imagined it in my dreams. Arthur had a nerve.

I blustered that he would have to ask my aunt if he wanted to take me anywhere. I was afraid he was merely teasing me, but then Arthur smiled.

"All right, Nell. I will."

He smirked confidently, knowing how much Aunt held him in great esteem. I turned back to the washing and strained my ears as I listened for the familiar chime of the sweetshop bell. Jessie gave me a sour look and went off with her basket.

****

We went on the train from Norwich to Yarmouth. The place was overrun with people from the city, who had come to loll on the sand and splash in the sea.

Arthur held my hand as he took me to the fair. I could feel the cold smear of sea spray on his fingers. His skin was rough, like the surface of a pebble.

We passed sideshows featuring a strong woman lifting donkeys, a fire breather who unfortunately set his grey whiskers alight, and a mermaid whose tail was a net full of fish scales.

A steam powered roundabout trilled with pipe music. Couples clung to one another as they rode on carved seahorses and kelpies. They were so vivid I expected them to rear up and gallop into the sea.

There were food stalls as well. We ate mouth-watering Yarmouth straws, a mix of cheese and bloaters, and drank scrumpy cider.

My heart always sounded like a war drum and my tongue and limbs lost all sense of rhythm when I was nervous. I could not find the words to tell Arthur how I felt. I liked him, even though his cheekiness often frustrated me.

However, here I did not feel as if I had to be on my best behaviour. We were another couple in the crowd, enjoying a moment of pleasure before we had to return to the drudge of work. I did not have to worry about my aunt's bawdy laugh or the other yard girls' unkind whispering.

My frantic heartbeat was drowned out by the crash of waves and my laughter. I was having fun.

Arthur noticed a small multi-coloured tent with pearls hanging over the entrance. We ducked under the curtain. The atmosphere felt different, as if we had shut a door to the revelries.

An old woman grasped Arthur's hand. I watched her gnarled fingers carefully trace each callus and line.

"Hopeful, but you will not get what you desire on this day. Patience is needed." She chuckled. "A breeze shall bring you to your greatest gift."

Then it was my turn. I reluctantly offered my hand.

"A fury of emotions." The fortune teller seemed to stare more into my eyes than at my palm. "As violent and conflicting as when a storm graces the sea. Courage, not patience, is required here."

****

The sky had turned to dusk, the sea reflecting the sinking, burning sun and its many red threads about to be spun into night.

As Arthur and I walked along the shore, we shared a bag of fair buttons and wondered over what the old woman had meant. My shoes dangled from my fingers.

I popped one of the biscuits into my mouth. My eyes shut at the sharp taste of ginger.

"I suppose we should go home soon," Arthur murmured, and I could hear the reluctance in his voice.

As the night had come, so had the cold. We drew closer together. My arm was tucked through his and he had draped his coat over my shoulders. I could smell the wisps of oak wood he used in his smokehouse.

Arthur had already dismissed the fortune teller's prediction. It remained with me, like a third person intruding in our couple. Courage, I thought, and it made me curl in on myself.

I had never had a sweetheart before. I did not know what Arthur wanted. Could I trust my heart to him? My elder brothers had always been so protective, constantly warning me of the fickle nature of boys or chasing off any who smiled my way.

Did Arthur truly want me? I could be a distraction. When he had my love, might he drop it into the sea to drown and walk away with another girl? If only I could hold him to me, as a child would hold a seashell to their ear, and be able to hear the whispers of his mind!

I glanced back at our footprints in the sand. Soon, we would leave and the sea would devour all trace of us.

Once we were home, the promise of this day would fade, returning to Arthur wheeling past with his cart and me uselessly sighing as I watched him from the window.

When I glanced at Arthur, he fondly smiled. The sea spray had darkened his pale hair and plastered it to his face.

"Lost in thought?"

I quietly nodded. He reached out to stroke aside the damp hair clinging to my forehead. The red curls tangled around his fingers, almost like seaweed.

"I think I like you here," he murmured.

From the look on my face, he knew that I had no idea what he meant.

Arthur explained, "Down on the ground with me. I see you each morning, watching. Before I knew your name, I used to call you my little bird a-peering from her nest."

He kissed me. His face was cold from the touch of the wind. I could feel a faint tremor in him, as if he too was afeared. I clasped his hand and kissed him back.

The sea seemed to roar, but then I realised it was the rush of my blood. I dropped my shoes so I could embrace him.

Harsh and brutal, reminiscent of the sound of shattering stone, a gull squawked. It broke me from my passion. What was I doing kissing a boy after one outing?

I pushed Arthur away. "We'll miss our train."

Without another look at him, I scooped up my soaked, ruined shoes and hurried back to dry land.

****

Several days passed, and I had been avoiding Arthur. I felt a fool who didn't know what she wanted. I no longer sat by my window each morning. To take my mind off my troubled thoughts, I had thrown myself into the housework.

"Though I'm pleased you've been helping me," my aunt said as we sorted through the glass jars in her sweetshop, "you've had a scowl carved into your face and Arthur's slunk off like the cat without its tail. What's a-diddling you both?"

I poured out the sherbet lemons onto the counter. "Nothing."

The yards were cramped and often considered unclean by higher folk. However, yard women like my aunt did not live up to their expectations. She was incredibly house proud and her front step was the cleanest on the street.

Although Aunt looked every bit the cheery, round cheeked sweetshop owner, she was as quick as a shadow. She would often appear when others least expected her. Uncle would sometimes say that her love of cleaning wasn't from wanting to see her reflection in a surface, but because she heard so much gossip when people were mardling nearby.

"I've seen that Jessie O'Brien in the shop with Arthur," my aunt said.

I paused in picking out a stray fudge. "Doing what?"

"Buying her sweets, of course. She was plaguing him for a day out at the coast. Something about a nightdress he had ruined."

I roughly ran my cloth over the jar, but said nothing. There was a heavy, stone shaped pressure sinking in my stomach. My jaw ached as I gritted my teeth.

Surely, she was wrong. I couldn't bear the thought of Arthur kissing Jessie as he had me.

Aunt would not give me any peace, she continued, "I was married when I was your age."

"I know." I also knew what Aunt planned to say next.

"Arthur's a nice boy. You're just shy. I was the same with your uncle."

"And what did you do?"

She smiled softly as she poured berry coloured sweets into a twist of paper.

"He had come to get some liquorice. I was restocking the shelves. The ladder was a bit rickety and I was having trouble keeping hold of a jar. When Sam passed by, I almost dropped it on his head. It could have been a funeral, rather than a wedding!"

I almost choked on my laughter in disbelief. "How did that get him to marry you?"

"We got to talking. He would always come see me, even if it was to call me gal fumble fist. What I'm saying is – get his attention. Talk to him. If it's meant to be, then it'll happen without you even realising."

****

Wash day came again. I asked Aunt if she might hang up what I had cleaned. In response, she lumped the basket back into my arms and bustled me out into the courtyard. Then I heard the shutters overhead open so that she could spy on what would happen.

There were some clothes still hanging on the line, from what had been left overnight to dry. A breeze wove through, causing them to dance.

I had hoped Arthur might be in his shop, but I caught him leaning against the smokehouse. Jessie was with him. I didn't want to see. I turned my back to them, yet I could still hear their conversation.

"One of the old boys at Palace Yard has a garden of shells. It must be beautiful," Jessie said.

"I haven't seen it yet," Arthur replied.

My fingers throbbed as I throttled the clothing, wringing out water over the cobbles. There was nothing wrong with them talking, yet the jealous pain in my stomach gnawed. All I could picture was Arthur at the fair with Jessie instead of me. My face burned and my eyes stung. I brought a shirt to the line.

"Perhaps we can go tonight?" Jessie suggested.

"Yes, I'll bring my sisters. They'll love to see the garden."

"No, I meant us. Alone."

Catch his attention, Aunt had said. I paused, about to unclip the pegs from a dry bed sheet. A gust blew by, tugging at my hair.

Should I dare? Would this one final chance give me the courage to speak my feelings plain to him?

My fingers slowly parted. The wind snatched the linen. I watched as it unfolded, heading for Arthur. My eyes widened.

That wasn't a bed sheet. They were my aunt's bloomers.

Above, my aunt squawked in horror at the sight of her oversized undergarments flapping about the courtyard. Arthur had not noticed. He was too busy talking with Jessie.

I raced for them with my hands outstretched. The washing basket was knocked aside. Before I could grab the bloomers, they wrapped around poor Arthur's head!

Arthur was struggling to free himself. Jessie stood there, too overwhelmed with giggles to help.

I caught up the lace frills and pulled them off. Arthur peered at me. His eyes were wide, face red and he looked so stunned. I found myself laughing as well.

"They're not mine," I managed to splutter.

I still clutched his face. The faint bristles on his chin scraped my thumb.

"Sorry about that," I murmured, distracted.

I kissed him, and this time I did not run away.

****

Across the uneven paving of the street, wheels jangled and rattled. There was a louder sound; the horses' clip-clopping hooves caught everyone's ears. Curtains were pulled aside and windows opened to see what was happening.

I waved to my neighbours as the carriage went past. A jolt nudged me into Arthur's arms. I nestled closer and held on to my bridal veil. The church was steadily rising in the horizon.

To think, what a pair of Aunt's bloomers could catch!

The Sea Stone

1841

For every heirloom and trinket in our family, Grandfather always had a story to tell.

He had promised my sister, Susanna, and me that we would hear the tale of the sea stone when we were old enough. Each day we came to visit we pestered him to tell us, but he would shake his head and make us swear to be patient.

This year, I had turned fourteen. Grandfather and a few cousins had come around for Norfolk dumplings and bloaters. He sat at the end of the table and I saw that his hands were empty.

As we ate, I kept on slyly glancing at him, wondering where he had hidden my present. Perhaps he hadn't brought one? Yet I had been good all week and no-one knew about the filched apples from the Reverend's tree…

When we were finished and the plates cleared away, Grandfather went to his slightly scorched, creaky chair by the fireside and lit his pipe. We gathered at his feet, watching as the smoke curled all about his head. He looked as though he had vanished up a misty mountaintop, with his thick beard a snow cap.

"My grandfather, Josiah Young…" he began, coughing as he always did. I once heard Grandmother say to Mum that she always knew the old boy was lying when he coughed, but I didn't believe that. "…once saw a mermaid."

One of my cousins quietly scoffed, but I leaned forward, eyes widening. This was the story I had hoped for.

"Josiah hadn't been a fisherman, like my father, myself and your fathers were. He had been a rippier, one of the men who took the net's catch and sold it further inland. In fact, Josiah was afeared of water, yet he loved to walk the beach each day's end to see the fall of the sun. That was where he saw it."

Grandfather blew away the smoke cloud and we realised his eyes were shut. After a few minutes, we thought he'd fallen asleep. We all called for him to continue, asking what Josiah had seen.

His bushy eyebrow lifted as he opened a single eye.

"Why, the mermaid of course! I can't be telling you everything. As the sky darkened to the colour of fire, he noticed a thousand sparkles, like light upon the water, but this was nowhere near the sea. It was back by the rocks, just barely peeking out. Josiah followed and there was the merwoman. The poor creature was trapped, with only a puddle of water to sustain her. She'd come in the hightide and got her tail caught."

I could picture everything: the panicked mermaid tugging desperately at her glistening tail while my great-great-grandfather stared down, his face agape with shock.

"The mermaid begged my grandfather for help. He freed her but, when he was about to gather her up, he realised what else helping her meant. He would have to step into the sea! But could he truly leave her to suffer?"

We all shook our heads. Grandfather smiled.

"Not Josiah. With a great heave –" And Grandfather stood and lifted my sister, who was the smallest. He pretended she was heavier than she was, struggling to carry her and pulling strained faces. Susanna kept on giggling. "– he pulled her into his arms and carried her to sea. His fear had not been completely swept away, though. He dipped his toe into that frigid water, felt the cold seep into his boot, and darted back out again. *I'll drown! I'll drown!* he cried, a coward once more."

He sat back down, placing Susanna on his lap.

"The mermaid, seeing how close she was to home yet having it out of reach, began to weep. Now, I don't know if any of you know this." Grandfather leaned in conspiratorially. "And most humans don't, but mermaids cry pearls. There was Josiah, with pearls rolling down his shirt and plinking down on the sands. So, he braved a single step into the sea and then another, and another. More and more, until he was waist high. The mermaid wriggled free and was soon happily swimming. To thank him for his kindness, she gave him a special stone.

Apparently, it would lead him to whatever his heart desired."

"Did it?" I asked.

"Well, Josiah always carried the stone with him to remember that night. One day, a hole in his pocket caused the stone to drop out and scatter away across the cobbles. A woman from London, who had arrived at our little town for her lungs, stumbled upon it and rushed after him. Soon after that sudden meeting, they married. When the stone was given to their son, he too was lured to his future wife through the sea magic. Whoever their heart desired, the stone brought them together. I might never have found your Gran if I did not have it."

Grandfather went back to his pipe, chewing on the end of it as he smoked. He was thinking of something, I could tell. His eyes drifted to look at the flames.

"I think it's time now," Grandfather decided. "Seeing as Hetty's the eldest, it's her turn first. Now, you mustn't squabble. My two sisters used to row like cats, as they were twins."

From his pocket, he pulled out a stone. He held it out to me. The stone perfectly fit my small palm and felt as smooth as water. The colour was every shade of blue in the world: a summer sky, the sea at night, my mother's eyes when she laughed.

I turned it over. Someone had carved a picture, and it reminded me of those winged fishes that came from distant shores.

I tucked the stone into my pocket, keeping my hand protectively curled around it.

****

As the years went by, the mysticism of the sea stone eroded away. Older and too busy drowning under my work as a net weaver, I did not expect the stone to leap out of my pocket and into the hands of my soulmate. However, I kept it with me as a good luck charm.

I sat at the seafront in a row of girls, women, mothers and widows. My hands, chapped from the salt tinged winds, wove back and forth as I braided another net. Soon, a web of it was draped across my legs like a second skirt.

When my fingers began to ache, I took a moment to rest and peer at the sea. Night was about to go on the prowl, with the sun seeming to dip into the glittering water. The sky was a tapestry, and someone had woven in threads made of sunset flames.

Once I had finished this net, I decided, I would go home. I snuck my hand into my pocket, checking the stone was still there. My fingers groped through empty space and then erupted through a hole at the bottom.

Disbelief and panic made me fumble through it again, expecting it to miraculously reappear. If it wasn't there, then where on the harbour had I dropped the stone? There would be no handsome man wildly waving it to get my attention.

"Are you all right?"

I looked up. A man stood there, carrying a net. He was about my age, with a face lovingly stroked by the sun and sharp bristles of oak whiskers. His dark eyes reminded me of a seagull.

"I –" I swallowed and forced myself to focus. "I've lost something. It's important."

He hefted his net over his shoulder to free his hands. "What is it? Perhaps I can help?"

"Thank you," I stammered, getting on my knees to search underneath my stool. "It's a stone. Not an ordinary one. It has a carving on the back."

We searched for a while, and asked some of the other weavers if they had seen anything. No-one had. Who would? How different was it from the scattered shingle? I couldn't believe I had lost the stone, it was the last thing Grandfather had given me.

The sun was finally claimed by the sea. It was too dark to look any further. I would have to go home and in bed dream of the stone being carried far off by the waves.

As we had searched, I had talked with the man who helped me. His name was Seb. He told me he had gone down to the weavers' row to have one of his nets fixed.

Needing the money, I offered to look at it in the morning. At least some good had come out of this day.

He picked up the net I had been working on. Something dropped out, loudly clattering. We stared at it and started chuckling.

It was the sea stone.

****

When the stone had done its job for me, I tried to give it to Susanna. My sister had laughed and shown me a sepia photograph of her in the arms of a young man with a cheeky grin.

"I'm sorry, sis, but I couldn't wait. His name is Edwin. I met him in London while I was working as a maid. He's a footman," she explained.

"And when were you planning on telling the family?"

"When I got a ring out of him."

She told me to keep the stone, as it might hurry up Seb with his own proposal. It never came. I didn't mind, I could wait. I wanted to know everything about him before I committed.

As time went past, the ships from the docks went out and each time I waved Seb away. He would be gone for months, trawling the Irish and Scottish seas for cod and skate. Then, when he returned, I would leap into his arms.

His smile made my heart lift and his hand within mine felt like the warmest thing in the world, even warmer than fire. I could not ignore the roaring waves of desire that crashed within me when he tightened our embrace.

Yet marriage meant change, and not for the better, for when Susanna married she moved to London to be with her husband. I dearly missed my sister, anxiously waiting for her next letter or visit.

****

It was the night before Seb's fleet, the *Stargazer*, was due to set sail again. As was tradition, the Reverend blessed the nets and then the ship's owner invited the fishermen for supper.

That morning, the nets had been draped over the pews. I stood next to Seb, watching the service, and my mind had been on other things.

I had pictured myself at the altar, dressed in white and the skirt made of the netting I braided so often. Seb had been opposite me, with his hair combed and wearing the smartest thing he owned. The vision had been so strong that I had clutched Seb's sleeve, unable to say anything.

Now, we were at the foy, and it was heaving with the men and their families as the food was dished out. A hearty meal of meat stew and hot-pot ale for there would be little warmth in their stomachs once they braved the sea.

I fanned my face yet it did little to cool me; the room was far too stuffy. My thoughts, still roiling over the church and what had come in the post today, seemed louder than the din. Seb must have guessed at what I was feeling, as he whispered in my ear to come outside.

We left the house to stand on the beach and breathe in the sharp sea air. The cry of the gulls and whispers of the shifting waves consumed the distant party noise. I tilted my head, letting the sea spray hit my face.

"Susanna didn't sound happy in her last letter," I confided in him. "She writes that Edwin leaves her for hours every night, and she knows it is not for work. I'm going to go see her. She must feel so alone, with just her and the baby."

I noticed there was a tenseness to Seb. His hand was buried deep in his pocket.

"Seb?"

He let out a long breath. His body relaxed and he nervously fiddled with his coat buttons. His smile was one of those lazy half-quirks that made me want to trace it with my fingers.

"I'll never treat you like Edwin has with your sister," he began to say.

"I know that, otherwise I wouldn't have chosen you." I hooked my arm with his.

"Hetty..." He hardly ever used my name. It was usually love or dear. It worried me.

Seb unhooked our arms and lowered himself on one knee. The ring, which was as thin as a fishing lure and had a pearl in the centre, was held up.

My hand stretched out to touch it, to feel that it was real, but I paused. This wasn't just a story my grandfather had told me. This was marriage, and fairy tales and magic stones could not hold it together.

"I..." I wanted to say yes, but what would one little word lead to? Would I be waiting for Seb every night, as my sister did with Edwin? "Can I think about it?"

His smile drifted away. "Of course." He stiffly stood. Traces of green from the seaweed scuffed his trouser leg. "Maybe when I come back, you'll have an answer?"

"I promise."

****

I watched Seb's ship cleave through the water. The sky was calm and the sea quiet. It was a good day to sail. However, when night came the sea awoke.

I had slept on while outside the waves hunted for ships. Finding one, they thrashed the small vessel, throwing it high into the air and dragging it back down. Waves came from every side with no escape. Like hands, they clapped around the ship.

The next day, I saw the washed-up wreck. The townspeople wandered through the shattered wood, searching for men they knew. But the sea had claimed them all, even the name of the ship.

We all assumed and mourned.

****

I walked along the coast, clutching my shawl tight to my cold flesh. During the long dark weeks, I had forgotten warmth. I started when a wave leapt up to nip at my toes. Angry, I kicked out at it.

The sea stone was heavy in my pocket, and it seemed to drag me down. I pulled it out.

"What use are you, if you can't keep him with me?" I cried bitterly.

The stone shimmered, as if mocking me. I wrenched my arm back and threw the stone as far as I could. Water splashed when it made contact, and then all became still and silent.

****

My hands were red raw from saltwater and too much scrubbing. I was in my uncle's shop, having just filleted the fish that would be put out for sale later in the day. Normally, I would be braiding, but I had grown sick of staring at the sea day after day, hoping even though there was no hope.

Seb still haunted me, though I tried to keep myself busy. Now that my sister had moved back with the baby, I at least felt useful, but seeing her made me think more of Seb.

How could I have thought he would be the same as Edwin? Josiah had risked the sea and drowning, why had I not risked myself with the man I had loved?

I was just about to go and take the herring into the smokehouse when I saw a gaggle of children rush past. Their faces were wild with joy. A pair of Scottish girls, who had come down to do the gutting work, had abandoned their wheelbarrow of fish. Their faces were the exact same as the children.

What had got everyone so excited?

I left the shop and hurried after them. They were heading for the beach. A crowd was beginning to form.

"It's the *Stargazer*!" someone shouted, a spyglass to their eye. "It didn't sink!"

I couldn't believe it; the *Stargazer* was docking. I pushed my way through as the oblivious fishermen disembarked to a cheering crowd and tearful welcomes.

At the front, I stood there, watching every man that passed. My hands were clasped together. I could barely breathe. The cloy of the sea was suffocating me.

Seb was the last off. His head was down, as he was examining something clutched in his hand.

"Seb!" My voice was ragged, like it was covered in sand.

I rushed up to him, near knocking him over with the force of my embrace.

"I'm sorry," I said. "I'm sorry that I let my fear get the better of me. It was yes all the time."

The kiss was tinged with sea salt. He pulled back, smiling. I reached up to push away the wet hair plastered to his forehead.

"You were calling me back home," he said, and gave me what he held. "I knew in my heart what your answer would be."

It was the stone, still glimmering every shade of blue.

Love Written on the Petals

1840

"My lady, you should not be out at night." *And certainly not climbing out of the kitchen window*, I thought to myself.

The young woman straddling the windowsill was in her early twenties, a few years younger than me. Her loose hair fell about her like curls of barley, the bound, harvested heads bouncing slightly as she struggled.

"You're not going to set the guards on me?" she asked, eyes wide and dark like poppy heads.

"We have no such things here in England, Miss. Perhaps you should climb back in."

"Not after all this effort." She held out her hand, which looked small and delicate in its white lace glove. "Uncle's had me locked away in the house for weeks. I want to walk in the gardens!"

"Shh!"

I would be for it if we were discovered. Less than a week I had been working here, and I couldn't lose all my prospects because of a misunderstanding.

Her imploring grin scrunched up the freckles on her tanned face. Somehow, I found myself grasping her hand and helping her out. Her boots crunched upon the grass.

"I'll take you around," I told her, "but only for a bit."

"Thank you...?"

"Caleb."

"I'm May."

"I know." Everyone knew about Lord Haynes' ward.

She clung to her shawl. The skirt of her dress was too thin, revealing the shadowed outline of her legs – she only wore her nightdress! Flushing, I glanced away, but not before noticing her shiver. I took off my coat and wrapped it around her shoulders.

"You're not in India anymore," I said. "The nights are even more unforgiving."

She was swamped in the coat and I smiled, taking off my wide-brimmed hat and putting it on her head. It dipped over her eyes.

I took her past the flower rows, where roses glimmered like glazed sweets and bluebells took on a purplish tint, wearing the shadows of the night. Spiders had been weaving, and there hung little bridges of webs wearing rain droplet baubles from the spring shower.

May knelt to stroke their petals, asking about their names and uses. While most would be drawn to the pomegranates in the hothouse, she was more interested in the common cowslips that Mr MacGregor wanted getting rid of.

"Oh, I hope not," she murmured. "They look so cheerful."

"Like you," I said, and I was rewarded with another smile.

I took her to the sitting area. It was too wet to use the bench, but we stood underneath the grove created by an overhanging willow tree. Between the wispy leaves were woven bushes and vines. The flowers growing there created a waterfall effect of purple and pink buds.

"It's almost fairy tale like at night, isn't it?" she sighed. "As though Titania had waved her hand and all of this arose in the span of a breath."

I had no clue who she spoke of, but I nodded to not look a fool.

"I think there's more magic when it grows," I told her. "Seeing a furled rose start to unpeel its petals is like someone taking their first gasp."

Only then did I realise she had taken my hand again. Quickly, I let go and saw I had soiled her glove with the earth coating my palms. She rubbed her fingers together.

"Thank you for showing me this."

The moon began to dip. I helped her climb back through the window.

We never spoke after that. A few days later, her uncle allowed her outside. There was no need for secret, moonlit wanderings.

****

May always appeared at her bedroom window to greet the morning.

As daylight painted reds and oranges upon her cheeks, I saw yearning widen her eyes as she hoped for a warm day, the bite of her lip as she noticed a cloud, then the flash of her teeth as the sun emerged. She looked down to see the garden and laughed in delight.

It was powerful, being able to tame trees and flowers. I formed them into something beautiful that a painter might put upon canvas. For her, I wanted to share that beauty.

Her smile was the reason why I worked until my hands pricked with welts. In sun, rain, I even tried to nudge flowers into surviving another winter's day. I clung to summer for her.

That night, though it often returned to me in dreams, was a year ago. I doubted she remembered my name.

May was the ward of a peer whereas I was a gardener. All I had were my rough, dirt-lined hands ready to work hard.

However, Miss May did not always have her jewels and dresses. Her mother had run off with an artist and the family cut her off. Then came the accident in India, leaving behind their young daughter.

Each time May opened her window, I wanted to shout up that I loved her. The words wilted on my tongue, afraid the fruits harvested would be bitter with her rejection.

Pitiful cheeping in the bushes caught my attention. Tangled in the brambles was a poor blackbird as tiny as my palm, its feathers sparse tufts.

"Hush," I whispered soothingly. "Greedy thing. After the berries, weren't you?"

It struggled, terrified. It'd wrench its wing if I wasn't quick. I wrapped my hands around the bird, thorns scratching my arms. Carefully, I pulled the blackbird free and it shot off unharmed.

I looked back, but May was gone.

"Caleb!" Mr MacGregor shouted. "What are you mooning over this time?"

"N-Nothing, sir."

He turned to the house and snorted.

"Not that I blame you. Go on, there's some ground that needs tilling for the master's newest acquisition."

One day, if I worked hard, treated the flowers and trees like my offspring as Mr MacGregor did, I'd be proud to earn the title head gardener.

As I walked past with my hoe, he said, "You'd best understand now that while it's fine admiring a rose, if you try and pull it out of the ground for yourself, you'll rip the roots and petals. Keep to your own."

"Yes, sir."

Did he think I had not already told myself this? Yet I was always letting my emotions rule me.

My father had been right all those years ago – I had no common sense.

****

There was something of the otherworld in the smell of turned earth. The damp pungency took me somewhere older and isolated, far removed from the roar of machines.

The other gardeners were cutting the grass, their silhouettes inkblots against the sun. The men slowly heaved forward the push mowers, backs humped like snails and the air punctured with their grunts.

I still found it hard to believe I was here, rather than on my family's farm. Back home there was nothing for me.

My father had been a distant figure, a soldier during the wars. After Waterloo he returned, but Mother started back as if he was a stranger. The scar on his face looked ugly because of his scowl.

Once, as a boy, he found me crying after a fall. More than his eyes or hair or laughter, it was the wire-like curl of his frustration I remembered most.

"What's that blubbering for?" he'd snapped. "If I'd spent my time weeping on the battlefield, I wouldn't have lasted long."

My mother was held to such exacting standards as well. When she laughed, it was cut short by his narrowed eyed disapproval. He scared us both away.

Lord Haynes offered me a job after seeing me working the fields. I owed him and Mr MacGregor everything.

So, why was I willing to risk it all over Miss May and her smile?

****

Always, May was bombarded with gifts from suitors. Jewels, dresses, rare delicacies...

I had my own gift for her. It might not be as expensive, yet I hoped the sentiment would be worth as much.

May's maid, an older woman called Pansy, had come to me with a book after I had asked her for ideas. Grinning, she said, "I believe this might help."

Inside were delicate watercolours depicting flowers from across the world. Next to the illustrations was writing, but it made no sense to me.

Father held no stock in learning, save being able to make his mark. Instead, I'd been sent to the fields.

I'd hated it when the rain pounded down, the horse snorting as its hooves slurped through the slurry. The rising irritation each time the plough struck a stone and I scrabbled to free it, mud raking frigid fingers up my wrists, the sharp blade of the tool cutting my hands.

And Father's voice, sounding behind me like thunder strikes, "There's always need for a man strong and willing. You'll never starve, lad."

It was the only time I disobeyed Father. Any chance I had, I snuck off to Sunday school. Books were covetously hidden in the cowshed. I only knew a few words. Still hungry to learn more, but not willing to admit my weakness.

Never mind the *language of the flowers*. I bet there were a dozen different interpretations on what a pink petal meant.

Mr MacGregor had let me use a small patch of land for my own growing. I had planted my message, nursing them for this moment.

Yellow carnations, amaryllis and hydrangeas.

Today was the day of blooming. I tarried beneath May's window, of no use to anyone.

Sunlight crept over the flowerbeds and, as if yearning for more, the open buds tilted their heads. The window opened.

"Good morning, Miss May," I called, taking off my cap. "I know how fond you are of flowers, and I wanted to show you my appreciation."

Would she understand? This was as far as I could admit my feelings, for decency's sake.

Pansy, fussing, threw a shawl over her charge. May barely noticed. Instead of the dawn, she was watching me. I grinned up at her.

Her gaze flicked to the flowers. My hat twisted in my hands.

I was too presumptuous. I would be thrown out –

Out of everything, I did not expect to see tears in her eyes.

"How could you?" she shouted, wrenching the window shut.

Leaving me standing there, mouth agape, wondering what I had done wrong.

****

Pansy was waiting for me in the kitchen. She roughly straightened her apron in a wringing gesture.

"Did you even read that floriography book?"

I shifted back as she leaned into my face.

"I thought I'd do it my own way." I wasn't about to tell her I couldn't read.

"She's close to crying up there. She thinks you hate her."

"Why would she –"

"Yellow carnations for disdain! Hydrangeas for vanity! Amaryllis for pride!"

I swallowed, then argued back, "How can they mean that? They're just flowers!"

"What matters is what she thinks they mean. It was your one chance,

Caleb. And somehow you've made it even worse!"

All that hard work, dealing with heavy rains, winds and hungry birds that had almost carried the seeds away, the sigh of an overbearing sun panting on the tiny saplings.

And I'd hurt May. My gut twisted, picturing her smile gone. I wanted to bound up and comfort her, admit I was a proud fool, apologise...

Cook eyed me, as if knowing what I thought. I'd be tackled before I made a single step.

Rankled, not wanting them to know how wrong I had got it, I growled, "It's only because that sweetheart of yours isn't back from his trawler, so you're interfering with my life."

Pansy's cheeks went red. She sucked in a breath so sharply it whistled. I rubbed my neck guiltily.

"You'll see," she said quietly.

****

A few weeks later, Pansy told me to wait by the water feature. It was of a Grecian woman with a vase balanced on her hip, lambs flocking at her feet.

I should have said no, but instead I waited in the pale night, watching the shadows of the dancers pass across the windows, trails of their high-backed dresses following them. May would be in there with suitors yapping at her feet.

It was another of her uncle's charity galas. She would meet someone of her station, hopefully an honest man. I'd finally be able to return to my gardening and bury this silly notion of love.

Yet all I felt was a hollow sensation – failure.

The door opened, music slipping out. I straightened in anticipation. However, it was another young woman, quickly followed by her sweetheart.

There was no point to this. I had work to do.

I left the gardens for the hothouse. This was where the master's exotic flowers and trees thrived. To stop it from standing out, vines had been trained to grow up the glass walls, making it appear in the grip of nature.

I went in and picked up a shovel. Every night I had to come here to stoke the fire in the stove, keeping it the desired temperature. The scratch of coals knocking together and the pop of flames roared in my ears –

"Caleb!"

Hastily, I dropped the shovel and wiped the sweat from my face. Then realised too late I'd smeared coal dust over me instead. At the even more irritated call of my name, I turned and faced her.

May stood with the moon bobbing over her shoulder. A threadbare cloak covered her lilac dress.

"Pansy told me you wanted to speak with me, but when I go searching I find you gone!" she complained. "If I was back in India, I'd get more sense out of a tiger. I've held out and hoped, but if you're not willing, then I don't see the point."

"What do you mean?"

"Figure it out for yourself."

She looked too lovely to dare to want her. To admit such a thing would mean ruin and strife for us both.

Keep to my station, find a woman willing to marry me or, better still, remain with only my shadow as company, just as my father had done. And I had left him alone and angry.

How was that stronger? Was it not better to admit all and face the consequences, rather than keep everything bottled up and push those I care for away? I should not fear my own tongue.

"I'm sorry about the flowers," I began.

"Did you mean what they said?"

The fury was gone. Her eyes were soft with sorrow.

"No!"

"It all felt like a dream, when my uncle brought me to England. Suddenly, I had fine clothes and pearls, but so many constraints. One day, I looked in a mirror and no longer recognised myself. I was afraid

I had changed into someone that girl would not like."

"You're still that girl. You've never made me feel as though we weren't equal." And that was what made it all the harder. "I do not know what all those flowers mean, only that they were beautiful and I wanted to make you smile."

May did smile, then. "A mistranslation."

Her hand dipped underneath her hood. She pulled out a pink rose that must have been tucked into her hair.

"You told me the names of the flowers I so loved. Let me tell you what they mean."

She stepped up until she peered at me, then slipped the flower into my buttonhole.

"For first love," she whispered.

I clasped her hand. My lips brushed her fingers.

For once in my life, I plucked up the nerve to speak what was inside of me.

****

We decked the church in myrtle, garlands of them hanging off the arch. Surrounding the altar was golden wheat from the recent harvest festival.

Few came to the wedding. We were a disgrace, a scandal, but at least we knew those here truly wanted to see us wed. May's uncle, not wanting to make the same mistake he had done with her mother, had not stood in our way.

Mr MacGregor tipped his cap to me. There were also the other gardening lads, all vying for the bridesmaid, alongside May's friends, agog that she had done what they had only dreamed of.

I'd sent word to my father, but had no response. I did not know where my mother was. It saddened me, I hoped for some sort of reconciliation, but when I looked at the pews I knew I had a family.

Then the doors opened and footsteps echoed along the stone floor. I risked a glance over my shoulder, finding myself swallowing in awe and terror. Her uncle led her up the aisle and Pansy grinned behind her as she held her bridal train.

May was decked in a veil that fell to her feet. Her bright eyes shimmered past the gauze film. As beautiful as ivy draped in frost. And yet I knew nothing could top the sight of her climbing out of a window, cheeks rosy and wearing only her nightdress.

We exchanged vows without a hitch. As I lifted her veil, she smiled at me, teeth grazing her lower lip as I cupped her cheek.

When it came to signing the marriage lines, I slowly wrote my name. It might be rough and jagged, but it was better than making a soulless X.

A surprise for May. I'd let go of my pride and asked Pansy for writing lessons.

It was May's turn. Her hands emerged from folds of lace and silk to hand me the posy. Pinkish smears stained her gloves from the flowers.

She didn't care. It was better that way; life was only real when we could dig our fingers into the soil.

I glanced at the flowers. Even with their negative messages, she had included the ones I had used. Woven with them were others: yellow roses for joy, jasmine for faithfulness, and rosemary for remembrance.

Daffodils and honeysuckle – a new beginning bound by love.

The Green Mists

1880

"You must never pick flowers near Willow Blyth, Matthew," Mother warned me. "Not unless you want a funeral, rather than a wedding!"

"What?" I thought I hadn't heard her right over the splashing. "Stop struggling, Jacob!"

Jacob fell still and crossed his arms, shivering. He sat curled up in the copper tub as we tried to wash him.

Outside, rain pattered on the window. Water inside, water out there, we were practically drowning in it, and not even the fire could chase away the chill.

"But it's cold," Jacob whined.

"Well, if you go running about in the fields where the cows have been, you know what you're going to trip in."

My nose wrinkled as I scrubbed his back even harder. Was the smell ever going to go?

"I didn't trip. Sarah pushed me!"

"And you pushed her back, so now her mother is doing just what we are." I sighed, but then chuckled, promising, "Once we're finished, we'll duddle you up by the fire."

"Willow," Mother went on, not about to give up. "I've seen you sighing over her when she skips past. I'll not have a pretty jibby like her in my house, dabbling in herbs and spirits. All the women with Blyth blood have been odd. I bet she dances with bogles when the green mists are in the air."

I couldn't help but snort in disbelief.

"Bogles! Women can't dance with creatures that don't exist. She's a lovely young woman. A little dreamy, I admit." I smiled knowingly. "You're just not fond of Willow's mother, seeing as she's from Norfolk."

Mother scowled, roughly rubbing the cloth over Jacob's mucky face. He spluttered against it.

"I don't see why Josiah had to go to Yarmouth for a wife. There were plenty of Suffolk girls here, and there still are." She'd remembered what she was getting at, and I had to hold back my sigh as she said, "You'll be twenty-seven in a month. I expected you to be married and gone years ago."

Frustrated, I snapped, "Perhaps I'll not bother. Seems more trouble than it's worth, especially as I have you lot to look out for." I flushed. "Willow hardly looks at me, anyway."

Jacob snickered. "With your face, I wouldn't either."

The cheeky little toad! I snatched the cup and poured cold water over his head.

****

Willow Blyth was the most beautiful girl in the village. She wandered the woodlands for herbs to make remedies for whatever ailed a man, not any of this witchcraft nonsense.

I could not stop thinking about Willow. Her very image was stitched upon my mind. I lay in bed, drowsily dipping in and out of sleep.

Willow had an easy smile, as if she had been born with her sunset red lips upturned. One of my sisters once told me Willow reminded her of our cat Dandy when she sat by the fire and eyed us the same way a heron waits for the shimmer of a fish.

Her hair was a mystery to me, as she always had it tucked underneath a bonnet. Once, I had caught the tantalising glimpse of a lock of hair, like a head of corn curling around her ear. I was often tempted to pluck at her ribbon ties, to see the whole wheat field tumble free.

I awoke mid-breath when I caught an odd smell in the air. It was not the last wisps of the blackberry syrup we had drunk with supper. This smell was a clean, sharp scent. The same as when I strode out across the fields after a heavy night of rain.

I looked out of the window. The sky was not dark or bright. It was every shade of green: the moss that crawled on the walls when the rain would not let up, or the grass that peeped through when winter ended.

The colours swirled and entwined. The mist seemed to crook a finger and beckon.

What on earth was in the air? I lifted up my shirt to cover my mouth. I felt buffle-headed, and wondered if I was still dreaming.

I pressed my cheek against the window to feel the cool pane on my flesh. Just barely visible in the mist, I could see the bend in the path which led to the Barley Bird Inn.

That was not all. I saw Willow.

Her face was turned towards me, almost meeting my eye. The hair she normally kept so primly under her bonnet now flew in the wind as wildly as the mist, as if she was part of this strange manifestation.

I opened my window. The air was faintly damp.

"Willow," I softly called, but she continued on. Had she not heard or was she ignoring me?

I clambered outside. Not caring that I was barefooted, I ran. Pebbles scraped my heels, while the muddy path squelched with each step.

Willow did not notice. Her entire body swayed, with the long tips of her shawl swishing to and fro, dancing to some unknown music.

I gently caught her arm. "Willow," I tried again, "what are you doing out so late?"

She turned to face me. Her hair twisted about her face, so all I could see were her eyes.

"Can't you hear them?" she whispered.

I looked around, straining to catch whatever was out there with us. There was the whisper hiss of the wind and the scratchy rustle of leaves.

"There's nothing," I told her, and she shook her head sadly.

"It was the same with my grandmother. Will others think me as strange as she was? Will everyone avoid me and whisper behind my back? Even fear me?"

Tears shuddered upon her lashes, the coal black of her eyes turning as watery as ink. I could not help myself. It pained me to see her weep. I cupped her face. My thumb swept across her cheek, wiping any tears that spilled.

"I'm not afeared of you. Far from it."

She clasped my hands. Her smile reared up.

"Then dance with me!"

And to keep her smiling, I obeyed. I would do anything for her. We spun and twirled, the mist scattering away from us.

This must be a dream, for it was like one of Mother's strange tales. I would awake to Jacob tugging at my hair to take him to see if the eggs in our tree had hatched.

Willow's face drew nearer. Her hair tangled between our entwined fingers, like vines that I could never be freed from.

Yet how could this night be a fantasy? Willow kissed me and I basked in her warmth.

****

When I woke up in bed, there was a dim recollection of walking Willow back to her home, and then returning here. It still could have been in my mind. There was no sign of last night's events, not even a wisp of pale hair caught in one of my buttons.

I went to my washstand. The shock of icy water brought back my reason, while the creeping sunlight chased off the rest of my dream.

Of course, it had been my imagination. I had yet to get Willow to say more than good morning to me, let alone dance with her. But perhaps such dreams were a good omen. A man could hope.

"Matthew!" Mother shouted from the kitchen.

I changed quickly and left my room. Mother glanced over her shoulder as she beat at some mixture in a bowl. She took in my rosy face and her eyes narrowed. My cheeks reddened. Why was it mothers always knew everything?

"Daydreaming again? Go be of some use and run down to the Barley Bird. Your aunt is coming around tonight, and I told her not to forget to make her raisin roly poly, but you know what she's like."

"All right, Ma."

"Take Jacob with you, he likes to hear Old Peter's tales. Perhaps you'll hear one that'll interest you."

I put on my cap and left, calling for Jacob to follow.

I'd go remind Aunt Lucy, but I wasn't going to listen to Peter. Half of his stories were about him barely escaping gamekeepers when he used to go poaching, while the others were fairy tales. I wasn't a child anymore!

****

Many years ago, Old Peter had sat down in the corner of the Barley Bird and taken root. Nothing could shift him, not even when someone had once cried fire.

He had his walking stick tucked between his legs, so that he could hold his ale in one hand and pie in the other. As the children settled down on the floor, Peter swallowed the food and drink in one go like a duck. He patted his beard dry.

I'd never actually heard the entirety of any of Peter's tales. After Father's accident with one of the new tractors, I had to take on more work to support the family. When my friends had sat there, shuddering over Grim Shuck, I was in the fields crow scaring.

Nowadays, I helped with the harvests. I was still working for the farmer who first employed me, and I'd probably be working for his son when I was closer to the grave.

There were times I wished something might change. Life was as predictable as sunrise and sunset. I'd had daydreams of running off, going around the world, but where would that leave my family?

"For hundreds of years," Peter began, dragging me from my moody thoughts, "the people were afraid of all manner of strange creatures. They believed that the fields were not natural soil, awaiting man's plough to till it, but alive with spirits.

"Bogles were what we called them. At winter, when the fields are left alone, the bored bogles get up to mischief. They are spiteful creatures and grant wishes with cruel tricks.

"Now, when spring comes, the earth takes a big ol' breath after months of being suffocated under the snow, and as it exhales a green mist erupts. That is how we know the fields are awake.

"There was one girl, Rosemary Blyth, who was as beautiful as the moon but dwain and waning. The winter was cold enough to turn your blood to ice, and there was no hope of it being a short spell. Young Rosemary wished that she might be like a cowslip and last long enough to breathe in the green mists. Surely, taking in the airs full of spring life and hope, she would grow stronger?"

Thinking he really was asking them, the children nodded wildly.

"Did she live?" Jacob asked, and then started coughing into his fist.

"Oh yes, the bogles must have heard her. When the green mists arose, she no longer coughed but laughed and danced. Men from all over came to our little village, but she only had eyes for a childhood friend. And in the shadow of their garden gate, there grew a clump of cowslips that seemed to hide away from the sunlight."

Peter sighed then. He rested his chin on his hands and peered down at the children, talking in a hushed, sombre voice. I leaned in to listen.

"But the bogles know their flowers. Cowslips do rise up in spring, but they perish at the first touch of a summer sun. On the first day of summer, when the couple were walking home, happy and in love, Rosemary's husband spied that little patch of cowslips.

"He plucked them from their home, intending on weaving them through her hair. The summer sun graced their petals, and Rosemary gasped her last. Her hair turned white and her flesh wizened, for her lifespan was as short as the pretty cowslips!"

****

"Are you all right, Jacob?" I asked a couple of nights later.

That cough had become much worse, and now there was a distinct ruttle in his chest as he breathed. Jacob wiped his nose on the back of his hand.

"I'm fine," he mumbled, voice thick with phlegm. "I'm going to see

Sarah. She found tadpoles in the pond by her house."

Jacob made to rush outside. I snatched him up and hauled him back to bed. His forehead was as hot as a used poker, yet he was milk-pale.

He grumbled, saying he was fine and wanted to go play. I tucked him in even tighter.

Mother was not here. She had gone to market in the town three miles off. If Jacob stayed still and rested, he would probably be better in a few days.

But what if he wasn't? I was in charge, and I had promised Mother I would keep an eye on him.

"Stay here," I told him. "I'm going to Willow Blyth. She might have something for that cough."

His cloudy eyes brightened. "The witch? Is she going to do a spell?"

"She's no witch... though I'd happily have her turn you into a toad if she could."

****

The Blyth family did not live in the village, but nearer the marshes. The perfect place to consort with bogles, according to some.

A candle flickered in the open window of the little cottage. I caught a glimpse of Willow as she crushed something with a mortar and pestle.

I did not have to knock, as she glanced up and saw me. She smiled.

There was a shimmer in her eyes, like stars in the night sky. It was mischievous, as if we shared a secret joke. It almost made me believe the dream was true.

My tongue twisted into a knot, and I stumbled to say, "My brother's sick."

"Is it a cough? Fever?"

I told her what was plaguing him and she got her bag. We hurried back. At the sight of Willow, Jacob pulled the bed covers closer to his face.

"You're not afeared of me, are you?" she said, sitting on the edge of his bed.

"No," he answered. "I'm scared of what Ma will do if she hears you've been in her house."

She felt his forehead and throat, murmuring softly and making him laugh. I stood in the doorway, watching with a smile. She'd be a wonderful mother if she ever had children.

Willow pulled out a bottle with a murky green liquid swimming within. Jacob grimaced.

"Is it crushed up beetles and toad spit?"

She chuckled. "It's thyme and honey. Drink some of this each evening and it will clear your chest. But you'll also need plenty of rest or else I really will have to feed toad spit to you!"

At that threat, Jacob swore he'd drink the concoction. I offered Willow a slice of what was left of the raisin roly poly as a thank you, but she shook her head.

"The light is fading. Your mother will be here soon."

"At least let me take you back."

She held out her arm and I happily looped mine with hers. As we left the house and walked along the path, I could not help but think of the dream. I even tricked myself into believing that the twilight had a misty green tinge.

We talked about the weather, hopes for this year's harvest, even about the Furman's lad running off with a gypsy girl. I did not mind. I got to see her lovely face. Although, her eyes seemed to be red and sore. I could hear a faint rasp as she breathed.

"You've not caught what Jacob has?" I asked.

"It doesn't catch that quickly," she tried to sound cheery, but her voice was rough. "It will go once I've had some chamomile tea."

This wasn't just a fancy. I loved this woman. When she had been tending to Jacob, I could picture her leaning over to kiss the forehead of our child.

She would probably think me a fool, yet I had to tell her. This might be the only chance I got.

"Willow, wait."

We stopped, and she eyed me curiously. My hands felt clumsy. I wanted to hold her, but what if she shoved me away?

There were a cluster of small, pretty flowers growing by her foot. I didn't know what they were. They were the same yellow as her hair, with green strips like tongues. Perfect!

I knelt and plucked the flowers, offering them. Willow's smile dropped. Her eyes widened.

"Willow?"

A quiver racked through her body. Panic reared up in me. Was Old Peter's story true? By simply picking flowers, had I killed her?

"Achoo!"

She clapped her hands over her face. Again and again she spluttered and sneezed, eyes weeping.

I threw aside the flowers and dug into my pockets for a cloth. She dabbed at her eyes and blew her nose with it.

"I thought I'd killed you!" I whispered in horror.

"What?" She rubbed at her streaming eyes.

"I..." I swallowed, feeling silly. "You're not going to keel over, then?"

I thought she was going to sneeze again, then she bent over and started to laugh.

"There's no curse!" she managed to choke out. "Flowers make me sneeze, but they certainly won't send me to my grave."

Willow hauled me onto my feet. She took my hand and we started walking once more. I was still a little shaken. Relief slowly trickled inside of me.

I started to laugh as well. I couldn't believe that, for a moment, I had been taken in by a fairy tale.

We reached the cottage. I was reluctant to let her go, wishing we could stay out here forever.

"Goodnight, Matthew," Willow whispered. "Perhaps, another time, we might dance again."

She opened the door and went inside. My heart hammered. The dream had been real.

And Willow had kissed me.

****

There were plenty more dances after that night, although I never saw the green mists again.

Willow might not be cursed, however, whenever she came to visit, Mother had the annoying habit of setting out flowers. But on our wedding day not a single posy managed to sneak into the church.

Red Admiral and Ringlet butterflies

Meadow Brown butterfly and hedgerow berries.

Tell it to the Bees

1877

"I swear I'll never marry without your express permission," I whispered to the bees. "So, there's no need to get into a snit and fly off."

I looked to my grandfather, who crouched by another hive with his smoker.

"Satisfied now?" I asked.

He grunted, expression unclear due to the mesh veil hanging from his hat.

"We'll see, Dorothy. You're still young."

You might turn out like your mother, went unsaid. I harshly tugged on my gloves.

Grandfather would never forgive her. She had been the one the bees loved.

When the skeps were still used, most destroyed the hive to snatch as much of the honey as they could. Not Mother. She would weave straw baskets for days, then carefully lure the swarm to the new skeps before claiming the honeycomb.

Just before I was born, Mother eloped with my father. It was disrespectful not to tell the bees of important events. The night she snuck away, they also departed.

Somehow, I had found my way here instead. Last year, my parents perished from a blaze that tore through the Norwich yards. Neighbours had pulled me from the wreckage.

Whenever I was abed, I swore I tasted the bitter grit of ash on my tongue. The room I rented seemed as empty as a harvested field. Writhing shadows resembled crackling flames.

I could not bear being alone. I needed family.

There were letters in a steel box; the only thing which survived the fire. They had been written by a grandmother I knew nothing of. A letter for each year, all twenty of them.

Why had Mother never told me of this? I'd pried each one open with trembling fingers.

With the last of my money, I travelled to Winterton-on-Sea. Tucked in the shadow of the church tower was the cottage.

As I opened the gate, I ducked beneath an overgrown canopy of deep purple flowers twisted together. Honey bees dived into the wide-open blooms.

Some crawled over the cottage door. So used to being lord here, they buzzed furiously as I rapped the knocker.

Even louder than them came the shout of, "I do not wish to be disturbed!"

Footsteps pounded and the door flung open. That was how I met my grandfather.

His face had been puce beneath the white sideburns and beard, his crown bare and reddened painfully by the sun. Two dark eyes screwed up to glare at me.

I might have run then, but having nowhere to go frightened me more. Stammering, I told him what brought me here. I would be willing to cook, clean, find employ, if he gave me a bed.

I had hoped to find a kindly grandmother to share my grief with. Instead, only my grandfather awaited. Grandmother perished last winter. There would be no more letters.

I expected to be sent away. However, he stood aside and offered me my mother's old, untouched room. I felt like an interloper, waiting for someone to throw me out.

A few months had passed. Day and night were spent in silence, our conversation a groaning floorboard or scraping of a chair.

Such a cold individual. I understood why Mother left.

And yet I continued to hope for some affection. He had shown kindness to a stranger, after all.

****

If I were to stay, I must acquaint myself with the bees.

My introduction to them came from a jar of honey. My spoon sunk in and came out with sticky, tawny strings which clung to the glass.

Honey coated the inside of my mouth. I had eaten it before, slathered on buns, mixed into tea. Before, it had been gritty, almost smoky, as though sucking in the city smog. This time, sweetness flooded my mouth.

Grandfather chuckled roughly. "Keep a bee happy and you'll always be able to taste it."

Ours was a strange household. Even when it rained, our windows were kept open. Bees had a habit of following us inside while we worked. I'd once tried flapping one out with my apron, but Grandfather shook his head.

"Chase out a bee and you shoo off the good luck they bring with them."

Such superstitions were a curiosity. I asked for more, then managed to coax stories about my mother and the bees. It was the only time he became animated.

These creatures consumed the garden, seeding them with life for miles. They climbed clusters of lavender spires or darted into bluebells, the drooping heads dancing as if ringing.

It would take us the whole harvest to do such a thing ourselves. The thrum of a bee promised vibrancy and succulent fruits.

This place was beautiful compared to the overcrowded sprawl of Norwich, which had been vast yet as claustrophobic as a tightening fist. It amazed me someone like my grandfather could create this.

****

One day, Grandfather complained his bones were aching.

"The honey still needs delivering. You do it for me, girl. The village will want a proper look at you."

We weren't the only beekeepers in the area. The local lord and lady had their own apiary, with dozens of hives compared to our five.

Our honey was the sweetest, though, according to Grandfather. I could understand his pride after that first taste.

The basket hung heavy on the crook of my arm, laden with glass jars glistening golden. A girl ran towards me, her own basket piled with loaves and pies. The baker's daughter. Mercy often flitted in the background during his deliveries.

"Miss Dorothy, is some of that for us? Our honey cakes have been selling –"

Echoing, louder than the chatter of magpies, was the dull ring of metal striking metal. I tensed.

I should know that sound. I'd be warned about it. It was the striking of a shovel: a swarm was coming. Their keeper could traipse wherever he wanted to track down his runaway hive.

It came quickly, like a giant hand sweeping overhead. A humming mass that pulsed with vibrations.

Mercy dropped her basket and shrieked, "I can't be stung! I can't –"

"Hush." I knelt and turned her to me. "They'll pass by, so long as you stay quiet."

She nodded jerkily, screwed up her eyes and pressed her mouth shut.

Bees flickered out of the corner of my eye. A fluttering sensation disturbed the top of my hair. Buzzing shuddered in my ear.

Some of the bees broke off to settle amongst the poppies fringing the fields. The rest moved on.

I let out the breath I held. "We're fine. They won't sting unless they're frightened. To sting someone is to trade their life."

A man my age hurried up the path while I helped pick up the fallen bread. Flour dusted his dark, tied back hair.

"Adam, there was a swarm of bees –"

With a grunt, the stranger easily heaved Mercy into his arms. He stared hard at me.

"You're the keeper's granddaughter, aren't you? You'd do well to keep an eye on your bees, rather than letting them run wild."

"How dare you!" I leapt up, a roll crushed in my fist. "Rather than haller at me, you'd see they came from the manor house. They're not my bees."

He meant to argue further. Just as I suspected, the man who looked after the apiary went rushing past with a net.

Mercy, backing me up, shouted, "See!"

Adam went a very dark shade of red. "I…" He tugged at his hair. "My sister got stung as a babe. She's feared them ever since, so I –"

"Perhaps, if you tell me who you are, I'll accept it as an apology."

"Adam Shaw, Miss." He dipped into a mock-bow, Mercy squealing in joy from the sudden descent. "I'm taking over the bakery from my father."

So, I'd be seeing more of him. As brusque as he was, I found I did not mind the prospect as I scowled at his handsome, tanned face.

I winked at Mercy. "I'll show you something so you won't be scared of bees, if your brother is willing?"

****

I took Mercy to the bee garden. Adam followed, but kept his distance while Mercy and I crouched before a hollyhock.

"Careful now, don't nudge the flower."

I never thought bees slept. As a girl, I had believed they buzzed constantly.

Inside, about three or four bees had settled around the stamen. They were tucked together, forming a fuzzy mass of black and yellow stripes. Like mice in a nest.

"Adam, you should have a look as well."

I had guessed at his anger and sudden reluctance. He held the same unease as his sister. I quirked my eyebrow, daring him.

Adam settled next to me. The warm scent of baking bread seeped into my senses. He snorted in disbelief.

"They normally seem such fierce little devils."

"It's all a tough front."

After that, while the seasons darkened into the fiery hues of autumn, Mercy continued visiting the bees. She helped me plant wild flowers for them.

Her brother often came, making out he was keeping an eye so she'd be no trouble. The baker's honey cakes were becoming known across the village for their sweetness.

Grandfather watched us, his cane gripped tight. When I clung to Adam's arm, I felt his narrowed, disapproving eyes upon us.

****

Adam invited me to a picnic on the dunes. While Mercy ran about the marram grasses, chasing dragonflies, Adam laid out plates of pork pies, ginger beer and the famous honey cakes. Palm sized bites the colour of amber, glistening on the crown.

"This is all rather thought out," I commented uncertainly.

"Well, it's a celebration. You've been here near a year and I've grown fond of you."

A flush crept up my neck, consuming my face. I grasped one of the cakes, biting deep into the springy sponge.

Its stickiness left an impression on my lips, almost like a kiss.

"Mercy, don't go too far near the edge!" I called, startling Adam.

He laughed, scratching his cheek. We talked of random things, fluttering around and not quite settling. As always, it turned back to the bees.

"My gran told me an unmarried woman could walk through the most furious cloud of bees and remain unharmed. I suppose that's how you got away that day we met."

He was trying to steer the conversation, darting to it as a wasp might its target.

"That sounds almost pagan," I teased. "Are you trying to get me named a witch?"

Adam leaned in much too close. I started to fluster, rushing out, "An unmarried man and woman are the best couple to tend them, according to lore. So, the church might condemn me, but the bees will still love me."

"And if I wanted to make an honest woman of you?"

"I'm already honest," I spluttered.

"You know what I mean. Would you marry me, if I was to ask?"

I almost dared him to propose and see what my reply would be. I held my tongue.

I did not come to this place to be married. I was here for my family.

Grandfather's iciness had not thawed. A dark thought entered my mind: *If I married, I could leave.*

It was the same with Mother. History would be repeating itself.

Mercy ran over before Adam could press me. We finished our food and packed up.

Rather than dally, I quickened my step as we walked home, soon escaping to the cottage. I threw myself into making candles with the leftover beeswax. The skies turned burnt orange between clouds with a bruise-like hue.

I did like Adam. I had kissed his cheek a week before at the harvest celebration.

I had never been courted, though. Was one kiss the first step and the next one straight into marriage?

I'd barely begun to know my family. Would I suddenly weave myself into another? It would be a livelier, happier household.

At such a thought, guilt pinched my stomach. I eyed my grandfather where he sat by the fire, quiet as usual.

I had made my promise to the bees and, in effect, to my grandfather. He would be abandoned again.

"Dorothy, fetch the book upon the shelf. The red one. Would you read it for me?"

I arose, wiping my hands. There was a small shelf carved into the flint wall, with books and yellowing papers crammed in. I gripped the book and wriggled it free. Another came with it, thudding at my feet and splaying open.

Tucked within was a small black frame. Carefully, I pulled out the monochrome photograph.

I recognised my mother, even with her looking so young. Behind her stood an older woman I could only assume was my grandmother.

She had a kind smile. I wished I could have met her.

Grandfather knelt, somehow infinitely younger than the man I knew. As if the lines, shadows and white of his hair had flaked to reveal this grinning man.

A younger man stood beside my mother, slightly blurred from turning to whisper to her. He looked like Mother, and in turn like me. An uncle, perhaps? I flicked to the book's title page, to the inscription: *Alexander Fairweather*.

"Hurry up, girl."

I snapped shut the book and joined Grandfather by the fireside. Haltingly, I read.

I knew he could tell something had affected me. The lines of his face deepened, but he said nothing.

Perhaps he did not want to discover the truth. I was just the same; I dared not question him about that happy, long ago family.

****

At crow time, I stared at the bracken creeping across my window. My thoughts buzzed along with my thrumming heart.

I could not forget Adam's proposal. When I pictured what might await me, joy wove itself alongside my apprehension. It was the strongest out of the two.

I should not have remained silent. He would think it a rejection.

I put on my cloak and crept out, heading for the baker's cottage. The flowers that were so bright in daylight were now nothing more than droplets of shadows. A lone foxglove shivered from a breeze.

I tucked a small jar of honey underneath the shuttered window. Tied around the lid was my answer.

As I returned home, I saw a light flickering in the window. I would not run. Reluctantly, I went inside.

Grandfather had lit one of my candles, leaving it weeping in a cup on the kitchen table. Shadows lapped him like waves, sharpening the bony jut of his face.

"Just the same as your mother," he growled. "As flighty as a butterfly."

"Do not speak of her that way!"

"I'll say what I like. Deserters, all of you. The moment you get the chance you run, and the bees will abandon me as well."

"What do you expect? You are cold and sullen. You –" The words caught in my throat. I almost called him a hollow man. "Who is Alexander?" I asked instead.

Grandfather stilled, wetness glimmering in his eyes. He sucked in a breath, the sound whistling.

"How do you know that name?" It did not come out as a roar, but a low moan.

"I found a photograph in one of the books."

His fist made to strike the table, but he stopped himself. The fingers uncurled.

"This doesn't concern him. Do not distract me."

I could not stand the almost darkness. I struck a match and lit the slumped candles on the windowsill.

"Alexander is at the crux of all this."

I turned back, expecting a fight. Instead, Grandfather had his head in his hands. In the flickering glare of the light, he looked frail and tired and ever so lonely.

I remembered nights after the fire when I would stare at shadows. Exhausted but unable to shut my eyes. Feeling every bump and ache, but also hollowed out within.

"Please, Grandfather, tell me about my uncle."

"It was over twenty years ago. Only nineteen when he left to fight in Crimea and did not return. I had such hopes for him and that was all I saw. Blind to my wife's grief and my daughter's anger. I did not want to deal with them."

And I could imagine why Mother took flight, the bees leaving with her. I myself had planned to run.

What had it been like for her, when before she had known a kind, caring man?

I hesitated, then put my hand upon his shoulder. “They’re gone now, but that doesn’t mean you should hide. Please don’t reject me as well.”

“You’re off to be married,” he muttered bitterly.

“So?” I countered. “The bees won’t mind once I tell them, or are you going to fly away?”

****

The church overflowed with flowers. Hawthorn crawled outside, glimmering with rain from that morning. Droplets scattered as bees settled upon the lips of the petals. Their buzzing hummed around us, almost in song, as Adam and I exchanged our vows.

At the party, we drunk mead and dined on wedding cake piped with the gleam of honey. I leant over to whisper in Adam’s ear.

We linked arms and snuck away from the celebration, back to the cottage and hives. From my basket I took out a slice of wedding cake.

“See, just as I promised. Those wedding bells are ringing for me. I’m to live with my husband now, but I’ll always visit and keep an eye on you.”

And Grandfather, I thought. It was a promise not just to the bees.

Grandfather would not hear, for he was back at the church. He had been the one to give me away.

I settled against Adam. He leant down to kiss me.

“Does everyone approve?” he asked.

“They’re pleased I’m happy.”

Bees were a most social creature. They considered themselves part of the family. Treat them like a stranger and that person would soon regret it.

The Cocoa Tree

1885

"Lettie, quick! Peter and Lord Nathaniel are fighting in the garden!"

I darted over my bed to get to the window. Alice already had half her body hanging out to see better. I gripped her legs lest she fell.

The two men circled one another, their jackets shucked to the ground and shirt sleeves rolled up. Our brother kept on bouncing on his toes, weaving his fists distractedly. Lord Nathaniel stalked, graceful as a fox.

"Has Peter reneged on his debts again?" I wondered, though it seemed friendly enough.

Peter might have a bloody nose, but he was laughing. Typical of him. I couldn't understand why he and his friends found beating themselves to a pulp invigorating.

Why were they allowed to be so rowdy? They were never told to be quiet, sit and read a book or do needlework. Not even as a little girl had I been allowed to go tearing about. My parents feared it would make me unruly to the core, thus losing all prospects of a decent marriage.

More blows were exchanged, then the pair shook hands. As Lord Nathaniel bent to retrieve his jacket, he glanced up and saw us watching avidly.

He bowed and I could barely make out his grin. Not that I needed to see to know.

At one of my friend's coming out balls I couldn't stop watching him. He was so handsome I believed I'd conjured him from my thoughts as I'd sat bored, my dance card empty.

Alice nudged me. "He's still in search of a wife."

I flushed, slinking away from the window.

"There's to be another ball in a few months," she continued. "If we can get ourselves looking our best, he's sure to ask one of us to dance… perhaps even more."

"As if! He'll be hunting for a dowry, not someone with mousy hair and freckles."

She reached over, pinching my cheek. "That's why ladies use powders. We'll make it so he can't look away. Make-up. Dresses. I've heard he likes a woman with a trim figure who doesn't stay indoors."

I pictured riding alongside Lord Nathaniel, traversing the country. Breathless and wild.

That was not what Alice had in mind.

****

By dawn, my elder sister was rapping on my door wearing a brand-new walking outfit.

I recognised her smile. It was a challenge. My heart thrummed.

With little else to do, Alice and I found ways to make exciting the dull tasks our parents described wholesome and character building. Singing, reading, painting, whoever could finish first or received the strongest praise from our tutors won. We'd done it since we were children.

How long would that short thrill last, though? Quickly chasing the latest fashion until our mother found us suitable matches. We would then have to come to terms with life as a dutiful wife. Her only tasks deciding on what soup was for dinner and dictating to the nursemaid how best to care for the children.

Our dresses had already been chosen for Hope's party. They could easily be adjusted to fit our waistlines, yet the sizes we ordered were smaller than what we usually wore, anticipating the changes of our hard work.

"Keep going, Leticia!" Alice called over her shoulder. "You won't get a man if you can't catch him!"

I didn't even have the puff to reply.

We had started our walking regime mid-spring, now we were in summer. The household had moved from the country estate to our address in the city.

I'd hoped Alice might have finally been satisfied by now. However, each day she still set off briskly walking. I wasn't about to admit defeat.

We weaved through the people on the streets. It was early morning, the sun turning the red sky into sharp shards of glass.

Salary workers strode through single file, so used to the journey that one was reading his paper without looking up. Apple and cress sellers juggled baskets, hands cupped to their mouths to cry out prices. One woman threw an apple and caught it to show off the bright green, unblemished flesh.

Street sweepers darted across the road, undaunted by the rattling wheels and stomping hooves of the horse drawn carriages. Laughing and shouting, their brooms knocked into one another like dogs snapping over territory.

The weather was becoming too much. No matter how much I fanned myself or the thinness of my pelisse, the heat felt like a hand upon my throat. Worst of all, my corset jabbed and chafed against me. The stickiness of my perspiration itched.

"You should have some airholes put in!" Alice told me cheerily. "It's a remarkable innovation."

"I can't go on," I whined, having to stop.

It wasn't as if I was unhealthy. Every morning I did my daily callisthenics. Peter was far worse with his snuff and brandy.

If I went out walking with Alice, though, it could last for hours. She would suck at her teeth in annoyance should I even suggest taking the carriage if there was the threat of rain. Her obsession had even extended to our meals, only dining on weak broths and rejecting anything with a hint of sweetness.

I was starting to worry for her. There was something more than simply winning at play.

As I caught my breath, I examined the building I was leaning against. I thought it was any other shop, but there was no hint at all of what it sold.

The window was concealed by an ornate red curtain with a tiny sign promising something would be *coming soon*. Curious, I tried peering in to try and make anything out.

The curtain shifted minutely. I thought I saw a flash of another's brown eyes, and then they winked!

I staggered back. Alice strode on ahead as I hurried after her, telling me I shouldn't waste time staring at shop windows.

I found it more interesting than what we were doing.

It hadn't been as bad when we were staying in the country. We had explored the endless stretches of marshlands glistening from the bright skies, awash with birds scattering from the rushes. Whenever Alice did listen to my begging and stopped to rest, we could sit and watch a wherry idling past, so far off the sail looked like a pocket of mist.

There had been so many new sights to try and capture in my sketchbook. I would rather be mingling with the people here instead of stiffly marching past, silent and distant.

****

After that day, I considered running to Father's library and locking myself away from Alice's nagging. I almost did, thinking enough was enough.

Even when I threatened to stop, Alice kept walking well until sundown. I didn't want to leave her alone.

Whenever we did our familiar, agonisingly dull circuit through the city, I kept my eye on that mysterious shop. There were subtle changes. Someone had painted the dark outline of a tree upon the window, the heavy shapes of some sort of fruit clinging to the branches.

Slowly, bit by bit, the curtains were pulled open. I barely made out the booths where people would be seated.

I sighed. The colours were rich tones of mahogany, not the pale shades of a tearoom or ice-cream parlour. No doubt it would be another gentlemen's club. Somewhere we were not allowed.

****

The day of the ball was getting closer.

"Just take a few inches off," Alice pressed.

She sharply tugged at my corset strings and I sucked in a breath. My voice went a little higher. I would have to resume my singing lessons, just as Mother wanted, to strengthen my voice.

"Now do me."

She darted in front. Hesitatingly, I tightened her corset beyond what it was normally. I flinched as she gasped.

"Alice…" I began. "I'm concerned this is more than you wanting to look your best. I know you have a habit of becoming overinvested –"

"It'll be fine once we get used to it," she hastily interrupted. "An inch or two isn't so bad. Hope says all the young women in her finishing school have gone even tighter."

I couldn't stand watching her struggle to breathe. Without her realising, I loosened the corset.

Before we set off walking, I forced her to sit and have a breakfast of stewed fruits and porridge. The skies had darkened, the air muggy. There had been a thunderstorm last night, but not even that had managed to cool down the city.

Alice expertly wove her way around disgruntled farmers herding their sheep to market as she pounded the pavement, oblivious to the upset she caused. A sheepdog strained at his rope, barking as I tried to keep up.

"I think…" I heaved. "I think the smog in the air is affecting me."

"Nonsense," Alice glibly replied. "We're going so fast it can't keep up."

An omnibus sped past, the conductor chasing one of his fares. One of the wheels glided through a puddle.

I scrabbled for my parasol, but it was too late. The icy burst of water slapped my side.

Two street sweepers stopped, leaning against their brooms, gleeful at some entertainment.

"What an absolute shame!" one announced to his friends. "All that lovely lace is ruined. She looks more like a marsh lily than a young lady."

My throat went tight. Suddenly I felt ridiculous, heaving and panting, feeling sorry for myself over Lord Nathaniel. What was the point of forcing myself into perfection for someone who had only looked upon me once?

Alice rushed over.

"Don't worry. We'll hurry home –"

"Enough." I hadn't meant to snap as I roughly grasped my hem and wrung it. "I'm tired of this. I'd rather box like Peter does."

Alice leaned away, hissing out a hush. "Do you want respectable people to hear? We'd be shunned!"

"Then they don't deserve our friendship, if they're so petty minded. I want to run and dance and not have others constantly worry it will ruin me in some way."

Through the exhausted fog, I dragged in a breath. The sweet scent of chocolate trickled into my nose, rich and tempting. It lured me into taking another guilty sniff.

The shop I had been so interested in was open. In the window was a land of sweets and cakes.

Profiterole mountains with chocolate and caramel drizzled peaks beckoned alongside ornate tarts topped with shimmering glazed fruits like stained glass. Upon a tray were thin flutes of bubbly skinned brandy snaps with heavy crowns of cream.

Then there were the cakes. I almost pressed my nose to the glass.

Chocolate cakes with fudge pieces and strawberries oozing into a lake of decadence. On simpler, elegant sponges were curled white chocolate shavings.

There were too many to choose from and not enough room in my stomach.

Alice's nose wrinkled, as though the weight would cling to her hips just from looking at them.

"We deserve a treat," I said, "seeing how much effort we've put in."

"And waste our hard work? No thank you! We can have tea and cucumber sandwiches when we get home."

I considered the two so quickly that my mind could probably

outpace Alice.

"I'm sorry, but I'd rather eat that right there."

And as I pointed out a row of éclairs in the window, a man leaned over to right one that had gone askew. His hair was the same colour as the chocolate smoothed over the pastries, his eyes a slightly paler shade of the walnuts upon the coffee cakes. Suddenly, I was even hungrier.

I wanted to go inside, but I was a state, there was no denying it. My nose was red, cheeks no doubt almost purple by now, hair unravelling and skirt past saving. Yet I wasn't going to run.

After the cold shock of water, the comforting warmth of brewing hot chocolate embraced me as I entered the shop. The amiable murmuring coming from the booths paused as I found an empty table.

I picked nervously at the buttons on my glove. I had hoped Alice might follow, if only to argue. However, she shook her head in disgust and walked off. I was on my own.

They wouldn't throw me out, would they? Although I looked more like some spirit who'd crawled out of the river.

The man I had caught a glimpse of came over. He wasn't annoyed, I hoped, I think merely curious. He set down a chocolate pot decorated with a smiling, rosy cheeked girl carrying bundles of wheat.

"Are you in distress, my lady?"

"No, I'm… I'm here to order," I said, a little breathless.

He beamed. "Welcome to *The Cocoa Tree*. I'm Ambrose Sidmouth. What would you like?"

"Something sweet. A chocolate cake with fruit."

"You'll want the *Cherry Kiss*, then. It has a succulent sweetness."

The slice of cake was a nice, thick wedge, with a single cherry sinking into the embrace of a spoonful of whipped cream. I took a bite and a burst of cherries danced upon my tongue as I hit the fruit layer hidden within the chocolate sponge.

A contented sigh escaped. Ambrose laughed.

"It is always good to see a beautiful woman who enjoys her chocolate… my lady."

I blushed, but before I could stammer something back Ambrose had to attend to the other customers. I was sorry to see him leave, although the cake was a decent replacement.

When there was a lull, he returned. He sat opposite, watching me eat with a soft, pleased smile. He was much too forward, yet I found I didn't mind.

"Do you make them yourself?" I asked, all I wanted to do was find out more about him.

"I've travelled the country sharing my love for cooking. I'm hoping to go to France once I have enough saved." Ambrose leaned in close and whispered, "Although, I'm considering staying longer if enough people enjoy my delicacies."

"I wish I could make something similar to this."

I glanced at the window. Alice had returned. She pulled a face and I pettishly shoved a larger spoonful of cake in my mouth.

Then she saw Ambrose sitting with me. Her mouth gaped. I waved.

The door hesitatingly opened, the jingle of the bell drawn out.

My sister and I always seemed to be in competition with one another. Perhaps this time I'd be the one to win.

A sweet treat wasn't so bad, especially if it led to better things.

I looked up mid-moan as I popped another mouthful of the delicious cherry cake into my mouth. Ambrose bowed his head slightly in teasing deference as he poured a frothing cup of chocolate for Alice when she sat next to me.

****

"Alice has finally stopped hoping Lord Nathaniel will return to England," I told Ambrose, draining the last of the chocolate from my teacup. "Who would have expected he was so heavily in debt he had to abscond from his creditors?"

The weather was still too mild to drink the chocolate piping hot, but cooled with some cream it was refreshing. I dabbed at my lips with my handkerchief.

It had only taken an éclair to get Alice to admit what had been troubling her. Even she had stopped believing we would have a chance at ensnaring Lord Nathaniel. It was common sense, really. If Peter was friends with him then it was certain he would be no good.

Alice was due to turn twenty-six soon, well past the age most women were already married. Hope had been whispering in her ear they'd be calling her a spinster soon, and I'd have no luck of finding a husband if my elder sister could catch no-one.

A match such as Lord Nathaniel would stop the whispers and Mother's disappointment. Alice would have done anything to succeed, even make herself sick through stress.

"But is that all I'm good for?" she'd mumbled, sniffing. "I can sing, yet that was only for dinner parties. I cannot truly do anything of use!"

"You can read, write, paint," I'd offered. "I've seen your paintings. I'm certain you can find something to work towards and not only for a husband. If we force it, we'll only come to regret our choices."

It had been what I feared as well. All our lives we were meant to be devoted to finding a suitable husband.

What if we failed at that? What if we wanted more?

"You were always the flighty one," she had said, finally managing to smile.

I had received a letter from Alice that morning. Four more young ladies were joining her finishing school for the arts and languages. She had also been getting closer to the piano tutor working with her. There were plenty of women wanting to find other pursuits rather than go husband hunting at balls.

Of course, each day her lessons began with a brisk walk to invigorate the mind… but Alice now knew when to stop.

The last of the shop's customers trailed out. The young woman Ambrose had hired started cleaning the booths. She knew not to gossip.

My mother had come here a week ago for afternoon tea and deigned it an appropriate place to meet with friends. Father had yet to visit. I think he had started to suspect my reasons for coming were for more than the angel cake.

I finished the last mouthful of croissant, brushing from my fingers what remained of the buttery, flaking pastry.

"That was delicious. Hopefully I won't burn the mixture this time!"

Ambrose chuckled. He stilled for a moment, then dared to take my hand.

"So disparaging! If you were to hear all the mistakes I made as a boy, you'd not be impressed."

He led me into the kitchen at the back, where he had been secretly teaching me how to fold and mix, finding the perfect balance between sweetness and richness.

We almost had enough saved. Paris awaited.

The Lucky Net

1870

"There they are, Seb!" Ethan, the youngest member of our crew, shouted. "The silver darlings are swimming!"

He clung to the rigging so that he swung above our heads. All I saw was his silhouette, coat flapping as he pointed at the dark waters. Stars sharply glimmered past the clouds.

"Come down," I called. "We're not fishing you out if you fall in!"

"You'll taint the catch!" someone joked.

Winds tugged at Ethan, dashing him back and forth. He hastily scrambled down, joining my side, as we threw the nets over.

Below, a glow gently undulated. Pale and shimmering, as though the moon had cracked and some of its light dripped into the sea. Night would soon be departing, the sky twisting into smoky hues.

Herring swam just beneath the surface, their scales silvery, tails flicking. Ignorant of us until we dragged them into the air. They thrashed, slapping against our arms as whole barrelsful came aboard.

I shuddered from the cold, fingers rough and knuckles cracked. Sweat rolled down my face while sea spray splattered my chest. Muscles taut as knotted rope.

Waves heaved against the ship, tipping it this way and that – making us all feel as powerless as a ship in a bottle, one that was in the hands of a tantrummy child.

There was a cry, and my breath caught.

Ethan teetered, too small to withstand the sea's hungry maw but not wanting to give up his catch. His body dragged over the side. I lunged, snapped my arm around his waist and wrenched us both back.

It was not enough. We were going to go over!

I clung on, not about to abandon him. Waves knocked against the hull. I braced my feet.

Then we sprawled across the deck, fishes flapping amongst us. I let go of Ethan, who fell to his hands and knees, shaking.

"You all right?"

Too winded to answer back, all he did was nod. I heaved him up and we went back to our work.

Only when the hold was full did the skipper cry "land home". We went below deck, glad to be finally lounging in our hammocks. Constant was the tilting of the room, rocked in the hands of the waves.

The pot cook was worrying at started to boil, smelling of thick, cloying potato and herring stew. My stomach growled, impatient. I kept busy by checking for breaks in my net.

Ethan dealt cards for Whist with some of the other lads. His head kept on lolling as he fought against sleep, and Jimmy always liked to slip a few cards up his sleeve.

My skipper, Olaf, jabbed me in the side. "You're a lucky thing, Seb."

I smiled carelessly, but I knew how hungry those tar-like waves were. I'd lost my father and brothers to them years ago.

"I've got someone watching over me," I told him.

"Then be sure to keep them happy or, if I was you, I wouldn't be sailing out again!"

Ethan pursed his lips, but before he could whistle up a wind by accident Olaf slapped his back. "You remember this song?" And he started hollering a shanty, drowning out the rumbling slurp of the sea outside.

We were going home.

I could picture gulls swooping over the Yarmouth rows, trying to dive into troll-carts to thieve fish at the top of the pile, women fixing nets on the quayside while Scotch girls gutted herring.

And my family would be waiting for me as I came down the gangplank. My darling wife Hetty and our daughter Susie.

Our nets were as wide as a sail, and there were so many we were always tripping over them. I had several, but there was one that I always kept an eye on. The net that led me to meeting my wife.

I'd met Hetty when I was looking for someone to mend my net. She carried a family trinket, a stone, that lured their intended to them. She'd lost her stone and I'd had to help her find it. Out of all the women there, even though her head was bowed and I could not see her face, something had brought me to her.

Nowadays, though, she laughed at the story. She called me a superstitious worrier. I thought it being sensible, as did most of the crew.

None of us on the *Stargazer* wore green – it was unlucky. Any eggshells aboard were crushed to smithereens, in case a foul spirit decided to sail within them and cause mischief. Some fishermen would not even step onboard if something went against their superstitions.

I found a few breaks in the mesh, where fish scales had torn through. I'd been trying my luck, but I knew a woman who could weave a few charms. The biggest joy would be seeing Hetty's smile and swinging my daughter up into my arms.

I joined in with the singing, "Up jumped the herring, queen of the sea!"

****

During the long journey back, we packed the fish. Once the ship had docked, I heaved cran baskets thick with herrings to the quayside. There was a shout of joy.

I paused before I turned, steeling myself, I suppose. Wondering who I would face this time.

Whenever I returned, it was like flicking through a book of photographs. Susie had been running in the mud with the dog when I'd last seen her. Now, she looked almost a woman, hair neatly pinned in a bun, clothes clean.

I was relieved to see some of her wildness still there, as she hitched up her skirts and rushed up to me, waving frantically. Her mother followed slowly behind.

It could be unsettling, seeing how easily a person changed when you weren't there to watch them grow. And nobody else noticed the differences.

As a boy, I'd been afraid I'd never really get close to anyone, that I was gone for so long I'd be set apart from my community. Although with my Hetty, I knew that'd never happen. My girls were my tie to the land.

As I got closer, I saw in Hetty's arms… A lump formed in my throat. I swallowed.

"Who's this little lad, then?" My voice dipped.

I bent down to peer into the swaddling. Between the folds I saw a pair of flushed cheeks and screwed up eyes. The last I saw of him, he was still tucked away inside his mother.

"Seb, meet our son Josiah."

She held him out. I wiped the salt and brine from my hands, then carefully took the boy, who was as small as a warp of herrings. His eyes opened and he blinked at me so curiously, most likely wondering who this stranger was.

We walked home, Susie taking one arm and Hetty the other. To think, I had never seen my children newly born in this world. I seemed not to have a hand in them, as though they simply sprouted into existence.

The town swarmed with holiday goers come off the trains. They were more familiar with this place than I was.

Home had not changed, though. They never moved the furniture. It was the only constant.

While we ate bloaters on toast I regaled Susie with my journeys, as wild as the ones her great-grandfather apparently told. When she heard about me and Ethan almost falling in, her cheeks paled so much her freckles stood out.

"He's – You were both all right?"

"The ship swung back, we pulled with all our might, and the mermaid let go of the net and swam off!"

She rolled her eyes. Before, she used to love my stories.

Afterwards, with the children abed, Hetty sat with me outside. We watched the gentle lap of the waves speckled with moonlight. Steam from our blackberry syrup misted about our faces.

"You could have drowned," Hetty said softly.

"But I didn't. My luck held, and it was thanks to the magic in your weaving."

I kissed her fingers. She managed a smile, but it was quickly gone.

"Wouldn't you prefer working on the mainland? You'd see us more."

"It's not the way." My brothers had been fishermen. My son would be one as well. "I'll be sailing out again in a fortnight. I need my net fixed, can you do that?"

"I'll miss you."

She leaned over and kissed me, the sea our only audience.

****

The scratchy tang of salt water permeated the church. The sunlight streaming in caught upon fallen fish scales, causing them to glisten gold. As the priest stood at the altar, the nets hanging behind him gently swayed. Blessed for another season.

Olaf put his head between me and Hetty, whispering, "There's to be no foy."

"What?"

The man who owned our ship normally hosted a foy: a meal for fishermen and their family. It was tradition. But Old Arthur had passed and his son had taken over, a mill owner from the city.

"He hasn't even bothered coming up from Norwich."

"It's a bad omen." I sucked at my teeth, wishing I had my pipe. "But we'll have to make do. At least we've got our nets."

A slight furrow appeared between my wife's eyebrows. "Yes…"

The people on the land were shaking off their superstitions, yet they did not see the fury and power of the sea as I had done. I knew that most of life could not be explained, so I clung to my charms and hoped they would protect me.

It was my only form of control over that beast known as nature.

****

The next day, I spied Hetty walking along with my net draped over her shoulder. I called out, but she was too far away; the gulls were louder than me.

She vanished around the corner and I rushed after her. When we were together, I snatched as many moments as I could. The day for pushing off was drawing nearer, like the tide.

As I got close enough, I saw her duck into a familiar shop: *Rowley's Net Repairs*. I used to go there before I met Hetty.

Through the shop window, a beatster squinted in the dim light at the net hanging off a hook. Her shale needle weaved as seamlessly as a spider with its silk. Impersonal and without care.

I wondered how long Hetty had been doing this. From the beginning? I might have been clinging to my charms, and all the time they were impotent. My knuckles rubbed against the bristles of my beard.

More people were calling me a fool, turning instead to the choking belch of train smoke, comforted by the thrum of machinery. They'd all forgotten about the waves.

Hetty emerged without my net. "Seb!"

Rosy patches appeared in her cheeks. She would not meet my eye.

"You've been lying to me," I said, trying to keep the roughness out of my voice, but she flinched.

"Not really. I…"

"Then why? All this time, have you been laughing at your husband? These folktales might or might not be true, but they matter to me! Do you want me to sail out one day and not come back?"

Her lips parted, then she gritted her teeth. Wetness glimmered on her eyelashes.

"How dare you suggest such a thing. Every night you're gone, I pray you come home safe."

"I'm not angry –"

"Then why else say it? I don't want to see you hurt! Or…" All the heat in her face went, pallor chalky. "Or worse. You are my husband. I love you."

We've not said it much. Always murmured in hurried snatches just as I was about to board.

I sighed, and the harshness in my voice softened. "I love you as well, but I don't expect my wife to lie to me. It makes me wonder what else you've fooled me about."

Her breath burst out in frustration, her hair fluttering.

"I have a daughter who wanders about in a daydream and a newly born boy. I'm the one raising them. We barely get any time together, and I'd rather be sitting with you than fixing a net."

She held herself. I wrapped my arms around her, chin nestled on her head.

"Perhaps that's the problem. We've been so long apart, we've never really been comfortably settled as man and wife."

Hetty went home, but I did not follow. I wandered past the anchored ships bobbing in the water. The masts seemed so thin, as though they might tip with a flick of the wind's fingers.

Ethan sat on the edge of the jetty, watching the *Stargazer*.

"Now, what are you up to?" I asked.

He started, flushed guiltily. "Looking for rats jumping off the ships."

"I think that should be cook's job."

"It'd probably be the smell of his cooking that'd send them running!" He laughed. "But it's obvious, isn't it? If a rat doesn't fancy sailing, then it must know something is up."

Ethan was the same age as my daughter. He'd almost lost his life that last voyage. As much as we talked about charms, it was luck that we survived. I'd been staying to keep an eye on him, just as my uncle saw me through when I first started.

"Well, there are a few other things you should watch out for…" I trailed off when I saw him watching me attentively. Put too much stock in lucky charms and you might be missing out on the most important thing. "More than anything, you need some common sense. Keep calm, obey your skipper and do not tempt the waves."

We sat a while in silence.

"Are you all right, sir?"

"I will be. I've argued with the wife about my charms. Were you waiting for someone?"

"N-No!"

I clapped my hand on the boy's shoulder. "Get home to your gran, then, before she starts to worry."

"And you?"

"I'm off home, too."

****

Yet I did not enter my house. I sat out back with my pipe. There was a curious feeling in my stomach, like a load of eels jumbled in there.

Along the way, I'd bought a St Christopher's medal from a gypsy, but the unease did not go. The trinket felt as insubstantial as a raindrop.

Had it always been useless clinging to my charms? I was powerless against the waves.

A figure wafted across the sands. Hetty was right; our daughter was too much of a dreamer. I whistled Susie over, and she settled next to me.

"Are you watching the skies for geese?" my daughter teased.

I knew the stone-like scrape in my chest from loneliness when the waves were howling and the winds bit deep into my bones. I knew it too well.

What about my family? They did not go still as figures in a music box did the moment I left, only thinking and feeling when I returned. They had whole other lives separate from me. That old, childish fear of being left behind resurfaced.

I wanted to be an old man. Watch my son grow and walk my daughter down the aisle. I hungered for the ordinary things upon the land.

Perhaps those tales of mermaids were true, in a way. To feed their families, the fishermen had to be constantly away at sea, but always longing to go back.

And Hetty was yearning for me to return to her. I should not have upset her so. Too stubborn and caught up in the old ways.

Susie stared at me, eyes empty and ever so pale as she examined my weary face. As though she knew my thoughts.

I never wanted Susie to marry a fisherman, because I knew the toll it took upon the heart. For both those involved.

Movement against my side. Susie was fumbling in my coat pocket. When I saw she'd taken my knife –

"Careful with that!"

Susie held out a lock of her hair, shearing enough to the length of her finger. Then she went inside, and a few minutes later she returned with a dark strand and Hetty's pale blonde. She knotted them together in the sailor's knot I'd shown her and hooked them to her necklace. She leant over and put it on me.

"There. That's all the luck you need."

Susie kissed my cheek and went inside. I arose as well. It was time to stop skulking about and apologise.

****

We were lined up before we set sail. Our skipper marched in front, getting us to turn out our pockets. I'd spent the last of my pay on cushies for the children. Jimmy had a few coins left.

"Throw it over, man," we called, and he did so.

"I'll wish for treasure to tangle in my net!"

Hetty waved me off, Josiah tucked under her shawl. Susie was waving to another – Ethan! She flushed when I caught her eye.

The *Stargazer* cleaved through the water, the town becoming as small as driftwood. We were leaving the rest of the world behind.

Perhaps this would be my last voyage. The sea no longer called to me as it once did. My thoughts were too occupied with the land I left behind. The grey in my beard was proof enough I was no longer a young man.

So, let my luck hold one more time. The others might mock my superstitions, but in truth it was my promise to come back home.

Nothing, not sea, adventure or promised riches would lead me astray.

As I worked, I noticed something about my crewmates: Jimmy, although unmarried, wore his mother's wedding ring; Olaf the navy jumper his granddaughters knitted for him; Ethan's pom-pom bounced as he swabbed the deck, from the hat his grandmother forced upon his head before he ran on to the ship. I touched the knotted hairs around my neck.

We all had reminders of our promises. These were our threads back. So long as we had them, we knew there was someone waiting for our return.

The Runaway Bathing Machine

1860

Lizzie knew she'd lose her position at the big house if she was caught. The rules were absolute:

Do not steal from the lady's jewellery box. Always be neat, honest and loyal. As gentle as summer warm heather, like a country girl with nary a thought or temptation.

A maid must never be someone's sweetheart, not unless she planned to marry and give up her position. At nineteen, Lizzie was far from a comfortable pension.

Ma had told her to stop dallying with Gabriel. The sailor had been there first, before Father's accident meant it was her turn to step up.

No more oysters were brought suppertime to make Ma grudgingly invite him in, Gabriel's hand sneaking under the table to hold Lizzie's. Little could be said with a look while sitting apart in church pews.

Now, Gabriel was off on the trawlers for cod. He might not come back at all.

Lizzie knew fate had put her and her mistress on the train to Great Yarmouth, where Gabriel's ship was moored. Her last chance to tell him he still had her heart.

Lady Ashworth was meant to be her priority. Lizzie couldn't stray.

Her mistress remained stiffly silent throughout the journey, observing the unrolling of bright blue sea and its skirt of sand. Her expression was shielded by a black bonnet, but Lizzie knew it would be a disapproving frown. For once, it wasn't turned on her.

The maid might have been deemed suitable enough to braid the woman's ethereal pale hair, apply her favoured powders and rosewater scent, but that was all she knew about her employer. As secretive as a church statue, the cook had told her.

When Lady Ashworth looked at her, Lizzie rigidly mimicked her straight posture.

"About that girl, Charlotte –"

Panic put a pebble in Lizzie's throat, and like always she gabbled to dislodge it.

"I'm sorry it happened, missus, especially with the vicar come 'round and wanting his umbrella. His face! It was right of your daughters to tell her to go."

Lady Ashworth shook her head and sighed. "Yes, of course. Maids shouldn't be courting. They become too dreamy, spill the tea and leave the fire to go cold."

Guilt stuck to Lizzie's tongue. She should have argued for Charlotte's sake, but the housemaid was found under the coats with the footman. There was no hope of passing that off as anything else.

A sensible woman would consider this a warning. How could Lizzie hope to get away with what she planned?

****

Lizzie leaned over the promenade's railing. Muggy salt winds ruffled her curls and lacey fringe of her cap. The sky was the dark colour of water when doing laundry in the copper tub, the sun a disc of soap dropped in.

Families laid out their picnic blankets, like patches on a quilt. Bathing machines were already pulled out to sea. Ladies splashed their feet on the steps, others were dunked in by their paid for 'dipper' for something more bracing.

Lizzie gripped her skinny arms, hoping Lady Ashworth wouldn't ask her to do that – they'd both tip in!

Further down the beach, racing and kicking up sand to dive into the waves, were the men and boys. Lizzie shielded her eyes, which narrowed upon the bobbing shapes.

Her employer rapped her with the end of her parasol.

"Don't waste time hoping for a peek. New rules are in: swimming costumes must be worn."

Lizzie flushed, rubbing her leg. "I wasn't!"

It was 6d to rent the deluxe. The hut on wheels was large enough to comfortably change in, offering seclusion for ladies to enjoy the waters without the scandal of being seen in their bathing costume.

"Are you certain you don't want to swim?"

"Oh no, missus. I don't know how. I'll sit and enjoy the sun."

Lady Ashworth climbed into the bathing machine. Lizzie's hand went behind her back, fingers crossed.

The hut swayed. Wind chimes jingled and the veranda, made from a tent and some poles, creaked and groaned.

"Just how old is this thing?" she asked the boy leading the horse, who shrugged.

"My grandfather used to drive them when he was a boy."

Well, it had held out all this time. The weather was fair enough.

"It's just my conscience wanting me to stay," Lizzie muttered under her breath.

The bathing machine rolled into the sea. Small waves lapped the horse's legs and it whickered.

"Boy! Boy!" another lady's maid shouted back at the groynes.

The boy, with his trousers tugged up, hurriedly waded back to shore.

"There's a little flag on top. It'll go up when she's had enough."

Lizzie was left alone. The hut seemed so quiet, like some derelict building.

She was abandoning her duty, stamping over what her family needed from her. All for a man.

Just for today, she wanted to be more than someone's maid.

"Sorry, missus."

Lizzie caught up her skirt and rushed into town. Gabriel had no idea she was here. She had to catch him before he set sail.

A walk across the pier. An ice-cream. One kiss. Then she would be content.

She forced herself not to look back. If she had, she would have seen the sloppily made veranda crack in half and block the door.

****

"Imagine needing a chaperone at sixty!" Chastity Ashworth complained upon shutting the bathing machine door.

Even after becoming a widow, she was still anchored by propriety. Her daughters constantly fretted over the looming entity known as Society. They thought they knew best, dictating what their mother should do and who with. Most likely, they'd prefer it if she sat collecting dust in the folds of her skirt like a forgotten figurine on the hearth.

In her youth, Chastity had imagined an elopement as some wild dash to Gretna Green, clinging to her husband's waist as Father's horse pounded after them. Instead, it would be quiet and respectable, the only ones making a fuss the seagulls.

She would have involved Lizzie as witness to the ceremony, but their conversation warned her the girl was no ally. A spy sent to stop her ruining the family name.

Chastity changed into a full body swimming costume made of heavy flannel. The dour grey colour apparently befitted her age. Tied beneath the skirt were weights to stop it from billowing and exposing her ankles to sea molluscs. She severed them with a penknife so she would not be slowed down.

Not even the maid would suspect her of swimming further along the shore, where her lover awaited. By the time Lizzie realised, Chastity would be married to her unsuitable man.

She gripped the handle –

The door would not budge.

Chastity tried again, her devious smile going stiff. The door opened slightly, yet something blocked her in.

It was admitting defeat, having Lizzie rescue her, but she would find another way of giving the girl the slip. She tugged the pull by the door.

Outside, the red flag flipped up. It ruffled in the winds.

The maid did not come.

Chastity's breath came out as a thin stream. Only a month ago, there were reports of young women being locked in by mistake, coming over with heatstroke and expiring on the steps.

Sweat formed a sticky ring around her neck. When she rubbed her mouth, dry, cracked flesh caught on her knuckles.

Shards of light scattered over the floor and she squinted, making out the thin lines of a hatch. The roof had a skylight!

Panting, Chastity clambered upon the dressing table, banging the hatch open with her parasol. She clung to the edge, heaving herself up. She drank in the rush of wind, but her heart continued thrumming in her ears.

The veranda was nothing more than debris. On a small hook by the door, the reins had been hung up.

She still had a chance of making her meeting.

Grimacing, Chastity snatched for them, the leather throng almost slipping from her shaking fingers. She had not seen, leaning against the reins, a broken post from the veranda.

At the sharp movement, it rolled off. She watched in horror as it tumbled hard into the horse's flank.

The creature let out a shriek. It reared, water spraying as its hooves stamped back down.

The horse bolted across the shoreline, dragging the bathing machine and Chastity. They thundered through the holiday goers. A group of men tussling in the water laughed and whistled at the display, only for the big wheels to douse them in a wave. Children chased after, screaming with excitement.

Inside, Chastity fell back, trying to hold on to something. Knickknacks rattled off the shelves. Empty perfume bottles smashed at her feet. The mirror on the dressing table swung wildly. A string of seashells looped over her shoulder.

"Never mind what my daughters think," Chastity whispered under her breath, horrified. "I'll end up in the papers!"

The reins dangled from the skylight. She grasped them again, clawing to the top, and tried pulling the horse into the safety of the buffering waters. She just managed to avoid a young girl staring agog with her bucket.

Someone shouted for the horse to slow. The person ran towards them, rather than away like the others. The bridle was got hold of.

Everything came to a halt. Chastity staggered into a chair, releasing the reins. She leaned forward, heaving.

Whoever had rescued her climbed atop the roof. She made a meagre effort to cover herself, upon realising her rescuer was a man.

"I knew it was you," he said, reaching in to pull away the seashells tangled in her hair. "You always loved to make an entrance."

"Jack!"

She grasped his hand and was pulled up and out of the bathing machine.

****

Of course, one walk had drawn out like the waves, for Lizzie didn't want to let go of Gabriel's hand. Ice-cream dripped, sugar gleaming on her nails.

He kissed away the vanilla, her face becoming so rosy the freckles seemed to vanish. That was as far as it had gone.

Lizzie's time was running out, yet she'd lost her nerve to tell him.

When she started as a housemaid, she had hated the early rises, scrubbing her hands raw, getting bossed by cook, but she still did it. All for her family. Only at night did she dare wonder what her future would be. A little cottage on the coast, a dog, Gabriel sitting with her by the fire. Children perhaps, quite far into the future.

Getting a fresh apron every Christmas at work didn't compare to when Gabriel held her tight and her heartbeat picked up.

The bobbing of a parasol caught her eye.

It couldn't be Lady Ashworth, could it? She'd be in for it if she was caught.

"Gabriel, hide," she hissed, pushing him behind a shrimp seller's cart.

Lizzie peeked out and realised it wasn't her mistress. The two women didn't even look alike.

"Lizzie, you've made me drop my ice-cream."

She giggled when she saw his face. "I'm sorry. It's ridiculous, I'm seeing my employer everywhere!"

Her nerves were frayed and trembling. Anxiety pushed her the rest of the way. Jolting forward, she pressed her lips to his.

"Will a kiss make things better?"

He grinned, his arm coming around to pull her closer. "You'll have to try again and see, won't you?"

They ran past promenading couples and stopped by a chapel, hiding in its shadow so they could hold one another. As Gabriel's cheek pressed against hers, she glanced up at the cross, but it was far too early for that.

The door opened. Of all people, a rumpled looking dandy stepped out. He wore an orange and blue striped waistcoat, plum purple jacket and a red carnation tucked in his buttonhole.

The man's eyes alighted upon them. "You'll do."

"What? I, no –"

Lizzie couldn't be seen with Gabriel, especially not stepping into a chapel! Her mistress no doubt knew she was gone by now.

The man took her hand, inclining his head as though paying her court.

"My dear, I would be forever in your debt if you honoured me with your kindness. I am about to marry a woman I have loved my entire life when all, a husband, daughters, the very world, has stood between us."

Gabriel, entranced by the vibrancy of the older man's costume, leaned over to whisper, "Go on, Lizzie. What if it was us who needed someone?"

"Might it be us? In the future?" she asked, because kisses were the most fragile of promises.

"So long as the sea is kind to me, I'll always come back to you."

The couple stepped inside of the chapel with the dandy. Seashells and fishing nets had been hung up. There was a briny undercurrent alongside fresh sea air. Gull cries sounded overhead.

The bride waited not in white but a dress tawny as a nightingale, with a hat of feathers and a small lace veil. She no longer wore severe black or a bonnet with its ribbon knotted tightly under her chin.

Her braid had been loosened, hair falling about in beautiful pale waves. She appeared younger because of her wide, flushed smile.

Lizzie's head began to swim. The bride was her mistress.

****

Chastity thought her heart wouldn't stop racing since her misadventure with the bathing machine. When she saw her maid, leaning against the good-looking young man with her, everything stilled.

They were in a small chapel without pews. She and her bridegroom had to stand either side of the christening font. The windows behind the pulpit dominated the walls, flooding everything in light. Coastal landscape stretched beyond, smattered with white from swooping gulls.

Seeing how surprised the maid was made her want to laugh. Then she realised the girl's shock came from seeing her happy. When had she become so dour and prim?

Jack grinned, the lines around his eyes deepening and the scar on his chin from an argument over cards stretching.

They had met at her coming out ball. He wasn't meant to be there, instead sneaking in to borrow money from her brother.

Chastity had escaped to the balcony, after the man her mother had in mind for her was being too ardent. It was either that or slap him with her fan.

There was Jack, leg thrown over the rail, his hat clamped between his teeth. Such a grand figure. His stories had enthralled her: duelling with Napoleon's men, escaping prison, spying for the government. Only half of it had been true.

Then he asked for a dance.

He might be charming and mysterious, but ever so smug. Almost in retaliation she rebuffed him. She spent the night wishing she'd accepted, forced to dance with bumbling men and listen to them drone.

Dreams of running off with Jack were as insubstantial as sea froth. Instead her parents brokered a dependable marriage to replenish their depleted coffers. There was no love there, though she'd learnt to feel fondness for Gregory. If not, the coldness of the house would have set into her bones.

Now Chastity was free. Jack had returned to the country after paying off his debts and called on her to see how she was doing. He still told too many tall tales, but was softer around the edges. He'd learnt to finally act his age.

She supposed she had made him into another man entirely in her mind. Some rogue who had made off with her heart. A fantasy. Somehow, she preferred the reality.

Their vows were made. Everything quick and blurred.

It was strange, considering she remembered every anxious intake of breath while walking to the altar during her first marriage. All she wanted to do now was rush and enjoy what came next.

When Jack kissed her, he seemed to slip her a spark of his gumption. No longer would she be dictated to. Not by her mother, her first husband, certainly not her daughters. She understood too well how brittle and precious time was.

From the way her maid clung to that sailor's arm, Lizzie was not above getting what she wanted. Chastity looked to where the witnesses stood.

The moment the ceremony had ended, Lizzie and her sweetheart had run off.

****

Like a rind of orange flicked into the fire, daylight burned away into smoke and ash.

Lizzie heaved off her shawl, wildly waving as the ship set off. She stayed there until *Dawn Breaker* was another star in the distance.

She sniffed, but played it off as sea salt in her eyes. She had promised Gabriel not to cry.

When she turned, someone watched her. Lady Ashworth. Something prickly and sharp like a shell lodged in Lizzie's throat.

She knew she'd done wrong. Time to face up and receive her punishment. Ma was going to murder her.

As she approached, her mistress smiled. It wasn't a kindly one, instead bemused.

"You've led me a merry dance! Jack's the other side of town searching for you."

"I'm sorry, Lady Ashworth." She supposed she was Lady something else now, considering what she had witnessed. "I…"

"Was gallivanting with a fancy man? I hope he isn't stringing you along."

"Gabriel would never betray me!" She lowered her voice. "I've known him all my life. It was his last day here, you see."

A tiny part of Lizzie wondered if she could get away with what she'd done by threatening to reveal her employer's secrets. Her lips pressed together.

Things would be changing at the household, but she wasn't about to ruin it with spite.

"About my job, missus?"

"I can hardly fault you for having some fun. After all, I had the same plan." Chastity held out her arm. "Come on, girl. I've had more excitement than just a wedding, no thanks to you!"

Laughing in relief, Lizzie linked arms with her mistress and the pair walked down the pier.

Rivoli's Gelato

1885

I expected some resistance when I returned to Cromer to open my ice-cream parlour. Father had caused plenty of strife before running off to London. However, I didn't expect my window to shatter, a flint scattering into the corner.

I snatched my cane, going to the gaping hole. Warm gusts of salty sea winds buffeted my shawl.

"You'll not frighten me away, Lucie," I shouted. "I've got just as much right to sell penny licks, and at least I clean mine!"

My rival wasn't out there. Instead it was a girl, flushed with shame as she made to creep down the dunes.

"Stop right there, Maisie Dawes. Does your mother know you're here?"

Lucie would probably congratulate the girl. Maisie's face screwed up.

"I'm sorry, Mrs Rivoli. I was only playing."

"Come now, don't weep. I'm sure you can make amends somehow." I pointed my cane towards the back. "You can start by helping with the ice-cream."

The girl nervously entered the cottage, as if she was Gretel invited into the ginger bread house. I suppose she would think a retired governess a sort of witch.

I had not gone for the usual vibrant pinks and creams for the parlour, instead keeping to flint and timber shades. It was easier to relax somewhere that felt familiar and homely, as if customers were friends stepping into my kitchen.

The ice-cream maker, a small barrel with a hand crank, sat waiting on the counter.

"I've done the chocolate, but I still need to finish the vanilla and cucumber."

"Do you do this every day?" the girl murmured, drying her face with her pinafore.

"It melts away otherwise, especially on a warm day like this."

Within the churn were two rings, the outer one packed with salt and ice. I poured into the centre boiled sugar, eggs and milk flavoured with vanilla bean.

"Keep it going now."

Maisie puffed her cheeks as she jerkily turned the crank with all her might. I beat in a mixing bowl brandy cream, custard and lemon juice with mashed cucumbers.

Thanks to the salt making the ice even colder, the vanilla ice-cream thickened into peaks. Maisie went on tiptoe, watching the process avidly. She scraped at the mixture with a spatula, creamy waves smoothing out.

She looked as I used to when I crept from bed well before sunrise to watch Father make hokey pokey.

Once it was done, Maisie scooped out the pale globes frosted with glistening ice. I quickly made the cucumber ice-cream, shaking in drops of food dye to turn it more vivid.

Maisie sat at one of the tables, swinging her legs. Her eyes darted around.

"There's one thing left," I said. "Then you can go."

I brought out a bowl, doling out a small portion. Maisie hesitantly tried the vanilla.

Her freckles crinkled as she smiled. The next spoonful was much bigger.

"I'll take that as a success."

Imagine, me giving ice-cream to Lucie Dawes' daughter!

It wasn't as if we were in direct competition. There were plenty of opportunities.

I had the best view, though. The sights outside my place were of crashing, crystalline waves crowned with white froth and seaweed caped sands. I'd managed to get cheap a rundown cottage on the edges of the sand cliffs, abandoned by a fisherman for somewhere further inland.

After Maisie had eaten, I sent the girl on her way. Then the shop sign was turned to open.

I glanced at the broken window. There was little I could do. For now, I swept away the glass and hung my shawl to cover the hole.

Out of the bad luck I'd had, hopefully this would be the worst of it.

****

Some of the locals visited the parlour. They could have bought something, rather than being so obvious in their nosiness.

They'd wanted to assess the stranger. So far, none recognised the girl whose father had run out on her to get away from his debts.

My past students would never believe I grew up here. Governesses might be sneered at, but they had at least fallen from respectable society.

It had given me an odd sort of glee to have families not even suspect I was only a common country lass, who'd made her way up through hard work and studying. They ignored a girl of my station in any other situation.

I did have some claim to Italy. My grandfather had left Tuscany after falling in love with my grandmother over here.

Father used to go out with him at wintertime to break ice from the marshes. They made ice-cream when the days were warmer, selling it from a cart I pushed for them.

The other children used to flock. I was everyone's friend. Of course, it wasn't hokey pokey but ecco un poco!

As I got older, I realised an ice-cream man's wage could not support us. Grandfather passed and Mother could not sway Father from leaving the card tables.

This place was going to be reputable. I wouldn't have to worry. Everyone loved ice-cream.

The shop bell jangled and I grimaced. The wherryman bringing my daily supply of ice came in, heaving a sack over his shoulder. Marsh mud still clung to his boots, going all over my floor.

"You're late," I remarked as I came over, avoiding the spots of muck.

"You can't urge a wherry into galloping like a horse," he said, chuckling. I knew that laugh.

He hitched his cap out of his face, glancing at me with puckered grey eyes. They widened.

"It's not Agatha, is it?" He gave me a familiar lopsided grin. "Only you would be stubborn enough to live this close to the sea."

He'd known in an instant. Beneath my powder I flushed.

"Jeb, I'm guessing?"

Out of everyone, it had to be him. Before I could say anything more, he strode over and lifted the gently billowing shawl.

"You've not been causing trouble again, Aggie?"

"Don't call me that," I snapped. "It's Francesca Rivoli now. And don't tromp about like you did as a boy. I'm... I'm respectable now."

Jeb's gaze flicked over my stiffly starched dress, the dull ochre gloves I wore. The light in his eyes made it seem he still saw the ragged skirted girl he used to go paddling in rockpools with.

"You've really done well for yourself. Your grandfather would be proud."

"I've got to make this place a success first."

He jerked his thumb at the window. "Seeing as we're old friends, I can fix this for you. No charge."

It didn't take long for Jeb to bring his tools. I went outside to peer down the path in case customers appeared. Almost as if I needed a warning so I could ferry him into the back if a group of ladies arrived.

I looked at Jeb, who was cursing as the hammer caught his thumb. His moleskin jacket was blotchy in places from being bleached by the sun. Sleeves rolled up to show the greying hairs on his arms and the scars from his boat work.

Summer was well underway. Like molten gold, daylight rippled over the waves. Shadows of distant swimmers bobbed, some holding on to their bonnets.

Lapped at by seafoam were the bathing machines, ready for the women to run back in. A maid sat by one of the wheels, fanning herself.

Little girls in lace dresses caught up their petticoats, wading tentatively. One girl toppled over when a boy knocked into her, wildly waving a crab pinching his hand.

Further along the beach, a group of holidaymakers plodded along on the backs of donkeys. A young woman pointed towards Rivoli's Gelato. I tensed, thinking, finally some customers.

The boy and his crab still flailed about. He barrelled through the riders, startling the donkeys into a panicked trot in the other direction.

****

Last night, rain had been beating against my windows, the waves crashing booms and the wind seething. I'd lain there, wondering if the slight rocking, groaning sensation was my cottage or a dream.

By morning, you wouldn't think there'd been a storm. The day shone in, hot and uncomfortable.

I draped my shawl over a chair. I did not go any further. Even though I was no longer a governess, I stuck to the sombre, heavy layers of my uniform.

I recalled what Jeb had said and tugged at my collar, irritated. What did he know? All he remembered was some dirty footed girl. The truth was we were nothing more than strangers.

Dabbing at my face with my handkerchief, I scrutinised the rows of ice-cream on the counter: cucumber, a delicate pastel green, glistened like wet grass; chocolate shavings oozed from the pale mint; the caramel sauce in another gleamed.

I'd been optimistic and made too much. Come noon, most of it would have melted away. What a waste.

I heard the shrieking of children at play, sounding no different than gulls cawing. I'd caught a few peering in curiously, but at the mutters of disapproval from my customers I had to shoo them away.

I sold nothing like the hokey pokey my grandfather used to make. I had a business to run. This was my investment. Everything I had to put up with, from my years of serving and being ignored, had been devoted to this place.

Putting on my bonnet, I walked until I found the children playing in the beach gap.

"There's an offer at the shop. All the ice-cream you can eat for a penny."

And they rushed over like beach combers escaping the hightide.

They kept on knocking into the tables as they raced one another for a seat. Ice-cream dripped and hit the floor. They were louder than my most unruly charges, yet it did not bother me as much as I thought it would.

****

Maisie didn't need to come in again. However, the girl did return, eager to make new flavours.

My bad luck continued. At least she was witness to this strangeness, so I couldn't think I was going mad.

The advertisements I sent to the papers were either lost or directed customers to the other side of town. Even though I labelled everything, somehow extra sugar got into the maker rather than salt, meaning the ice-cream wouldn't set.

Today, I was more hopeful. A walking tour had stopped off at the parlour, discussing whether to go as far as Sheringham.

These ladies sat over bowls of jasmine ice-cream moulded into seashells. Daintily, they prodded at their treats. Parasols were tucked underneath chairs. Their delicate pastel jackets and lace collars made it seem as if they were separate from the heat outside.

Only one slightly fanning herself with her hand betrayed she was affected. As pretty as my ice-creams, but when summer came they started to melt.

A scrabbling, squawking sound came from the unused chimney. Spoons paused midway as all looked at the tiny puffs of soot falling.

The ladies sprang away as a too inquisitive seagull burst in. It soared above them, frustratedly squawking at finding ceiling instead of sky.

The ladies ran off, shrieking, and without paying. It took me and Maisie an hour to finally catch the creature and free it outside.

I sank down in a chair. Maisie was busy not letting the abandoned ice-cream go to waste.

"Don't be sad, Mrs Rivoli. We'll have some good luck soon."

"It seems as if someone doesn't want us to succeed. Perhaps having something new to brighten the place might do some good."

I brought out Agnes Marshall's *The Book of Ices*, flicking through. The flavours seemed too obvious; we needed something exciting.

"What is your mother doing, Maisie?" I asked.

The girl shook her head, slapping a hand over her mouth. "I'm not allowed to tell," she answered, muffled.

"I'm sure you tell her everything I do."

"Well, you never got me to promise not to."

The bell rang, then crashed to the ground. Jeb came in with my ice, stooping to pick up the bell. Another thing for him to fix.

"I heard what you did for the children," he said. "That was a nice thing to do."

"It would have gone to waste," I told him stiffly. "Maisie, go and put the book away."

"Yes, Mrs Rivoli."

The girl actually bobbed a curtsey. I forced down my smile, turning back to Jeb. He quirked his eyebrow.

"Mrs? I didn't realise you were married."

"I'm not." I put on my gloves and packed away the ice. "It's what they start calling you when you get older."

I tore the bag open harsher than I intended. When had they started referring to me as Mrs? It was at some point during my forties, as if I'd been consigned somewhere cold and distant.

"Good."

I stared at him, hard, and he waved his hand.

"It's good you're as free as you used to be. I was curious, as I'd seen no lover lurking about."

"I've never encountered such excitement." I smiled, though my eyes were still narrowed. I caught hold of his wrist. "Look how sore your skin is! Don't you bother taking proper care of yourself?"

"There's no point. I'm always on the water, pulling out reeds, breaking ice or catching a slippery eel."

"It's a wonder your fingers aren't webbed."

He grinned. "Was that a joke?"

I found up my pot of hand cream. For some reason, I began rubbing it in the back of his hand. At least he didn't tease me as he usually did. Instead he had a strange expression. The closest I could name it was fondness.

"It gets quite cold making the ice-cream," I found myself explaining, "and my hands kept cracking."

It was soon over. He put back on his cap.

"Thank you, Aggie. Why don't you come and walk the jetty with me later today?"

Had he planned to ask me from the beginning? I noticed he wore a much smarter coat than usual, and his boots had been cleaned.

"I'd like that. Don't be late, though. I hate to be kept waiting."

Once, as a girl, I'd told him off, saying he'd be late for his own wedding if he kept this up and no girl would have that.

****

Jeb and I walked along the narrow wooden jetty. The slight rains had dried and the wing-like arch of a rainbow left a faint imprint on the deep blue sky. We watched as crabs were hauled in by fishermen, pot traps full of snapping claws shimmering with seawater.

As we returned to the parlour, I linked my arm with his.

"It was… fun," I reluctantly admitted.

My little cottage was starting to appear. The marram grasses surrounding it were buffeted by a harsh wind. A gull crouched upon the thatch roof.

The joy I'd felt started to ebb. I couldn't help but sigh.

I'd come here with such high hopes, but I couldn't even succeed

Grandfather's dream. My dream. Whatever impish spirit was plaguing me didn't want me here.

There came an almighty groan. The bird shot off, its empty nest tumbling down.

Beneath the cottage the dunes were coming away! The grass toppled to the rocky beach, more and more breaking apart, the cottage teetering.

Jeb grabbed me when I made to move. "You can't do anything."

"It isn't that," I gasped, heart thudding in my head. "Maisie's still in there!"

Jeb let go, rushing to the door. He wrenched it open, started shouting, but the cottage slid as easily as mud going down the slope. Within moments the cottage was gone, shattering upon the sands below.

Then Maisie was walking up the gap, poppies clutched in her arms. I wasn't sobbing, I wasn't, but I choked out her name and held out my arms.

She came over, looking curiously at where the parlour had once been.

"I know you said to wait for customers," she said, "but you wanted something pretty, and then I thought about these."

"It's fine."

I took one of the flowers. The red petals hung limply, smearing sand and dirt on my glove.

My hopes were gone. Forty years of service. My pension.

****

Jeb heaved the bright flower and shell painted cart forward while Maisie rang a little cowbell.

"Gelato! Ecco un poco!" she called. "We have vanilla and raspberry – my favourite!"

"Stop your hinting," I said. "You'll get a scoop once you've earnt it."

The little imp ran into the schoolhouse, bell ringing furiously, and rushed out the other children. They swarmed around the cart, waving coins found on the road. I served up what was demanded.

Soon enough we were walking home, Maisie already dropped off at her mother's shop. Almost every carton was scraped clean.

"See you tomorrow, Missus?" Jeb said.

I might not have got up from the ground had it not been for him. Jeb had arrived outside Lucie's shop after that disastrous day, where my rival had been reluctantly allowing me to stay. There had been the cart, hurriedly made up and painted.

He was never one to give up.

"Of course. But first." I opened the smallest pot I had tucked aside, full of peach ice-cream. "I remember you always used to pester Grandfather for it, but was too late to get it before it was gone."

"Must be why I still have all my teeth," Jeb joked, taking it from me.

The first bite, his eyes shut. This was what I had always wanted to see with my customers: that first taste of joy.

"Thank you, Agatha."

Jeb clasped my hand. Then he leaned over and kissed me.

When we pulled apart, I remarked, "You're letting that melt."

I was smiling, though, as we pushed the cart to where his wherry was moored.

I might have almost lost everything, but the most important things of all were safe.

The Wherryman's Daughter

Part One

Charity spied her father from where she knelt amongst the reeds and rushes. Owen stood at the tiller of their wherry, the *Marsh Lady*.

The moon was a smooth pebble throbbing with light but, like waves slowly dragging across, night mists covered it. The painted white snout on the wherry, used to help other boats spot her in the gloom, had been covered with ropes.

Wavering, Charity dug her feet into the riverbank. Mud smeared over her skirt and legs, yet a bit of dirt was better than tipping into that dark, grasping water.

Her father could not sail the wherry alone. She should be there with him, helping guide the boat through the river bends.

He had not dared to ask for her help, though. Her father knew she would have disapproved of his reason, and demanded he give the goods back to whomever had got him into this wicked business.

At the stem of the wherry, there was the hunched figure of another man. She could not tell who he was, as his face was concealed by his downturned hat. He was too big and hulking to be her cousin Alf. Could he be the smuggler or just another one of his lackeys?

Oh, Father, she thought, gritting her teeth, *why do you do this?* Couldn't he see he was the one taking all the risk, while some unknown person reaped the profits?

Charity was tempted to stand and call for him to take the wherry home. However, she knew he was too stubborn. If only her mother were still here, then she would have been able to get him to listen.

She crept further along. Rain still glistened on the grass. Damp reeds stuck to her cheek, tugging like a child desperate for attention. Annoyed, she scraped them away, shivering as the cold crept past her shawl.

A misstep, and the squelching splash of mud seemed to echo. Her lips snapped together as she held her breath, waiting for her father to cry her name.

The brim of the stranger's hat twisted in her direction. Her pale blue eyes seemed to stand out even more as they widened. Breath spluttered out of her as her heart writhed, wanting her to run.

Do not call out, Charity prayed desperately in her head. *I am nothing but a shadow, a trick of the mind.*

Then a barley bird shot out from a bush nearby. The stranger and her father chuckled, though it was empty of humour.

Her father turned back to the tiller. They were just as nervous. The sound of the boat cleaving through the water and the groan of the oak body pierced the silence.

A bright leaf green flag at the very top of the mast fluttered and danced at the slightest of breezes. It curled around the little tin *Marsh Lady* vane: a woman with a hat of feathers and a long river weed dress.

The wind blew Charity's way and her nose wrinkled. No matter how long she worked on the wherry, she would never be fond of the whiff of tar and herring oil that the sail had been dipped in.

The *Marsh Lady* slowed. This was it. She had an idea of what her father planned. Although they were far from the fields, there would be one man sowing the crops, as men down the Copper Rose Inn said as they laughed into their tankards.

Heaving and grunting, straining his already weak back, Owen lifted up a cask of something. Brandy, most likely. There was a rope attached and she knew a stone was tied at the end.

Last week, she had curiously watched him pick stones from the path back home from church. He even had such plans on a Sunday!

The cask was pushed overboard, and it made a deafening splashing sound. He stiffened, anxiously turning his head side to side. Was he checking that the customs and excise men weren't about to leap out of the water?

After a while, he started up again. Charity quietly counted under her breath as each cask struck the water. One, two . . . thirteen!

None rose. They were weighted down and hidden until someone came to dredge up the booty and carry it down to Norwich.

The *Marsh Lady* continued on. Charity hurried home, scowling.

She had seen all she needed to prove her suspicions. Now, all she had to do was figure out how to get her father safely away from the smugglers.

****

"Have you seen anything strange these past few nights, Charity?" was the first thing she heard that morning, upon opening the front door.

Her fingers tightly clenched the door handle to try and contain the tremor in her hand.

Josiah Thiske, the local customs man, stood there with his hat in his hand. He was only five years older than her, twenty-nine, yet he had a sunken, craggy face. Sharp winds had whittled his skin from when he had hunted for smugglers along the coast.

He was smiling at her, revealing the crooked, chipped front tooth that looked like a fang. Apparently, it was caused by a Dutch smuggler who had struck him with his cosh. It gave him a hungry, wolfish look.

A shiver was scraping up Charity's back. Was she the prey? Had she been watched and followed as well, as she had done to her father?

"Strange, Mr Thiske?" Her voice quavered.

His eyes, as grey and misty as gun smoke, narrowed.

"Odd noises. People out of their beds when they should be asleep."

Charity reached for her hair, about to tug at it nervously, but managed to stop herself.

"Only the foxes yowling, although…"

"Yes?"

Was he leaning forward to hear her better or anticipating a confession?

Charity met his stare. "I thought I saw a hulking shadow bound over a hill. You don't think it could be the hound Black Shuck?"

He sneered. "I hardly think, in this day and age, we should believe in ghosts. It is another trick used by smugglers to frighten people indoors, so they can do their foul work undisturbed."

"Then perhaps it was a dream."

He accepted this, leaning away. His gaze seemed to eat up her face. Then he suddenly took her hand.

His thumb ran across the delicate flesh as he remarked, "Such soft hands! I find it difficult to believe you do tasks best suited for your cousin. Are you not unhappy working on that troublesome vessel?"

With a sharp tug, Charity freed herself just before he placed a kiss on her hand.

"Whatever suited my mother suits me. Good day, sir!"

Charity slammed shut the door. She leaned against it, hand to her face. She was never certain if his sweet words were true or if it was a snare to catch her.

"Are you well, my love?" Aunt Mariah called as she came down the stairs, tying up her dark, greying hair in preparation for the work ahead.

Charity managed a genuine smile for her. "It's only a slight headache. How many breakfasts today?"

Charity would be eternally grateful to her aunt. When her mother passed from illness last winter, Mariah had let Charity and her father room at the inn.

"Three," Mariah answered. "A young man came while you were abed."

"At that hour?"

Charity set up the chairs, not meeting her aunt's honey eyes. Mariah always seemed to know her thoughts, tempting her to tell her secrets. Charity was worried. Had the stranger seen her sneaking along the river?

"The silly boy got himself lost finding the village. He was absolutely soaked and had to be put before the fire. From what he'd said, he had fallen into several deeks!"

"Poor man! Is he not from around here?"

"London, he said, though it might have been Loddon. It was hard to tell as his teeth were chattering so much. He had a dog with him as well."

Aunt Mariah went into the kitchen. Soon enough, there came the buttery, salty smell of frying bloaters.

Charity's mind wandered. She pictured the traveller, trying to guess who might appear. All she could conjure up was a man in a top hat with smuts on his cheeks and a bulldog at his heel. City people were a rare, intriguing sight.

The next one awake was her father. She eyed him disapprovingly as he ambled over.

"Late night?"

He dismissively waved his hand and went to sit at one of the tables.

Charity sighed. What had happened to the man who had leapt out of bed, eager to explore the marshes with his wherry? Without her mother, he was fading. He was like a wherry in the centre of a lake, and the wind had departed just as the quant tumbled from his hands and splashed into the water.

The deep autumn leaf colours of his hair and bracken beard had blown away into the dull hues of winter. He wore his long brim hat, pale blue neck scarf and marsh slimed boots every day, not caring how tattered and frayed they became.

Charity resumed watching the stairs, and next came the new guest. He looked very young as his cheeks were clean shaven, although there was a scuff mark upon his face. His cap was shoved down on his head while his dark hair curled around the edges, like wild, spiralling roots creeping out of a pot.

"Hello," Charity called. "I hope a chill didn't settle in your bones?"

He flushed, and she realised that the mark on his face was a birthmark. The blemish was the shape of a poppy. It wasn't ugly, more like someone had left a kiss on his cheek.

"Is it all around the village?" he asked.

"I'm afraid we don't have much else to talk about."

"I didn't get the chance to say sorry to your mother for trailing so much water in here."

"Oh, it's fine. My aunt likes having guests. Breakfast will be out soon – that'll warm you up."

"Thank you..."

"Charity."

"I'm Tom."

He had a nice close-mouthed smile, soft and gentle. It made a girl want to lift it into a grin.

Tom sat down, near her father. When she went to them with the food, her father now sat next to him. She could not help – oh, why pretend? She was curious. She listened in as she served.

"Does the barge come by often?" Tom asked him.

Owen spluttered around his pipe, smoke pattering like rain. "A barge! You might as well call a mouse a cow! The *Marsh Lady* is far daintier than a brutish barge."

Tom stammered an apology. Grudgingly, Owen forgave him, after he had bought him another drink.

"What exactly is it you want me to do, boy?"

Charity smiled faintly. Her father did not look so worried now. No matter what, he always loved to talk about his *Marsh Lady*. Hopefully, this Tom could distract him.

"Would it be possible for me to ride with you?"

"Why? You want to try your hand at the tiller?" Owen glanced at his hands, which were small and pale. "I don't think you'll like it."

"I'm a painter. I wanted to see the rivers," Tom explained.

"We're a trading wherry, not a pleasure yacht." But Owen's lips were twisting up.

"I'll pay, of course."

"Your first time in Norfolk?" Owen asked. "And on a wherry?"

Tom nodded. "I do hope I don't fall into the water!"

Again, Charity thought to herself.

"The crew on the *Marsh Lady* are a steady hand." Owen patted him lightly on the shoulder. "You'll have not seen my mate. I'll have to warn you – you'll fall in love by the end of the journey. All the men here have."

Charity's eyes widened as she blushed. The poor young man looked so confused. It was rare that a woman helped steer a wherry, unless she was the wherryman's wife. Who was he picturing would appear?

Another man entered the inn. Charity stiffened, but relaxed when she realised it was not Josiah Thiske.

Lord Rosewood, local squire, tipped his hat to her as he leaned against his walking stick. Those watery tadpole black eyes of his were glimmering. She might not have thought him the same age as her father, as his face had a roundish, smooth look. Only his dark hair had streaks of white, like milk streaming through treacle.

Why was he here? Charity's eyes narrowed. Really, if anyone was the head of the smugglers, it would have to be someone with money and connections.

Aunt Mariah emerged from the kitchen, smiling. She straightened her apron and tucked a loose curl back under her cap.

"Keep an eye out for me, Charity. I need to speak with Lord Rosewood about a legal matter."

Charity nodded, and her aunt and the lord went into the backroom. Her father caught this as well – the scowl on his face!

Owen drained the rest of his drink, clapped Tom on the shoulder and followed. Within moments, raised voices could be heard in the other room.

Charity leaned in, listening. Aunt Mariah was speaking, but before she could hear, something scrabbled at Charity's feet. A rat, she near shrieked, yet it was too big.

A little dog crouched, wagging his tail. She could not tell what breed he was. In truth, he looked more like a rabbit the colour of sawdust. His ears stuck up and a burst of white curls erupted from his chest. His eyes were dark, like droplets of ink.

He put his paws on Charity's leg and tilted his head. She scratched the back of his ear. He made a happy grunting noise.

"Whose dog are you, anyway?"

"Bramble!"

The dog's ears stuck up even more, if that was possible. He bounded over, stopping by Tom's feet.

"What is he?" Charity asked.

"A mix. Some West Highland Terrier, I believe. Are you the

wherryman's daughter?"

"Yes. Why?"

"Is your father coming back?"

"I'm sorry. He gets distracted easily."

She could have lied, but she was tired of making up excuses. Too many and she would slip up or, as her grandmother had always warned, her tongue would fall out.

Tom's face fell. She felt slightly mean having to disappoint him.

"Is there anyone else who sails the wherry? This could be my only chance. It might rain tomorrow."

There weren't that many people to keep an eye on. Only Old Curve Joe was in the corner, but he could take an hour with a single drink.

Her family needed the money. She had never ridden the wherry without her father, yet it was his own fault he wasn't there to stop her. It would serve him right for being contrary and vanishing each night.

Charity smiled at Tom. "Welcome aboard the *Marsh Lady*, then."

****

"Can you not see he's only using you? No matter his promises, he'll not marry you," Owen argued, his boot against the backroom door so that no-one disturbed them.

It was as though history was repeating itself. His voice had been younger, yet the words were the same.

Some of Mariah's hair had come loose. She angrily blew it out of her face.

"Enough of this nonsense," she said. "You'll strain your heart for no good reason. There is nothing between Lord Rosewood and myself. It is in the past and forgotten."

"We're only talking about the inn," Augustus added. "Nothing scandalous at all."

"There's more than that going on," Owen said suspiciously, eyes narrowed. "Weren't my warnings back then enough?"

Years ago, in Mariah's youth, there had been a festival. The fairest girl would be crowned harvest queen by the squire's son. Augustus had placed a kiss upon her cheek, set the wheat crown upon her head and danced with her.

Mariah had thought it a dream, one to tuck into her heart. A cherished memory for when the drudge of her life became too much. Then Augustus came to visit, and she had learnt he too felt something kindle in the joy of that day.

Her father had noticed as well. To him, all the Rosewood men were rotten. He had whipped Owen up in a frenzy, and there'd been a fight.

Augustus had fallen. Even thinking of that night made Mariah shut her eyes in horror.

Ever since, Augustus had needed a walking stick, yet he never turned her brother and father in. He had still wanted her. He was willing to forgive.

However, Mariah was sensible. For all their sakes, it was better they remained apart. She had married someone of her own class, who her father approved of.

Yet Augustus had been her first love! Her feelings for him simmered beneath the surface, wondering what might have been.

After her husband's death, she had strived to be strong for her son Alf, to keep the Copper Rose running. It had been too much. A year ago, Augustus had found her weeping in the stable.

They had barely spoken for years, yet he had let her cry upon his shoulder. The kiss had come to them just as easily.

"Please, Owen, I do not wish to quarrel with you," Augustus urged. "Why don't I lend you some money? Mariah has told me –"

"I won't be bought by you," Owen snapped. "You leave my family be. Your meddling will only cause us strife."

Her brother had held on to his mistrust and prejudices, just as she had held on to her love. With a sharp sound, which might have been him refraining from spitting, Owen walked out.

Mariah sighed, "Oh, how I hate lying."

Augustus pulled her to him and stroked her hair. "Then stop. Tell them we're going to be married."

They were acting no better than thieves, skulking in the shadows. She had her son to think of. Would he despise her, believing she had betrayed his father's memory?

Her husband had given Mariah her sweet hearted, loyal Alf. When she looked back on her marriage, she had fond memories, but they were just memories. She herself was still alive.

Perhaps it was better to stop this, before they were found out. Mariah made to speak, to tell him this would be their final meeting. Augustus pressed a kiss to her work-worn knuckles.

"Do not fret, my harvest queen. I'm no longer a boy. I won't be bullied by your brother this time."

And all her protestations and worries fell away.

****

Although the sun had risen, mist still clung to the sky. It had turned faintly golden, like waves of wheat flying in the air.

Alf cried out, shoving his thumb in his mouth. He dropped the hammer and barely missed his foot.

As if mocking him, the fence he had been fixing rocked from the fairest of breezes. He grasped it before that too fell.

What a day! Alf roughly wiped the sweat on his forehead, pushing aside the red curls stuck there. He was covered in aches and bruises, and he had forgone breakfast to get this finished.

When he surveyed the fencing surrounding the inn, he had hoped he would feel some sense of accomplishment. Instead, all he felt was dismay.

"Why am I so useless?" Alf muttered to himself dejectedly.

He wished his father was here. He needed someone to teach him. His father's face was fading from his memories. Soon, all he would be left with was the distant sound of his laugh.

Uncle Owen had been a help. Alf was doing well on the wherry. However, he would be seventeen soon. He had to be the man he was trying to become, not the boy with a scruff of beard who was always messing up. His mother only had him to rely on.

His gut clenched with guilt. She wouldn't be happy with what he had planned.

It was for the best, though. The inn was falling apart and they weren't making enough.

Things were going to get better, Alf promised himself. He just had to be patient and keep his mouth shut.

"Alfie!"

He turned to see his cousin Charity waving wildly as she ran over. A man and dog were following her.

"Who's this?" Alf asked.

"Tom here wants to ride the wherry."

"Without your father? You sure you're strong enough?"

"It'll be fine. At least I can reach the gaff line."

His smile turned into a scowl. "All right, then, longshanks."

"Wait here," Charity told Tom. "We'll bring her to you."

****

Winds gently pushed the *Marsh Lady*. Charity helped it along with the quant, the pole pressed hard against her shoulder as she gritted her teeth and used all her strength.

Tom waited at the riverbank. She felt all the effort was worth it when he gaped in amazement.

The wherry cleaved through the mist. Its body was painted bright green. The black sail was its cape, like a bit of torn out night sky, and it fluttered in the emerging summer day.

The rivers here were particularly thin, with low bridges in the way. Charity's grandfather had made the *Marsh Lady* especially to be slim and graceful.

"Hop on!" Charity called, and Tom and Bramble clambered aboard.

Charity glanced back. She was half-afraid she might spy her father chasing after, shouting for them to stop. The other half was hoping for this, as at least it meant he had been galvanised into doing something.

Alf sat at the tiller, heaving his back against it to guide the boat. Charity stood by the winch, calling out directions. Tom leaned on the side with a sketchbook on his lap. The wherry was swift but gentle.

Bramble had shuffled on his back in a pile of rope, contentedly lounging in his sunspot. His fur had deepened into a fox-like, orange colour.

They were approaching one of the low bridges. She waited until the very last moment, then warned, “We’re lowering the mast!”

They dropped gear. The counterweight rose as the sail lowered. The pair wobbled slightly, unused to the weight of the mast without Owen. Tom quickly helped take some of the load from Charity.

The *Marsh Lady* slipped beneath the bridge. Charity ducked her head. Her hair clung to the lichen growing on the underside of the stones. Briefly, a hand of darkness closed around them. All they heard was the lap of water and their breaths.

Then they were easing out and sunlight burst into their faces. Men bent amongst the sedge, sickles gleaming as they sliced. Coots bobbed in the water, lazy and unafraid of the drifting boat.

As they lifted the sail again, Charity squinted at something glimmering on land. Someone astride a horse watched them with a spyglass. She knew the rider from the horizontal tilt of his wide brimmed hat. Her skin prickled as her smile died.

Wherever she was, Josiah Thiske always seemed to be near. He was like a shadow clinging to her heel, unable to be shook off.

****

Once they had disembarked, Alf waved the others off with a laugh. Charity was trying to take a peek at the sketches Tom was hiding.

Alf started cleaning out the cuddy, the small cabin inside the wherry where the skipper and mate slept. Uncle Owen didn’t have to know about their impromptu trip.

When he had finished, he sat on the steps and took out his letter. It had come that morning from Great Yarmouth; however, he hadn’t read it. There was no point.

As a boy, he had preferred sailing in the wherry. Reading had never interested him, and his schooling had suffered. No matter how hard he tried, he could only make sense of a few words. With Amelia's elegant, complicated handwriting, it was impossible.

He heard the familiar hoofbeat of a horse.

"Mr Thiske," he called in greeting as the customs man dismounted.

Josiah Thiske was a learned man. Alf had gone to him as he thought he'd be the least likely person to blab to the others.

They sat on the cramped cuddy bunks. Josiah broke the letter's seal as Alf jiggled his leg impatiently.

As he read the contents, Josiah asked, "Who was the stranger on the boat with you? Is the old man not fit for the job anymore?"

"Owen would rather fall in the water than let someone who isn't family sail her. Tom's a city boy come to paint the Broads."

"Charity seems fond of him."

"Tom's staying at the inn," Alf said. "She's probably keeping him sweet for Mother's sake."

"Just so long as it's only that."

"Hurry up, man," Alf urged. "What's she written?"

"Don't be impetuous."

As if trying him, Josiah slowly returned to the beginning, and began reading, "My dear Alf, I must be with you. I can wait no longer. If I do, then I fear it will be too late, and we will never meet again."

It was strange hearing sweet Amelia's words in Josiah's dull tone. Yet Alf shut his eyes and pictured her, imagining her feathery breathed voice.

She was a small woman, with pale hair, grey eyes, small pink lips always smiling and freckled cheeks that were always blushing. To even suggest he would not see her wrenched something out of his chest that he did not fully understand, and it frightened him.

Alf had been taking shipments of timber from Yarmouth to Norwich when he had spied her watching the boats, dressed far too finely in a cream dress to be there. She'd get her impractical shoes dirty.

He hadn't paid her much mind, assuming she was waiting for some high-ranking officer from one of the Navy vessels.

Then there'd been the cry of – "Look out!" – and her parasol, which had been blown by the wind, struck his head and knocked him out of the wherry. Uncle Owen had been too busy laughing to help.

Amelia had grasped his hand as he struggled up the bank, not caring how muddy and soaked she became.

After that, they had begun seeing one another. In secret, though. Amelia was the daughter of a lawyer, whereas Alf was no-one.

"Father wants me married by the end of the year," Josiah continued. "I have no choice. He has chosen the son of his business partner. I do not want him – I want you! Please, I must hear from you soon. Father suspects our meetings, that is why he is pushing this. I fear I will become a prisoner if I go against him. Send word, my love. Come and rescue me."

Alf's throat was dry. He leapt, as though he would go to her now, and his head cracked against the low roof. He clutched his forehead. *No*, he thought. He had to be calm.

"Mr Thiske, will you write my response?"

"If you agree to let me know if that Tom bothers Charity again."

"Fine! Fine!"

Hurriedly, Alf told Josiah what to write, often having to cross out and start anew when he changed his mind. His thoughts were thrashing about with half-made plans, most of which were no good.

Even though Alf had no titles or prospects, even though such a marriage would be scandalous and derided, he would marry Amelia. He would work and do whatever was necessary to ensure he could be worthy enough for her.

Once Josiah had finished, the man left him. Alf leaned over and covered his face.

At that moment, his tiny village seemed so far from the fishing town.

****

Charity was anxious throughout the rest of the day. She had made her decision and now she needed nightfall.

More people came into the inn: farm labourers wetting their whistles from sweating in the fields, merchants stopping off on their way to town, and even a walking party. She bustled back and forth with ale and steaming dumpling swimmers.

There was barely any time to speak, thankfully. She was too distracted to manage a conversation.

Slowly, dusk came. A vivid purple sky engulfed the thick undergrowth of clouds. People began to retire.

Old Joe was still hunched over a drink, possibly the same one from earlier. Oddly enough, he watched Charity, but said nothing as she ushered him out.

Tom bid her goodnight. She noticed with a smile that a furry tail peeked out from under his coat as he snuck Bramble upstairs.

Charity blew out the candles, trails of smoke tapering into the darkness. She counted, straining her ears to catch the warning creak of a step on the stairs, the coughing groan of someone awakening. All was quiet.

She put on her cloak and lit a lantern. In her pocket she had put away one of the kitchen knives, hoping it would be strong enough for thick rope.

When she turned the door handle, it let out an almighty groan of protest. Charity stilled. There was a skittering sound, but it was too light to be human.

She opened the door slowly. Cool night air crept in.

Charity steadied herself, then something yanked her. Bramble clung to the hem of her cloak.

"Let me be!" Charity hissed.

Bramble tugged harder, grumbling and growling. Each time she tried to open the door, he dragged her back. How could such a little dog be so strong?

Footsteps creaked down the stairs. Candlelight flickered.

A person's shadow fell across the wall. It was too tall to be her aunt.

Charity placed her hand over her lantern, hiding her light. She urged them to return to bed.

What if it was her father? He would guess at what she was doing, and her plan would be ruined.

The person lifted their candle, sharply illuminating their features.

The Wherryman's Daughter

Part Two

Tom Sparrow stood at the top of the stairs, gripping a dripping candle. Shadows crawled over his face, yet his dark eyes shone like pearls from the flame.

"Release her, Bramble."

Grumbling, the dog let go of Charity's cloak. She shook off some of the drool with distaste.

"What are you doing?" he asked, voice rough with sleep.

He was without his coat and his nightshirt was hastily tucked into his trousers. Charity flushed.

"I fancied going for a walk."

"Give me a moment and I'll come with you."

She laughed, hoping to send him scurrying back to bed with mockery.

"This place isn't your bustling city, sir. The only thing that is a danger to me is a will-o'-wisp."

Tom did not shift. "You're up to something." His eyes narrowed. "Tell me or I'll wake the whole inn up and we can all find out."

"Don't you dare!"

In response, he tilted his head, waiting. Charity scowled.

Why did he have to be so interfering? Her father must not find out what she planned. Yet she could not let a stranger meddle in her family's affairs.

Tom being a stranger might benefit her. He knew no-one else here. More importantly, he would not know the smugglers. Try as she might, she could not do everything alone. She took a steadying breath, knowing her decision could lead to all manner of consequences.

"My father is in a great deal of trouble," she admitted haltingly.

****

Charity and Tom sailed along in a rowboat. The oars sunk into the cold, dark water, then, as they rose, moonlight shimmered on the tumbling droplets. The creeper, a grapnel comprising of three hooks, was at their feet.

"There's one," Charity pointed out.

Bobbing in the water was a clutch of speckled tawny feathers. She knew this had not fluttered off from a duck's breast.

They came to a stop by the marker. The creeper splashed into the water, and Charity dragged it across the riverbed until it snagged upon the hidden cask. Together, they heaved it up and Charity sawed off the rope attached to the stone weighing it down.

A dragonfly fluttered over the river's surface, sending tiny ripples. Soon, there were thirteen casks squashed against them. Charity sighed as she pushed aside a strand of damp hair.

"I still don't know what I'm going to do with this."

The boat knocked against the bank, reeds bowing under the weight. They climbed out and pulled it fully onto land.

"You've got me now," Tom told her, and she could not meet his eye until the warm bubbling in her chest subsided.

"I'm tempted to pour them out into the water. Let it all float away."

However, that would be of no help at all. If all else failed, she could use the casks as leverage against the smugglers.

They used a wheelbarrow to carry the casks. It rattled much too loudly, compared to the murmurs and chitters of the insects and creatures watching them.

"We should tell someone about this," Tom said, grimacing as his boots squelched.

"It's not safe," she argued.

There was a cracking sound when she hit a rock, and she had to stop to free the wheel. Mud smeared over her skirt and hands.

"Neither is this. Men have killed for less. Your father is too heavily involved, but you could save yourself. Give evidence at the Yarmouth Custom House and –"

"And condemn my father?" She leapt up, furious. "How dare you! I would never betray my family. They're all I have. I'll not be ordered about by some stranger!"

A button plinked on her shoe. Charity blinked in surprise, forcing the anger and fear to simmer down. In her hand was the knife she had used to cut the ropes. The blade was tilted slightly and had nicked his coat.

Tom stared with wide eyes and teeth clenched. He wasn't breathing, anticipating what she would do.

Fumbling, Charity drew the knife away. He let out a great breath of relief.

"I swear I'll not speak of this," he said. His fingers went to where the button had once been. "I've been warned."

He was off then, back to the Copper Rose. Charity did not follow. She covered her face.

As usual, she had let her anger get hold of her. Think of what might have happened had she slipped! Tom had been kind enough to help, and all she had done was insult and threaten him.

"I should have apologised," she whispered to herself.

She could not worry about upsetting Tom's feelings. As much as she liked him, she barely knew him. She had to think of her family and their safety.

Charity's arms ached as she dragged the wheelbarrow through the night, jostling and jerking from the uneven terrain. The brandy sloshed as the casks shook.

All that remained of the old church ruin was its round tower. Hardly anyone ever went near enough to peer inside, only using it as a landmark while on the way to market.

At that moment, in the dark, the ruin looked like a tall man in the distance, with his shoulders hunched against the wind and the hood of his cloak pulled up. She half expected it to move, the giant traveller blowing into his hands.

When she reached the battered, rotten door, she had to slam into it to get it to open. She stashed the casks into an alcove, going back and forth, until the cold shivers along the back of her neck turned into beads of sweat. Then she pulled a frayed, damp bitten sheet over them. For now, only she knew where they were.

Shuddering, she pulled her cloak closer around herself. She paused, breath forming a hard ball of ice in the base of her throat.

An orb of light danced amongst the rushes, skipping over the water. It could – *it must be* – a lantern, but the misty glow around it made her stomach lurch. Every nerve and hair went taut, sensing something unnatural.

A twig cracked and she ran, abandoning the wheelbarrow. She did not stop until she reached the inn.

Candlelight flickered in Tom's room, but as Charity crept back inside she heard nothing from him.

****

"My Esther came in as pale as moonlight last night, and shaking like a breeze," a man murmured over his drink, flecks of foam and tobacco ash coating his beard.

Alf cocked his head, listening. There had been a strange atmosphere in the Copper Rose Inn that morning. It was as if everyone's unpleasant dreams had stayed with them into the new day.

"What happened?" the man's friend asked, chuckling. "Did the sight of you scare her?"

"Something out there did. She'd been foraging for mushrooms when she saw a light by the church. Fey and strange, and it came from somewhere other than the living realm. She thought it was her brother come to watch over her. She swore she heard him whistle *The Pretty Ploughboy*, just as he always did."

The other man spluttered, "But we all know where he went!"

"Maybe he got away, maybe he was hiding –"

"For ten years? He made a fool's mistake thinking he could get the smugglers to leave him be if he went blathering to customs, and he paid for it. Tell her if she hears that whistling again to run straight home to you, because it'll only lead her to the riverbed!"

Alf snorted, and couldn't help but say, "Was the ghost giving old Shucky a walk, then?"

The men glared at him, yellowed teeth clenched around their pipes.

"Don't you go mocking things you don't understand, boy!"

"Maybe the light will have to come and give me a scare," Alf chuckled. "Though it's probably a snipe calling for a mate."

A cat could go prowling through the fields, and the next day there would be fervid tales about a monstrous beast after the chickens. They were too easily bored here and saw everything in nothing.

Good, Alf thought, mopping up the dripping with the rest of his bread. A few tales would make things interesting and keep people in their beds.

****

Secrets were like keys tucked away in people's chests. The longer they remained hidden, the more the keys turned until they became too painful to keep in the lock.

Augustus Rosewood must have felt much the same way. Even though he had spent many years parted from his beloved Mariah, now that he had her he found it difficult to keep away. He could not resist sneaking into the backroom of the inn just to see her smile.

"You need to stop coming here," Mariah warned Augustus. "Others besides my brother will start to notice."

Augustus's smile was carefree, as though he did not care about the consequences. It frustrated Mariah somewhat. Everything always came so easily for him.

"You worry too much, my harvest maiden. It is normal for a man to stop off at his local inn for a drink, when he's spent most of the morning overseeing petty squabbles and work in the fields. It would be suspicious if I stayed away." Then there was yearning and impatience in his eyes. "None of this would matter if you told everyone. You've already accepted my proposal!"

"I know I did, but..."

"We cannot marry with no-one save God to see. You fret too much. So long as you are happy, I'm certain your family will relent, even Owen."

"You're very optimistic!"

She clutched his face, going on tiptoe. He stooped.

"A few more days," she promised. "Give me time to get the courage to speak." And, even though in the next room people were laughing and talking, she risked a kiss.

The door slammed shut. Mariah and Augustus wrenched themselves apart. She was terrified she would see her son standing there, shock and horror twisting his face.

However, it was Owen. His bushy eyebrows had risen up, hidden beneath his hat. Not for long, though. His small eyes narrowed, until they were like two pebbles.

He snarled, "So, I was right."

"Brother –"

"Don't try to make excuses, Mariah. Can't you see how bad he is for you? He's got you lying to your family, turning you against us."

Owen's weathered, reddened hands formed into fists. Augustus took a step to intervene.

Mariah moved in front of him. Her eyes flashed. Enough was enough.

"The only person causing strife is you!" she shouted. "I am tired of your sulking. I am a free woman. I can choose who I wish to marry. Yes, marry! I won't let Father's jealousy of the Rosewoods twist me from beyond the grave."

"We only wanted what was best for you," Owen argued.

"No, you wanted me to keep to my station. Enough. I let you stay here because I felt sorry for you, because I know how family should be treated – with kindness. If you cannot get over your spite to wish me good luck, then I… I'll," Mariah began to falter.

A muscle twitched in Owen's cheek. He cleared his throat.

"I'll not give him the satisfaction of seeing me thrown out. Charity and I will be gone by the morning. We won't be here when it goes wrong, and it will, and you'll not find us when you're in need."

Owen stared down at Mariah, waiting for her to give in. She did not.

No more words were wasted. He stormed out of the room in disgust.

Mariah started at the slam of the door. Her cheeks were red. She was panting. Tears shone with the anger in her eyes. Then she covered her face and sobbed. Augustus wrapped his arms around her, but she pushed him away.

"I cannot have my son hate me as well."

"So, you'll sacrifice your happiness instead?"

"I was happy before you came back into my life. Go."

She did not watch him leave.

****

"Charity, girl, sit by me a moment," Old Joe called.

Charity had been serving in the Copper Rose as usual. She set down his beer and sat next to him.

"What do you want with me?"

Joe had been in the back of the inn for most of Charity's life, and for Mariah's. His hair and beard were completely white, but eyes so black that they were like two wells dug into snowy fields.

Most people did not notice, though. Always, their eyes were drawn to the painful curve of his back.

He had been a young man when the smugglers of his time got him to lug tubs of Geneva. Every night he had done this. The weight had been too much. Like most retired tub men, his body had suffered the rigours of his nocturnal work. Charity doubted the smugglers had been kind enough to recompense him.

"I saw you that night."

She stiffened, remembering the stranger on the wherry who had hid his face.

"And?" Her voice quavered slightly as she tried to hide her panic.

"I've told no-one," Joe said, "but they already know what you've done. The smugglers want their casks back or they've promised retribution."

"I don't know anything about missing casks."

She tried swallowing, but the nausea would not go. She tucked her hands beneath the table, to hide her fidgeting.

"I'll not waste time dancing around this. Do as they want, and nothing will come of it. Be sensible, girl. They're worse than the lot I ran with. Got no proper ties around here – they don't care who they hurt."

Joe drained the dregs of his drink and left her. Even though sunlight flooded the room, she felt ever so cold.

Charity's mind warred between doing what the smugglers wanted and rebelling. How could she trust their promises? And if she obeyed them she would be complicit as well.

As she struggled to decide what to do, Charity flew through the guest rooms, tidying and making the beds. Even with everything that was going on, she still had her work to do.

She paused in Tom's room. There were papers scattered about, and a muddy pawprint on one told her exactly who the culprit was for the mess.

She had only meant to put them in a neat pile. The sketch had caught her eye by accident.

Charity was not certain when Tom had drawn her, though it must have been on the wherry. Her face was half-turned to the artist, lips parted mid-laugh.

It was an almost unfamiliar sight. When had she last truly laughed, without the dullness of worry?

Charity still had not apologised to Tom. She needed as many allies as she could get.

****

Charity had to beg Alf to take the wherry out again.

"Lover's tiff?" he joked, as they stopped off in front of the inn.

She turned back to scowl at him, then she grasped Tom's

outstretched hand and pulled him aboard the *Marsh Lady*.

Alf noticed that the pair were a bit distant, compared to last time. Besides polite talk, the laughter was gone. Charity was fiddling with her hair like she used to as a child, when she knew she was in the wrong but wasn't willing to admit it. Stubbornness ran through the family.

Yet here, with the murmuring quiet of the Broads – the lap of water and drone of midges – there was no need to clutter the atmosphere with pointless words. It was better to get to the point.

Alf strained to listen, curious as to how yesterday's friendliness could sour so quickly.

"I'm sorry about last night," Charity said. "What I did… I wouldn't have hurt you, but I have to look out for my family."

All that could be heard from Tom was the scratch of his pencils, then he said, "I understand."

"Then you…?"

Alf stared at them, waiting. Tom lifted his head, and he was smiling.

"I never really had anything against you to begin with."

Charity let out a relieved laugh. The wherry ride felt a lot more relaxed.

Alf did not have a clue what they were on about. He smiled to himself, pleased as he watched them fall into comfortable conversation, their cheeks red. His promise to Josiah tugged at his memory. Alf shrugged his shoulders, pressing his back to the tiller.

This was Charity's business and he wasn't about to interfere. Let Josiah find out for himself.

****

Charity hummed cheerfully as she returned to the Copper Rose. Everything would be fine. She wasn't alone to deal with this. Whatever she decided, she would have help.

The inn was crowded, as it always was between day and crow time. Charity took the baked herrings and beer from a grateful Mariah.

In Old Joe's usual spot now sat Josiah Thiske. The customs man raised his hand and Charity was forced to go over, arms full of jostling tankards.

"Which one is yours?"

"I didn't come for the drink," he told her.

He was watching her again, in that way which made her squirm. She remembered once, one harvest festival, he had given her a tiny brooch in the shape of a brame-berry. While they danced he had questioned her about her cousin and father, not actually saying but near enough suggesting smuggling. At first, she had thought he was sweet on her, but he was only after information. He could not be trusted.

Josiah took the drinks from her and set them down. Realising they weren't being served, the others curiously held their empty glasses to their mouths and glanced at them out of the corners of their eyes. No matter how subtle they were being, Charity's neck itched from the sensation of being watched.

Josiah stood, looming over her, and then those long legs suddenly folded to kneel. There were murmurs and whistles from their audience.

Charity's mouth was dry. She found it difficult to swallow. Her eyes ached slightly, no doubt as wide as plates.

He was pulling something from his pocket. A tiny carved wooden box. Someone started clapping. She was transfixed by the triumphant smile on Josiah's face, and it was a smile that did not give her joy.

She did not even wait for the ring to be revealed. "No."

The applause cut short. All that could be heard was the creaking of the inn's timbers. Josiah wobbled slightly, still holding the box, incomprehension screwing up his features.

His cheeks blazed red with fury. He gritted his teeth, eyes narrowed. Someone, one of the young farm lads, tried to stop his splutter of laughter.

Josiah strode out, cursing beneath his breath. Charity had angered a customs man, the worst thing she could possibly have done. She tried to swallow the ball of nerves in her throat and almost choked. They were all staring at her, anticipating more drama.

Charity grasped the tankards, but she could not meet anyone's eye or listen to their well-meaning words. She thrust the drinks back on the counter, one tipping over.

"I'm sorry, Aunt Mariah!"

And she too ended up running off. She went to the staithe where the wherry was moored.

The *Marsh Lady* needed its sign repainting, as some of the gold lettering had faded. She could at least do that without anyone bothering her.

Out of everyone, she did not want to see Tom. What if he had heard Josiah's proposal? Then she told herself not to be ridiculous. What Tom thought didn't matter at all.

She had hoped she would be alone, but Alf was knocking about in the cuddy. He must have had the same idea as her, as he held the little pot of paint, getting gold splatters all over the floor. Alf only realised she was there when she prodded him with the paintbrush he had been searching for.

Charity still had the brandy casks to deal with. She would have no luck with customs, as her only avenue was the now irate Josiah. She had to find some way to get the smugglers to leave her father be.

Her suspicions still lay with Lord Rosewood. If she wanted to have the upper hand, she had to know everything she could about the man.

"Alf," she began, sitting on the cuddy steps so he would have to step on her to get past, "do you know why the squire has been coming to the inn almost every day?"

"For the drink, why else?" Alf shrugged, disinterested.

"He keeps on sneaking off with Aunt Mariah and Father."

Alf rubbed his thumb over a carving near his head. It was almost worn away, yet no-one had dared to cover the small heart bearing the letters A and M. They both knew Lord Rosewood's first name. Alf scowled.

"No, he doesn't. You're seeing things."

"Is he a smuggler? Is he getting Auntie –"

"I don't know!" he snapped. "He's got nothing to do with my

mother."

Alf thrust the paint pot into her hands and stepped over her. She shouted after him, but he wouldn't come back.

She could not trust any of her family to be honest! Sighing, she dipped the brush and went to repaint the *Marsh Lady's* name.

****

Night had arrived. The stars shone sharply in the dark sky. Moonlight glimmered on the murky waters of the Broads.

"I've not got a clue where the casks are."

Owen's voice was no louder than the whisper of crisp leaves; desperate that no-one else inside the inn would hear him. His door was shut and the candles blown. He had finished packing and was about to go to bed when his visitor arrived.

He squinted in the darkness. The other man kept away from the window, preferring the shadows.

"Your daughter has been sneaking about, taking things that do not belong to her."

"No!" Owen hissed, eyes wide. "Charity's a good, obedient girl. She wouldn't. I swear."

But Owen knew his daughter too well. He prayed he would be believed. He needed to keep Charity safe. If she was taken from him as well, then he would be lost.

"Why don't we ask her now? Rouse her from her bed?" The malice in the man's voice made the words ragged. There was a gleam of metal from his weapon. Owen flinched.

The smuggler turned, making for the door.

"I won't let you!" Owen cried, and lunged for him.

He clung to his back, trying to drag him down. Should he shout louder? Bring everyone bursting in? His own guilt kept his mouth shut.

They struggled. Owen had spent his entire life tackling all kinds of weather and the heavy duties of wherry-life. His body might as well be a tree trunk. Yet he was weary and without hope.

His enemy thrust his elbow into his stomach. Owen spluttered, staggering and falling over his pack. He was held down. Rope bound his wrists and feet together. Owen made to call for help, but a dirty rag was thrust into his mouth.

****

Even though Mariah knew she should resist, one cajoling word from Augustus was enough to change her mind. He made her think of herself for a change. The upset her brother had caused was receding.

They had snuck away from the inn, and were now cloaked in the gloom of the church ruin. It had been their meeting place in their youth. It was a romantic notion, to wander amongst happy memories and look to the new ones they were about to make.

She noticed some of the grass had been trampled. The door was slightly open.

"I think others have made this their secret place," she said, smiling gently.

"Perhaps their luck will be swifter than ours."

Augustus stood behind her, leaning down to kiss the nape of her neck. She laughed, then covered her mouth lest someone heard them.

"I'm going to tell everyone tomorrow," she decided. "I am tired of lying, and I do not want to fight with my family. Alf will understand. And if he doesn't, well… we will come to an understanding."

"I'll stand by you all the way."

Mariah reached for the door. She looked back for another kiss.

She saw something over his shoulder. Her face twisted in horror.

"Mariah, what's wrong?"

She clutched Augustus. "The Copper Rose is on fire!"

And the pair rushed to that point in the distance, where smoke billowed and flames danced.

****

Charity had gone to bed early, fretting over what she must do. A mound had formed upon her bed, comprising of her whole body tucked in so tight that she resembled a spiral seashell.

She was dreaming. Not a pleasant dream, either. Her mind had latched upon one of Old Joe's smuggling stories. They had seemed distant, then, like a shadow of a person. Creatures that posed no real threat.

A ship was coming to shore. Charity wavered upon cliffs so dark and rearing they were like smoky imprints on the night sky. Wind and rain flicked her cheeks. Seafoam clung to her hair.

The moon peered alongside her, peeping past the misty clouds. A ship cleaved through the sands, sending shells and stones scattering. Its sail was torn and fluttering, ripped by the cannons of the revenue cutters. She could not read the ship's name, as barnacles concealed it.

Shadowy figures shambled down the gangplank, heaving underneath burdensome loads. Barrels were braced against their backs, giving them a hunched, snail-like look. Oilskin bags overflowing with tobacco hung from their necks. To the smugglers, these tub men were no better than the cattle in the fields.

They staggered their way to the carts, where great piles of seaweed dripped like ribbons drenched in ink. The goods were enwrapped in them.

Lanterns swung and crashed. Customs men rode out from the darkness, as wispy as wraiths, their eyes streaming with stars.

The smugglers raised their weapons, flintlocks spraying sparks like struck fireflies. She smelt the harsh burn of smoke as the shots cracked.

And yet, just as easily as blowing out candleflames, the figures faded. The tide came in, sweeping away all the rage, misery and spoils.

Warmth flooded over her feet. Charity stirred.

"Aunt Mariah?"

She wiped at her eyes and tried to stretch her legs. They would not move. Something pinned her down.

A rough tongue lapped at her toes and she almost shrieked. She threw up the blanket.

"Bramble!" she squeaked, laughing at the ticklish sensation of his whiskers. "How did you get in here?"

Charity once had a cat that was more like a hot stone than a creature. It was on nights such as this that she missed her and the weight that had pressed against her stomach. She reached out to scratch one of his ears, but the dog leapt down, turning a circle.

"Don't be silly. Come here," she urged him, patting the spot on the bed next to her.

Yet the dog did not leap into her arms. Whites showed in Bramble's eyes. He whined low in his throat. His claws clicked against the floor as he paced.

"What's wrong?"

Charity struggled out of bed, about to wrap her arms around herself. The room was not cold. Charity coughed into her fist, yet the tickle in her throat remained.

Still half in dreams, she could have sworn she saw a grey snake slither by. Then it broke apart and she realised, feeling sick, that it was smoke.

"Fire," she whispered, as if it might go away if she named it. Bramble barked and it broke her from her daze. "Fire!"

She thrust open the door. Flames snapped this way and that. A grimy smoke curled everywhere. She could still see the stairs at the end of the hall. Charity heaved Bramble into her arms, clutched the hem of her nightdress, lest it catch alight, and dashed for them.

One of the windows had burst. How had she slept through all of this? Half of her body was flushed with heat while the other side felt the cool night air. The piercing cold of her sweat made her shudder.

A shadow blocked her way. It wavered, completely shielded by the mask of the blaze. She knew it was person. Taller than her father, but that was all she could tell.

They held out their hand, yet they clutched the shaking, splintered bannister as if they would stop her if she tried to get past. Bramble's ears went back.

She should run into the person's arms. However, while behind her everything burned, every sense within shouted danger was before her.

Her eyes were streaming. "Move," she tried to cry, but instead spluttered.

The stranger snarled, sounding just like the flames. Their hand darted out, intending on dragging her. Smoke parted, about to reveal his face –

Bramble's head darted forward, clamping down on the soft flesh between the stranger's thumb and finger. There was a cry, and the figure fell back and vanished into the darkening smoke before she could see who they were.

Charity hurried downstairs. The kitchen was engulfed in flames, gnashing and spitting like the jaws of some beast. She rammed herself against the front door. Wood splintered.

She fell outside and began crawling until she no longer felt heat lashing her back. Panting, she collapsed on her side, face pillowed by damp strands of grass.

Her vision blurred. All she could focus on was a small beetle scuttling a few inches from her nose.

Names were appearing in her mind, followed by an urge to find them. Bramble kept on tugging at her sleeve, yet her body would not obey her. She did not want to see.

Voices shouted, followed by the pound of feet. Water splashed as the villagers futilely tried to stop the flames.

Smoke tapered into the steadily paling night sky. The Copper Rose Inn slowly crumpled into a mound of ash and blackened memories.

The Wherryman's Daughter

Part Three

The burnt ruins of the Copper Rose Inn had begun to smoulder. Men wiped smuts from their cheeks and sweat from their foreheads as they staggered back to survey the damage.

Nothing could be salvaged. Gone were the bedrooms, the kitchen and everything else that had been there the night before.

How could all of it have been taken so easily, as if the night had grasped it in its hand and whisked it elsewhere?

A village woman knelt by Charity, who still lay upon the grass.

"Here, girl, get up," she urged. "Are you hurt?"

Charity licked her dry lips. When she tried to speak, the words rasped like kindling. She was helped up.

"No burns?" the woman asked.

"No," Charity choked into her hand. "I can barely breathe."

Bramble fussed around her, woofing gently, until she let him crawl into her arms. His ears flicked beneath her chin. Even his furry warmth could not stop her shivering.

The shock of her escape from the inferno had made her like glass. Only now was she beginning to fracture and fully understand what had happened.

"Father," she realised. Her eyes had gone near black from horror. "Aunt Mariah – Alf –"

And Tom's name whimpered in her mind, but would not pass her lips. Had she been the only survivor?

People crowded around. The other guests and Old Joe were standing there. Everyone was safe, save for the people she most needed to see.

Then Alf struggled to the front and crouched down to hold her. He was wearing his coat and cap. He hadn't even been inside.

"What happened?" he demanded. "My mother –"

"I don't know!" she sobbed dryly, harshly rubbing her face,

wondering where her tears were.

Bramble barked, tail wagging. He jumped away and the crowd parted to reveal Tom heaving Owen along. They were both singed and staggering, wheezing with every breath they managed. Tom's dark curls stuck to his grimy, sweat slicked face.

Owen sank to his knees. Even though Charity was shaking and her head swam, she rushed over to stop her father from falling.

"It wasn't natural, that fire," Tom choked. "I found him tied up in his room. We barely managed to get out."

Had Tom not saved him, Charity would have lost her father. "Thank you," she gasped. "Oh, thank you, Tom!"

He held one of her hands, chafing it between his. "Don't cry. We're all right."

All she could focus on was what could have happened.

Lord Rosewood appeared with Mariah, panting from their running. His nose curled from the irritation of the smoke.

Charity's father had been left to die. Their home had been destroyed. It was the fault of the smugglers. It must be.

And the sight of Lord Rosewood made flames leap inside her. No longer did she shake from the cold, but shuddered in fury. She bared her teeth, cradling her father in her arms, and pointed one judgemental finger.

"You did this!" she snarled. "You are behind the smugglers!"

Her throat felt scratchy like tree bark. Tears seeped down her flushed cheeks.

Disbelief screwed up the man's face. He was about to argue, but Mariah spoke first.

"Do not be ridiculous, child," she snapped. "Augustus has been with me. He would do nothing to harm this family, because he will be marrying me."

Owen groaned, eyes fluttering. Charity's arm dropped.

"What is going on?" a voice called.

Josiah Thiske pushed his way through. His coat was half-buttoned, hair coming free from his hastily tied ponytail. He glanced briefly at

Charity, but his mouth curled and he turned aside his head.

"Smugglers have burnt the inn down," one of the men cried hysterically, whipping the drama back up again.

"This is unacceptable," Tom said. "They cannot be allowed to get away with this. The land guard needs to be summoned."

Like a dog having its territory encroached upon, Josiah's lip lifted to show his jagged tooth. "You, sir, do not give orders here. I know what must be done."

The customs man looked at the dizzy, fearful and exhilarated faces of the people. All of them needed someone to blame.

He grasped Old Joe's arm, pulling. Weakly, the man struggled.

"He wasn't –" Charity tried to say, but no-one listened to her.

"We all know what you used to be," Josiah called, for everyone to hear, "and no doubt you've gone back to your old ways. We'll see who you've been answering to." And he led him away.

The arrest had brought some calm. People wandered back home, yet there were those who no longer had any beds.

Augustus Rosewood smiled grimly back at the hostility on Alf and Charity's faces.

"I'll call a doctor for Owen. I also have an empty cottage on my estate."

"We cannot pay," Charity said.

"I'm not asking you to. Soon, we'll all be family." He ignored the looks they gave him. "Come on, Alf, I'll take the other side."

Together, Augustus and Alf helped Owen to his feet and carried him away. Mariah walked alongside, fretting over her brother.

Charity looked back at Tom, who was holding Bramble and watching the wreckage.

"What about you?" she asked.

He smiled reassuringly. "I'll manage. Don't you worry. Get to bed now, before you freeze."

"I'm glad you're safe."

"So am I."

****

Most of the other guests moved on to the next village or town, with a new story to add to their travelling tales. Tom remained.

As he was a stranger, many did not want him in their home. In the end, he managed to get Josiah Thiske to allow him to bed down on his floor, as his outpost was government property and welcome to all.

Charity was glad not to be party to their interactions in there, but it meant there was little chance of seeing him. There would be no more wherry rides.

Rosewood's cottage had once belonged to the gamekeeper, who had returned to Suffolk due to a family matter. It was quite spacious, but seemed cramped compared to the inn.

Mariah and Charity were sharing a room, while Alf slept before the fire in the kitchen. He seemed not to mind. Alf had a talent to be found snoring anywhere, once even on a patch of thistles.

Owen had been confined to the other bed. The coughing had subsided into wheezes that resembled stone scraping flint.

Charity could not bear to see her father suffer, and yet she would not leave his side. If she had thought he looked wan before from his misery, she now faced worse.

Every wrinkle and weather wearied scar on his flesh had sunk in, giving him the appearance of wood half-whittled into something and then left forgotten. She brushed some of his hair aside, thinking ash still clung to him. Then she realised they were fresh grey hairs. She went back to holding his hand.

"Father," she begged, "why do you keep silent? Joe's rotting in prison, and he was only helping you. If you tell Thiske who the smugglers are, then we might be able to stop them. He might offer you a deal."

At least, Josiah might if Charity reconsidered his marriage proposal, even if such a thought made a queasy lurch leap in her throat.

Her father squinted at her flushed face and worry bitten lips with eyes that looked like two crushed blackberries. He sighed, pursed his lips tight, and found he could not meet her stare for long. His eyebrows furrowed in despair at his cowardice, yet he would not do as she wanted.

Charity sniffed, blotting at her cheeks with her sleeve. "I almost lost you because I let you get away with your night time sailing. Not anymore. I'll stop them, even if you're too much of a mule to help!"

She had to get away. Charity left the room, passing the doctor.

Always eager to show how generous he was, for if Rosewood could not earn appreciation he could certainly buy it, Augustus had called for his own personal physician to tend to the ailing wherryman.

Doctor Hughes checked Owen over, just as he had been doing these past several days. He tutted over something he heard when listening to his chest, head shaking dismissively.

Mariah stood in the doorway, watching with blotchy cheeks, a furrowed brow and her thumbnail tapping against her lower lip. Tempted to chew on it, just as she had done when they were children and Owen was awaiting their father's punishment for some minor trouble. The wherryman shifted uneasily, feeling like a horse confined to the stable.

"What's the bother, doctor?" he asked.

"Give me a moment," the man replied, too busy feeling his pulse. "A good job takes time."

He ignored Owen's grumbling and stood, leading Mariah out of the room. The door shut.

The wherryman sucked at his cheek in frustration. How dare they keep things from him! It was his body, his health, and no-one would keep him ignorant.

His irritation was loud enough to quiet the small voice of worry that it might be something he didn't want to hear.

Screwing up his face, Owen forced himself up so he could be closer to the door. He strained to listen, half-teetering over the edge of the bed.

In the other room, the doctor put away his stethoscope. He smiled reassuringly at Mariah.

"Some smoke inhalation. Rest, light foods and plenty of fresh air, and he won't have to fear giving up his wherry life for good."

"Thank –" But she could not finish. Mariah wept, futilely wiping the tears away. "Forgive me, I'm being foolish. I should be happy."

"You've had a great deal to cope with. I doubt you've had a moment to sit down and let it sink in. I could prescribe you laudanum to help you sleep."

"No, I'd rather not. Thank you, though." And she led him out.

However, all Owen had heard of their conversation was: "... fear giving up his wherry life for good" and then his sister's sobs.

He fell back upon his pillow, mouth agape. He knew what it meant – the end. A lump swelled in his throat, which he could not swallow down. Every ache in his body clamoured to be the most painful, and he fretted over which one would finish him off, unless all were conspiring together.

He could already picture the misery on his daughter's face as she stood by his grave. Charity had been through too much because of his selfishness. The last time they had all truly been happy was when his wife had been alive.

Jane had been the sensible one. He could not even be glibly cheered that he would see her again, because all he could focus on were those he would leave behind. His daughter knew how to care for herself, but she needed someone to care for. It was her way.

And Mariah would be alone. Alf would watch out for the family, yet he was a young man already testing the ropes of stability. She needed someone to rely on.

Owen pressed his fingers together, thinking over all the things he would have never considered beforehand.

****

"Mr Sparrow, what are you doing here?"

Charity could feel three pairs of eyes on her back. It would have been four pairs had her father not remained in bed with a tray of dinner.

The rest of the family had been about to sit down for theirs. Seeing as Mr Rosewood had supplied the ingredients, it was only polite to give him a seat as well, although it wasn't proper for him to be there before the marriage. Now that Mariah's relationship with him was common gossip, secret meetings were impossible, forcing them to fall back on common courting etiquette.

Charity still did not trust Lord Rosewood. She watched him with a narrowed eye. However, her aunt had placed her joy in his care, and Charity was at least willing to try and trust him for her sake.

No-one was quite certain what Alf thought. He had been quiet, and seemed to be ignoring the older man unless spoken to directly. Perhaps he was hoping it might all go away.

Tom stood on the doorstep, wearing too baggy clothes borrowed from Josiah. He peered over her shoulder.

"I'm sorry for disturbing you. I'll come later," he said.

"No," Charity said quickly. "Join us. There's enough left for one more. We still haven't thanked you properly for saving Father."

She was desperate for any excuse to see Tom. Since the fire, the thought of losing him as well had left her feeling icy inside. She still had not found a way to make that sensation thaw.

Tom sat next to Alf, opposite Charity. Bramble cantered in and sat by each person's feet in turn, head tilted expectantly and eyes wide until someone relented and threw him a scrap.

"I suppose you'll be going back to London soon," Charity said reluctantly. "I'm sorry about your drawings. Were any of them salvageable?"

"I'm afraid not. However, I won't let this stop me. I have a job to do. I can buy more materials. You'll still see me stumbling about the Broads."

"Good." She matched his smile.

Bramble moved away from licking the gravy from Alf's fingers. He sat by the door, scratching his paw against the wood. Within a few moments, someone was banging. Bramble barked, spinning in excitement, while Augustus went to answer.

"Heavens, child, you're near frozen – come in!"

He led inside a young woman wearing only a thin muslin dress and spencer jacket the colour of autumn leaves. Her hair was pale and had fallen loose, clinging to her ashen face. She clutched herself. The hem of her skirt, which was only suitable for a drawing room, stuck to her boots and was grimed with mud and water.

Alf's chair scraped back. "Amelia!"

He rushed over, quick to take her hands and bring her before the fire. He gave her the rest of what was on his plate, waiting until she had eaten and stopped shivering before he let her tell her tale.

"I've been knocking on people's doors, searching for you," Amelia whispered. "I saw the state of your home. I'm so sorry."

Mariah crossed her arms. "Alf, what have you done this time?"

"Amelia is the daughter of a lawyer," he explained. "I met her at Yarmouth. We've been engaged ever since."

Mariah opened her mouth, about to admonish him, but she realised she was in no position to talk. She was frustratingly forced to hold her tongue.

There were plenty of downsides to marrying Augustus: she couldn't always be right when it came to her son.

"I take it her father does not approve?"

"He found your letters, Alf," Amelia said. "He was furious. He sent the servants away, then began shouting that I had ruined the family name and my sisters' prospects, that no-one would have me now.

"He locked me in my room, and said when he returned he would have a more suitable husband – a much older man with some property – and I would not be able to leave the house until we were wed. The man is a brute, we all know about him from the social circles. I broke my window and climbed out. I've been walking ever since. A tinker was kind enough to take me some of the way in his caravan."

"You'll need rest, then," Mariah sighed softly, briefly wishing she had accepted the doctor's offer of laudanum.

Amelia glanced over all she had disturbed for soon, hopefully, they would be family. Her eyes fell on Tom.

Only Alf noticed her reaction, as his hand was upon her shoulder. He felt how she tensed. He was about to ask her what was wrong, when she shook her head and mouthed "later".

Mariah led her to the shared bedroom, commenting that the girl was thin enough so there would not be too much of a squeeze in the bed. The rest of them cleaned up what remained of dinner, then Augustus, Tom and Bramble left.

Alf settled down once Charity said goodnight, watching the embers flutter into nothing. He did not shut his eyes.

The bedroom door opened. Amelia emerged, wearing a borrowed nightdress. She glanced back, checking the other two women were asleep. Then she rushed into his arms.

"Are you upset I'm here?" Amelia said miserably. "I'm sorry, but I had to come."

"It's a pleasant surprise," he reassured her, stroking the hair from her face.

Her mind was on other matters. "Who was that man, the one with the mark on his face?"

"Him? That's Tom, an artist."

"No, he's not."

Knowing the others were only in the other room, Amelia whispered in Alf's ear her suspicion. His face went slack in disbelief, then horror. He clasped her hand, kissing their linked fingers.

"If this is true," he said, "then we need to leave. Can you manage another journey?" She nodded. "Good. Go to sleep. Say you don't know where I've gone if they ask where I am."

"What will you be doing?"

"Getting what I'm owed."

Alf went to a small cupboard that no-one else had bothered to investigate. He unearthed from his hiding place a lantern.

It's a strange one, Amelia thought to herself, examining the spout which seemed too long and thin to allow the flame to be visible. She knew not what he planned, and it worried her.

"Get to bed now," Alf said, kissing her forehead. "I'll be back before dawn, and then we'll be away."

He opened the door and stepped into the night, where fell a light drizzle which made the bright moon seem watery.

****

Charity waited until Amelia settled next to her again, counting every sigh and snuffle until they turned into gentle snores. Then she climbed out, changed, and quietly slipped into the night. She had edged around the shadows on the floor before the dampened fireplace, where wisps of smoke crawled, thinking Alf still lay there.

She was afraid she had left this for too long. For nights she had been agonising. Amelia's tossing and turning was a welcome relief, as it was usually her unable to rest.

Poor Joe was still being questioned by Josiah's superiors. However, she knew the customs man would be out hunting for the others involved in the smuggling.

Wherrymen were punished severely if they were caught using their vessels for carrying smuggled brandy. Josiah would still be smarting from her rejection of his marriage proposal, and he already suspected her father. With proof, he would have the right to break the wherry into pieces and burn it. She could not allow the *Marsh Lady* to suffer such a fate.

The wherry bobbed in the gentle darkness of the waters. Gold lettering glimmered in the boat's reflection. The mast had been pulled down, and the woman shaped weathervane did not fly.

She carefully freed the sail, her hands becoming sticky with traces of tar and herring oil. Then she carried out the bedding and the personal things kept in the cuddy: her father's wood carvings, her mother's bracelet, and Tom's drawing of Charity that she could not resist taking when she had found it in his room. All that she could not carry she hid a small distance away, buried in the shadows of a cow shed.

Her grandfather built this wherry as a replacement for his wrecked keel. Her mother had grown up crawling about on the deck, and given it the name *Marsh Lady* when it had just been called the boat. Then Owen had been hired to be the new ship mate, and he had married her mother and Charity was the next child to grow up on the unsteady dip and rise of wherry life.

It may look like a boat that was perhaps too old; however, to Charity it was all she had left of when they had been a true family, without strife or secrets. She could not let it burn away as well.

Charity knew where each of the bolts for the detachable slipping keel were, as it had been her job to check them every journey. Her gut churned in rebellion as she pried them out with a slurping pop. Water gushed, splattering on the hem of her skirt. Steadily the level rose, spilling across the deck, submerging the oak body.

Charity leapt out when she pulled free the third stopper, pushing her boot down on the edge to force it to sink faster. Overladen with water, the boat tipped, going nose down, until the fingers of the river grasped the *Marsh Lady* and no more could be seen above the surface.

Charity's throat burned and the corners of her eyes stung. Her teeth scraped over her bottom lip as she scrutinised the water. All that could be discerned in the slow murky lap was a shadow.

She would tell everyone that she had discovered the *Marsh Lady* missing. They would assume it was stolen and hopefully look no further. It might at least dissuade customs temporarily, as a wherryman without his boat was a useless smuggler. They would have to focus their attentions on more important members of the smuggling gang.

The pathway back to the cottage was a long, lonely trek. Hedges framed her, berry bushes picked clean by the birds. The leaves rustled from the wind and sparrows settled in their nests.

Midges swarmed before her. She tried to wave them away, but there were too many. They followed, making her blink and cough. Some caught in her hair and she had to shake them out.

Ragged clouds clotted together and the shape of the mass reminded Charity of a sail-less boat. It was the *Marsh Lady* with her mast pulled down, sailing in the sky, going who knew where.

Charity swallowed. It was a sign of something, but she did not know what. The wherry was sailing away from her, where she could not follow.

She hunched up, suddenly feeling smothered. An owl shrieked in the distance and another creature, a fox or dog, howled in response.

Each of her footsteps crunched too loudly on the dry ground. The starkness of the night told her how alone she was. Yet every sense within made her not want to draw attention, creeping just as a creature did.

Charity used to run around here as a girl. She had never been frightened before, but now she looked over her shoulder.

I hate the smugglers for making me feel this way, Charity thought, sadness and anger churning together.

She passed another snake-like bend in the river. Light brighter than the stars and moon bobbed along on the opposite side of the bank. She stopped.

The night she had seen the blazing orb near the church felt like such a long time ago. During that, she had told herself it was her mind, a reflection in the water, anything but the nonsense of ghosts. She had thought, had in fact hoped, that she would not see it again.

She wanted to run, yet her feet disobeyed. The light swung, arching and sending shadows skittering away. Cold and nerves prickled over her face. The rest of her body was painfully tense, expecting the light to leap across the watery divide and engulf her.

It dipped suddenly, crouching amongst the parting rushes. Her eyes narrowed, as she could have sworn she saw – yes, there it was – a hand scrabbling in the dirt. The light turned this way and that, hunting for something.

Charity remembered searching for the feather-markers her father had left to mark down where the brandy was. The more she watched, the finer the details in the darkness became.

She could make out a figure hunched on the bank, clutching a lantern where the light came from. Just barely the glow caught upon the person's face. She saw the pale cheek and barely-there beard.

Her mouth pursed, then opened to cry out.

****

Alf's foot sank into the muddy bank and he wavered, gripping a handful of rushes before he lost his balance. The lantern he clung to in his other hand jerked and the flame within shuttered.

His breathing was erratic, slight shivers ran across his arms while the water crawled up his legs. He had to screw up his face to hold back a sneeze from the tickle in his nose that had been bothering him the past ten minutes.

Wandering the rivers and barns in search of the missing brandy had seemed an easy enough task for the first few nights. And he had got a perverse sort of pleasure from terrifying people into thinking a ghost was haunting the village. After five nights of stumbling into deeks, having to dig through the mud to retrieve his shoe, and an unfortunate encounter with an irritated coot, the jaunty whistling had stopped.

There were few places to hide casks, surely, they had to be here! He had been hunting for a marker, a clutch of feathers just as Uncle Owen had shown him when making fishing lures. Nothing at all.

He'd gone rooting through barns and near got his head kicked by a horse whose sleep he had disturbed. Alf had even tried the church ruins, but the door had been stuck from damp and rot. When he had put his shoulder to it, a loose stone overhead had started to groan and scrape, and so he had given up. He did not want to become an actual ghost, staggering about with a lantern and bleeding head, endlessly searching.

But he might as well be one if he could not find the casks. If he didn't, then the money he was owed would not be forthcoming, and he could not take himself and Amelia away.

Although Amelia had told him her father had most likely cut all ties from her to lessen the damage of the scandal, Alf was afraid the man would be coming down with a hunting party. And, with the inn gone, his mother would need the money even more. He was not going to leave her beholden to Lord Rosewood's care.

He didn't even know who had taken the blasted things, only that somehow Owen had lost them. If he did not find them, there would be nothing for him.

His throat went tight. The inn fire had been no accident. The smuggler was impatient. It was Alf's fault, because he had been useless as usual and not done as he had been told.

He was too involved to break free, and he hated how he felt like a fly squirming on a spider's web. In frustration, he dashed his hand across the surface of the water.

"Alf, you swine!"

The voice seemed to slap him it was so loud and near. Startled, he made to get away, but the mud held on to him and he had let go of the rushes. He tipped back, arms waving, cry caught in his mouth –

His side hit the river in a motion rather like a felled tree. Water crested over him, then crashed down. It tunnelled into his mouth and he choked, thrashing, feet kicking as he tried to keep above the surface.

He worked on a wherry and yet he could not swim!

Now the furious shout had gone higher into a panicked cry for help. His coat became as heavy and grasping as knotted weeds. He could not escape.

Hands gripped his underarms and heaved him onto the other bank. A fist banged his back as he coughed out the water he had swallowed. He still clung to the lantern, which had gone out and was spitting out a gush of water as well.

Charity knelt next to him. Her arms opened, and he thought she was going to hug him. Instead, she gripped his shoulders and shook him harshly, until he thought he felt water sloshing in his head.

"You stupid, stupid boy! You could have drowned. You could get yourself arrested! Those smugglers burnt down our home, how can you work for them?"

He tried to speak, but she kept on ranting.

"Give the boy a chance to say something," Tom panted next to him.

His curls were dripping water down his face and neck. He had been the one to dive in and rescue him. "Shouting isn't going to make him want to talk."

Charity paused, only to say, "And how did you know we were here?"

"I was worried about you," Tom explained. "I saw you going out alone, so I followed to make certain no-one was going to jump out and do you harm."

Her cheeks went red, even Alf could see it in the darkness, but then her eyes went back to him and it was more likely due to her fury.

"Well?"

Alf squirmed, wishing his teeth would stop chattering and that his clothes weren't weighing him down. His wide eyes flicked from between his cousin to Tom.

"A year back, a man came to me and offered money if I was willing to go out at night and carry a few bags and barrels to a horse and cart headed for the city."

Charity groaned and whispered his name in disbelief.

"What else could I do?" he said. "You did not see the bills Mother was getting. The inn was falling apart. And I needed money if I had any hope of making myself respectable for Amelia."

"Never mind your reasons," Tom said. "They were good enough for you. Who asked you to do this?"

However, Alf turned aside. His shuddering racked his entire body.

"He threatened to harm my mother if I said a word. I've already seen the inn burnt down."

How could one man terrify so many people?

The Wherryman's Daughter

Part Four

"There's no hope for me," Owen told himself miserably.

The wherryman had put on his cap and blue neck scarf, thinking getting dressed would galvanise him into leaving his sickbed. Still, he remained bound, a pile of pillows keeping him upright.

Although his appetite had moved on to calf's foot jelly, and his cough had left him, Owen knew it was only his body fooling him. An ill-timed wind might ferry him off before he had a chance to settle his earthly ties.

His gut churned in frustration at what he planned, at having to relent. Yet all that mattered was his sister was cared for and happy.

Then why did he want to spit?

The door opened and Mariah peered in. He had not told her he had overheard her conversation with the doctor, preferring not to upset her.

While he admired the brave front she had put up for his sake, he was a little disconcerted at how cheerful she was. He had hoped for at least some grief.

Owen beckoned her inside. As she entered, Augustus followed.

"What's this about now?" the other man asked.

Infuriatingly, Augustus did not return Owen's glare, instead smiling genially at him. No doubt Mariah had told him everything, and it galled him to have the man's pity. Owen clenched his teeth and told himself, yet again, this was for the best.

"Alf and Charity –" Mariah said, but Owen held up his hand.

"I'll get to them in a moment. I wanted to tell you that I have come to a decision," he announced as grandly as he could, swaddled in blankets with a red nose and watering eyes.

"Oh?"

"I might have been too… rash," he conceded, "in my opinion of you and Rosewood. You are both free and in love." The words were now not coming to him so easily. "It would be wrong of me to stand in the way of this marriage. So, I give you permission."

Instead of joy, Mariah's features went tight. "I was never asking for your permission. What's brought this on?"

"I know how badly the fire did me in. I won't be here forever, and I'd rather know you were safe and happy. All I ask is that you look out for Charity."

Mariah and Augustus shared a look. The squire was about to speak, but she shook her head.

"Of course, brother. Charity will always have a home with me."

Owen tugged at a strand of wool from the quilt. "I'm glad for that." They waited, and then he was babbling, "You're not one for being patient, Mariah. I'm sure you're both desperate to be married. Before I fall apart, call the priest to wed you... I'd be honoured to give you away."

Even if it was to Rosewood, he thought darkly, but again repeated the mantra: so long as she was happy.

Mariah pressed her knuckles to her lips. Owen thought that finally she might weep for her poor brother.

"You promise?" she asked.

"I do."

A snort came out. A smile appeared.

"You always were such a dramatic boy. Do you remember when you had a cold, and you told us you'd be whisked off by the end of the night?"

Owen spluttered, "Do not joke so when –"

"The doctor told me you were hale. Nothing is coming for you, not until all your hair is white and your teeth are gone!" She laughed, bending over to kiss his whiskery cheek. "But I'm glad you changed your mind."

Owen groaned. He might as well be dying! He'd been tricked by his own doubts.

Yet he would not break his promise. He smiled, knowing Mariah would have her own way whatever he did. At least she had forgiven him.

****

Charity, Tom and Alf returned to the cottage, dripping the entire way. They passed Mariah and Augustus leaving.

When Charity asked them what they were doing, she quickly stumbled on the words, hoping to distract her aunt from what they had been up to. The couple shared a smile.

"We need to speak with the priest." Then Mariah noticed the state of their clothes, face screwing up in confusion.

"Charity and Alf were showing me a fen-nightingale, and we took a tumble," Tom said.

"Then hurry inside and get yourself by the fire. Lots of tea as well. Owen has gone back to sleep, so don't disturb him."

Alf found a change of clothes for himself and Tom, then slunk off to speak with Amelia in private. Luckily for Charity only her hair had got wet. She toed off her boots, legs stretching in relief as she sat before the fire.

"Thank you for saving my cousin."

She shut her eyes, faintly heard the slop of falling clothes. Propriety meant this should not be happening, but with the wind hissing outside she was not cruel enough to throw Tom out. They were all too worn out to care about decency.

****

In the other room, Alf roused Amelia. She gaped at him.

"You're soaking wet!"

"It's all gone wrong," Alf said. "There's no money. All that lying and stealing for nothing. I've failed everyone."

"Do not start that. I never cared about the riches you promised in your letters."

"I cannot even write!" he admitted. "I thought I learnt more on the rivers, but now I'll never be respectable."

"Just stay by my side, that is all I need." And Amelia tugged at his sopping necktie to pull him down for a kiss. "I love you, not whether you can get a job as a clerk."

He wrapped her in his arms, ignoring her squeak when she realised she was getting wet as well.

"But that father of yours…"

"We'll go to the next village and get married before he can catch us. Then there's nothing Father can do."

Alf opened the bedroom window. Cool air blew in and he shivered. He climbed out and helped Amelia. Hand in hand, they ran.

By daybreak, they would be man and wife.

****

"What was Alf doing out there?"

Charity looked over her shoulder. Tom was doing up the buttons of the shirt. Shining rivulets ran over his shadowed face.

"Come here." She picked up a towel and rubbed his hair gently once he sat beside her. "My entire family seems to like getting themselves in trouble. Alf was pretending to be a spook."

"To frighten people away? Is everyone in this village involved in smuggling?"

"I guess so." She sighed. "I don't know what to do. I'm afraid that whatever choice I make, my family will pay."

She paused, peering up at his face. His hair stuck close to his forehead, eyes half-narrowed from the water that had seeped into them. His hands went over hers, their fingers intertwined.

Charity only had to tilt her head. Their noses brushed together, then their lips met. He even tasted of the frigid river water but, slowly, her warmth consumed them both.

"Charity," Tom murmured. "You do not have to worry. We'll sort this together."

She made to kiss him again, but stopped. There was a knot in the pit of her throat.

He had not spoken in that posh London accent she liked, because it made her imagine someplace more exotic than her little village. It had been the same accent as hers: a Norfolk man.

What else was he lying about?

She pulled back. Lightly, he clung to her arms to stop her from running.

She saw the jut of his Adam's apple as he swallowed, and knew nothing he said could make her pretend she had not heard him.

"I did not lie about my name," he said, as though that would make everything better. "I was sent here."

"By who?"

His wide eyes stared into hers, urging. Her eyes narrowed.

"Who sent you?" she demanded.

"The Yarmouth Custom House." He gritted his teeth at her gasp. "They thought if I came under a pretence –"

"Under a lie!"

"– then the villagers might be more accepting. Not even Thiske knows."

And she had told Tom everything. Tonight, when he had followed her, was it to see where she had hidden the contraband? He must know she had sunk the wherry to keep it out of customs' clutches.

"You're a customs officer like Josiah."

She still felt his kiss upon her lips. Roughly, she wiped her mouth.

"I swear –"

Charity would not listen to anymore lies. She shoved hard against his chest.

"Do not come near me again." Her head pounded from lack of air. She leapt up, thrust on her boots. "I trusted you!" Yet it was misery sharpening her voice, not anger.

Sense no longer held any meaning. Instead, she ran, leaving Tom in the cottage.

She needed to get the brandy casks. If they were gone, then nothing could link her family to the smugglers. If Tom tried to say otherwise, then she would lie and lie until her voice went.

Her shawl flapped about her shoulders. Winds tugged her loose hair, flicking it into her streaming eyes. Mud squelched beneath. She thought at first Tom followed her, she could have sworn she heard him shout her name, but it was only the groan of a tree trunk going against the wind.

Figures walked ahead of her hand in hand. She ran faster.

"Alf! I need to speak with the smugglers," Charity heaved. "I'll give them the casks back. I'll beg them to leave us be."

Alf had been using the smuggler's lantern to light his way. He gave it to her.

"Flash it five times, then he'll come find you." Alf grimaced. "You might have more luck, considering…" Yet the only thing he said was, "Take care of yourself, cousin."

She let them go, wishing them luck. It was better they were far from here. She wished she could leave as well.

By covering the lantern spout with her shawl, she managed to make the beam flash. Fives flashes danced across the water, ripping through the darkness. Charity swung around, sending the signal in several directions.

A silhouette wavered in the distance. His long coat flapped wildly, hat pushed down. He was coming for her.

Charity held the lantern close, like a child trying to clutch a star for comfort, not knowing what to expect or fear.

As the glare of the light softened, the flame oozing into the wax, the shape became clearer. Charity stiffened.

For months she had seen that tall, thin shadow out of the corner of her eye. Watching her. Making her want to look ahead and rush onwards.

The customs man. Josiah Thiske.

Her tongue felt like a stone was atop it, mouth slightly agape in horror.

"Put that down," the man snarled, hand raised to shield his eyes. Charity did so.

"You?" Then he straightened. "Who has made you do this? I thought I had finally found my smuggler, only to discover a girl playing at adventure."

Charity's lips pursed, her anger bubbled, and yet she had to be meek. Her family's safety depended on this man's mercy.

"I came upon this lantern, sir, and some brandy casks. I did not know what to do." Her voice shook. It frustrated her how weak she sounded.

Josiah's eyebrow rose, his lips quirked into what must have been a smile but it was gone quickly. "I don't do deals with liars, my girl. You've stolen from your family, haven't you?"

Charity shut her eyes, head bowed, and that was his answer.

"Take me to the brandy. I cannot promise there will be no repercussions, but it would be better to throw your lot in with me. I am still fond of you, Charity, and I do not like seeing you upset." He held out his hand. "Give me the lantern. I might be able to use it to lure my prey."

His bare fingers brushed against hers as he took the lantern, then she pointed the way and they set off. There were no others out there, only animals in the fields. Sheep huddled together and cows blearily blinked at the light.

Soon dawn would come and the village would wake. It seemed a different world at that moment, with only shadows and the rush of water, as though daylight would never come.

There was something wrong. Something she saw, yet could not understand.

Josiah should know where the church ruin was, everyone knew the landmark, yet he would not let her leave. He was keeping her in his gaze, perhaps thinking she was lying. She wanted to be with her father, to see him one last time in case they were all arrested.

"My father is an honest man, only he is led so easily by others. They would have threatened..." Then, when that elicited no sympathy, "He will not last long in prison."

"I do not care about that old fool, Charity. I have never been welcomed in this village."

"If you had a local wife, you would be... I was too rash when you proposed to me. I have never thought much about marriage before." Only her wherry and the Broads, that was where her heart lay.

Josiah laughed, and it sounded like the tumble of stones. "And now you have changed your mind!"

Of course I have, she wanted to snap, *you hold my family's life in your hands!*

"You did not truly court me. It was unexpected."

"Oh, so you wanted kindness and flowers?"

It was his hands, she realised, as she eyed them gripping the lantern's handle. They were without their gloves. Even when he had rushed from his bed on the night of the fire, he'd had at least one glove on.

His hands were pale, the fingers very long and the nails without any dirt or sign of hard work staining them. They were so lifeless that it made the vivid red mark all the clearer. She thought it was blood, but it was in fact a bite mark between his thumb and finger. Small punctures ran along the wound, and in her mind's eye she pictured Bramble's fangs.

The dog had bitten the man who had tried to grab her in the Copper Rose Inn. She had always assumed that man to be the smuggler – someone who meant her great harm.

She looked up. Josiah stared back into her uncomprehending eyes. His grip tightened, the bite mark flexing.

Charity stumbled on the uneven terrain. It was her shawl that failed her. Josiah grasped the tail of it fluttering behind and jerked her into his arms.

Her foot dug into the heel of her shoe, prising one off. It fell to be lost in the grass. However, she was unable to break free. His hand clamped over her mouth.

"I do not want to dirty my hands any further," he growled in her ear. "Hush your tongue, and you'll get out of this alive."

He saw the fear in her wide eyes, the lantern light gleaming in them. Josiah dragged her to where the church ruin was.

"Why are you doing this?" she spoke quietly, once his hand fell away.

He took her to the rotting door, which he heaved open with a strike from his boot.

"I am owed. For years I've half-froze on the coast, been beaten, shot at, despised and mistrusted by my kinsmen. And for what? The man on the field does not care where his liquor comes from, so long as it burns going down."

Inside were the brandy casks. Spiders had already begun to make their claim. Josiah tore aside the fledgling webs.

He shoved Charity inside. She fell to her hands and knees, grit digging into her palms. He grasped the uneven doorframe to block her escape.

"If you harm me," she promised, "no-one from this village will suffer you. There'll be no way to be rid of the brandy."

"And it'll all be for nothing." He was panting. "But imagine how amicable they would be if I had someone trusted singing my praises. No need for threats or bribes, then."

"Fine, I – I'll tell them how wonderful you are, only let me go!"

"But you'd be whispering in someone's ear – that boy Tom's – as soon as I looked away. There are better ways." In the shadows, his fingers curled and uncurled in a fist. "I threw the ring in the river, but the offer still stands."

"Your wife? How –"

"You would be implicated in anything I do. Your fortunes tied with mine."

After all, she would be just the same as a boat – her husband's property. Revulsion crawled through her like a hundred scuttling spiders.

"I would be a good husband, Charity," he said, voice falsely sweet, "so long as you obeyed me. With my side business, we would have a decent life. Far more comfortable than having to look after an ailing wherryman."

She remained silent. His gritted teeth showed every scar and line twisting on his face.

"One chance. I'll give you the time owed I should have in the first place." It was frightening, hearing his forced cheer, knowing it was wavering into fury. "When I return, we will see whether you'll leave this place."

And he left, blocking the door and engulfing her in darkness. She was trapped, with Josiah Thiske her only means of freedom.

Yet the shoe Charity had lost was still out there. A wet, black nose snuffled into the boot. Then something furry darted in the direction of the church.

Charity sat on her haunches, holding herself to control her shivering. She wished Alf was there or her father or aunt, even Lord Rosewood. More than anyone, she wished her mother was there.

Outside, the church ruin had always seemed stupendous, a giant turned to stone. Now within, crouched amongst the casks, the walls circling her were too narrow, like a snake tightening into a coil.

A scrabbling sound came from behind the casks. Charity heaved the brandy aside, finding a small hole and a certain someone's snout poking through.

"Bramble," Charity choked in relief, as the dog managed to get his head in.

She held out her hand and he nuzzled her knuckles, tongue flicking out to lick her scrapes.

Someone up there was listening. Her mother had always loved dogs.

Yet how could he help? Charity felt in her pockets. She still had the drawing of herself that Tom had sketched. Dirt stained her fingers, and she managed to mark out a message. She stuffed it under the dog's collar.

"Go to your master," she begged the dog, hoping he understood. "Away!"

The dog pulled himself free. She put her face to the hole, watching him disappear in the grass.

She was staking her life on a man who had lied to her. However, that kiss… No matter his lies, the kiss had felt real enough.

****

"There's no sign of your daughter, Owen. I fear the worst."

Tom had not taken off his coat, as he was heading out again. Mud coated his shoes and he picked off a rush that had caught on him.

He had been searching for Charity since she had run out of the cottage. In the mists, he thought he had caught sight of her, yet by the time he had reached the shadow there was nothing there.

The woman could not have got too far. Where was she, though? He scratched at his cheek, agitated.

She was not safe out there. He couldn't stand not knowing where she was.

He should not have lied.

Agonising over what he had done would do them no good. He had been so close to finding his quarry. He had his suspicions, yet without witnesses his superiors would not want to admit there was a problem.

The wherryman had slid down, sunken into his pillows. All trace of his burgeoning health had drained away to a chalky pallor. The flesh was as cracked and delicate as autumn leaves.

"He's got her," Owen moaned brokenly. "I should have taken her away. Warned her."

"I have summoned the land guard," Tom said, "but I cannot wait for them. You must tell me all that you have seen."

He'd roused the old man after Charity had run. With each passing hour the man became frailer. Whatever was going on in his mind was a far better interrogator than Tom could be.

Owen covered his face. "All of this was for her! I wanted her away from the water. It took her mother, and it'd take her as well. It's not an easy life. Last winter, we had work to do and the weather was bitter. My wife had been so strong before, but the cold caught upon her chest. I knew the same would happen to my girl if she kept living on the wherry."

"I do understand, sir, but it does not help your daughter. This is for her to hear. Give me a name!"

"The customs man – he caught me smuggling a few bottles of gin. Instead of reporting me, he offered me the chance of making more money."

"I tried Josiah's post, yet no-one was there," Tom said, going to the door. "He must have somewhere else he uses as a hideaway."

"Please, find her."

Claws scratched at the door. Tom let Bramble in, kneeling to see what was attached to his collar. He thought the drawing had been destroyed by the inn fire, yet the message was clear. He rubbed the dog under his chin.

"Good boy!"

****

Charity struggled to her feet. Someone was approaching.

Stone scraped her palms as she heaved up a large chunk of rubble. The door slowly dragged open. Lantern light burst into her eyes, making them weep and screw up.

"Well? What is your answer?" Josiah demanded.

Charity bared her teeth. She saw the brandy casks and she thrust down. The stone splintered apart the wood. Liquid glimmering a dark gold splashed across the floor.

"I'll never marry you!"

He lunged to stop her as she went for another one. She thrashed like an eel. Her head knocked against the lantern and it fell.

Glass smashed, the spout crumpled, and the flame within leapt free. It danced over the brandy, the wood, and kicked into a larger spark. Flames sputtered, a flutter away from her skirt. Smoke pooled around them.

"Out! Get out!" Josiah heaved.

He dragged them back, the door bursting open. They fell, scrambling amongst the grass and debris.

The dawn burned as it emerged, the darkness turning to a murky ash as bright oranges and yellows flared across the sky. Shadows of men on horses charged forward.

Cursing both Charity and himself, Josiah made to run. Wild

barking sounded. Bramble darted into sight, flinging himself at his coat and hanging on, slowing the smuggler's escape.

The land guard streamed into view, surrounding Josiah. Their swords and flintlocks were raised.

"Josiah Thiske," Tom Sparrow called, astride one of the horses, "you are hereby under arrest for arson, attempted murder, kidnapping and smuggling. You will be taken to Norwich, where you will be incarcerated at the castle to await the next assizes."

A soldier leapt down and bound Josiah's hands. Others went to put out the fire and retrieve what remained of the contraband.

Tom heaved Charity up so that she rode with him. She rested her head upon his back, so exhausted she barely heard what he said.

"I am sorry for lying to you, Charity. I swear from now on it will always be the truth."

****

The jailer of Norwich's castle upon the hill led a group of boys and girls down to the cells.

"A coin for every prisoner," he called. "We have residing in our fine establishment a horse thief, an agitator, and a customs officer who fancied a nip of the brandy he was supposed to be seizing."

He raised his light, and the crowd peered avidly into the cells. Most prisoners turned away.

Josiah Thiske bared his teeth to the jeers. He had been stripped of his uniform, forced to wear rags that itched with fleas. His hair and beard had grown unruly. To the spectators, he looked more like a feral creature than a respectable government official.

Soon those taunting him were hurried away. The cart had arrived to take him to the assizes.

It would have been better if he could pay the guard for fresh clothes and a shave. The funds he had managed to sneak in had been used to bribe the judge. He knew he would be found guilty. All he could do was ensure that the punishment would be a lesser sentence than hanging.

He was taken out of the cart and led into court, where the jury stared at him. They were of no import. His gaze was fixed upon the witnesses.

Might Charity have come? He had threatened her, yet it was understandable – if only she had been good and obeyed! He had pulled her from the fire. He could have easily abandoned her.

The young woman was not there. Instead, striding up to the stand with the aid of a cane, newly shaven and wearing a fresh neckerchief, was Owen.

The wherryman looked Josiah in the eye. No harm could come to him now. So long as he answered the judge's questions, he'd earn himself a pardon for his role.

"Well, sir," Owen began with relish, "I was an honest man scraping a living when Josiah Thiske began threatening me…"

The sentence was given: transportation. If Josiah survived the arduous journey, there might be the chance of a new life. However, he would never see England or Charity again.

****

Tom Sparrow jumped down from his horse. Bramble, who had been tucked into his coat for the journey, shot out in search of rabbits.

The customs man walked along the riverbank, watching a duck swim past. Dragonflies settled upon long dewy strands of grass, ignorant of the frogs eyeing them. An orange sun was setting, casting flames upon the water, purples streaking overhead.

He loved his hometown Yarmouth, even if he was woken at the crack of dawn by the ravenous shrieking of seagulls. Most nights he watched ships glide across the dark waters. While he had not sketched much before his undercover role, his desk was now choked with sketchbooks and pencils. Sketches full of fishermen, herring, the Custom House, and yet they seemed bland in comparison to his work here.

Tom had kept his distance from the village. He did not want to jeopardise the trial, and he was not certain of the reception he would receive. He had lied to Charity. The hurt had been sharp in her eyes, and he knew how stubborn she could be when riled.

He could not avoid her, though. He was no coward. Tom owed her an explanation.

Villagers had gathered at a spot in the Broads, surrounding two horses. Bonfires lit the darkening night, making the passed bottles of ale glisten.

He saw the flick of long dark hair, turned crimson by the firelight. Quietly, he joined Charity. She was speaking to her father. The wherryman was looking heartier, cheeks ruddy from beer and the cold. Old Joe, the man Josiah had wrongly arrested, was with them, absolved of all charges.

Mariah and Augustus Rosewood were dancing, completely lost in one another and looking younger than they were. A man stood and eyed them, hand on his hip and a young woman clinging to his arm. He seemed amused, though his eyebrows were furrowed in exasperation. Surprisingly, Tom realised it was Alf.

"I thought my cousin had chased you off," Alf chuckled. "I've only just dared come back myself. Amelia had enough of me sighing… I missed my family too much."

Alf and Amelia had matching rings, plain ones made of wood. The young woman wore a grey dress and cream shawl, and looked a stranger compared to the socialite Tom remembered staggering into the cottage. She smiled warmly at him when their eyes met.

"My father has cut me off completely. My Alf and I have been living in Hemsby, fixing nets and fishing for herring. I'm glad you weren't involved with that vile Mr Thiske."

They moved away to join in the dancing.

"I was hoping you'd come," a voice said softly.

He should have known Charity had realised he was here from the beginning. Felt the prickle of her eyes upon the back of his neck.

"Not going to run me off?" he teased.

"You were there for me when I needed help."

Comfortably, they watched the festivities. He wanted to ask her to sit, so he could sketch her again. It wasn't the right time, though.

Her fingers nudged against his. "My aunt's wedding will be soon."

"Am I invited, then?"

She ducked her head, biting down her smile. "Perhaps. You'll have to promise something… That you will dance with me."

"I'll not leave your side."

Cheers. The horses were moving, pulling at ropes that vanished into the water. The surface rippled. Then, like a bird cresting, the wherry emerged. Small waterfalls spilled from the sides, weeds tore away. Slowly, the wherry scraped onto the bank, pushing apart the rushes.

The gold lettering on the side had faded, grimed with mud. It would take time to dry, to clean completely, then the sail would be reattached and the *Marsh Lady* would sail the waters again.

Tom grinned, pleased the wherry had survived. He had only been involved briefly in this family's home and lives, yet he was not going to forget them.

And something told him he would not be so easily forgotten by the wherryman's daughter.

Wheat and farmland in the Hemsby-on-Sea area.

Discarded crab shell and seagull on a jaunt.

Coastal scene near Scratby and Herring Gull.

Winterton-on-Sea church, Holy Trinity & All Saints.

The Harvest Maiden

1861

We must give our thanks for a rich and bountiful harvest. When the fields of wheat were a vast tapestry of unwoven golden threads, which begged to be plucked up and spun, our village marched through with sickles and scythes.

Nothing would be left, no bed for the nesting field mouse or the harvest spirit. This was why we made the corn dollies with the final sheaf of wheat, so that the spirit had somewhere to replace her stolen home.

Some tales told that our harvest spirit was a woman who danced amongst the fields with a vase of rainwater, while others believed the good crop came from the sheer will of the villagers.

"Mirabel!" my cousin called.

I looked outside. Mary was picking raspberries from the bush by the garden gate, her apron held up to cradle the scarlet jewels.

I smiled. "Does the baby fancy something sweet, then?"

Mary laughed. "And brame-berries, with a dollop of cream."

Sunlight threaded through her copper curls. She wiped sweat from her forehead.

"Where's your bonnet?" I asked. "Mother always says heat brings a baby quicker. You need to hold on a bit longer, until she's home. I can barely manage a corn dolly, let alone bringing a baby into the world."

"Your brother had best hurry and get better. This baby wants to be born!"

Mary let herself in, and I could hear the larder door bang. I expected my freshly baked pie would soon be spirited away.

Now, with nothing to distract me, the corn dolly awaited.

Our harvests had been fertile and plenty for many years. The reason for that luck was because the same family made the dolly.

The Thurlow women were known for their intricate weaving. My grandmother, aunt and mother had all honoured the harvest with their own version.

It was my turn this year. The harvest would be in two days. However, the talent hadn't been passed to me.

Although the sun was bold and beckoning, I remained in the shadowed bake house of my room. With straw I had taken from the fields, I tried to plait the corn dolly I had seen my mother do.

The straw prickled against my fingers with a sharp, ticklish scratch. No matter what I did, the straw snarled into a fury of knots or unravelled in the last, frustrating second. I kept on trying. I couldn't give up.

Each place had its own style of dolly. My friend near Cambridgeshire made bells, Suffolk people had their horseshoes, while ours was the dancing woman. I would trade all my pretty ribbons for the simpler shape of the Yorkshire candlestick!

The doll had to be hollow, to let the spirit creep inside, yet that meant I needed to be gentle. I did not want to crush it by being too rough.

My hands moved faster. I worried at my lip, excited.

Had I done it right this time? Would I save the harvest?

Just as I proudly lifted up the corn dolly, it fell apart. The head rolled into the tiny vase and the arms snapped off.

I was so close! I scowled at the dolly.

"Is it because Mother's away?" I muttered, annoyed. "Well, I'm sorry if I'm not good enough, but we're stuck with one another!"

"Stop your sulking, Merry," my cousin shouted. "The Suffolk lads have come!"

My miserable, sorry for myself frown lightened. Even though I needed to practice, I couldn't resist a glimpse at Jacob.

I tucked the doll underneath my bed. I didn't want anyone to see how awful it was.

I hurried to where my cousin stood at the open kitchen door.

Our village squatted on the line dividing Norfolk and Suffolk. The animosity between our two counties was not so deeply buried in our soil.

Most of the young men had run off to the towns for work and excitement. The squire often hired labourers from further afield to help at harvest time.

They had just arrived on the horse and cart. We watched as a group of young men leapt off, laughing and mardling with one another.

They meant nothing to me. I knew who I wanted to see.

There he was! I never had trouble finding Jacob. His laughter always hooked me. The breathy, barely restrained sound was like gusts rushing through the fields and causing them to tremble.

Jacob pulled off his rabbit skin cap and flapped his flushed face. He turned and I smiled, waving. His own grin was a lazy one, as it was too hot for anything else.

Jacob's crinkled up eyes weren't one colour. The left was a dark green, as the freshly grown leaves were upon a tree, while the right was an orangey brown, when the leaves began to fade in autumn at the heralding of winter.

He winked at me, and I hoped he would stay for the festival this time, so we might share a dance.

I remembered what came before.

I could not waste time flirting. I had to go back to the quiet loneliness of my room and try to make another doll.

There would be no dancing with anyone if I failed.

****

The crows had left their nests and their feathers formed the night sky. I lay in my bed, surrounded by a horde of scattered dolls that looked more like chubby piglets.

Everywhere I looked, one of them stared back. I shut tight my eyes, forcing myself into dreams, yet they were as bad as the waking world. The dolls grew tall and monstrous, as shadows do in children's nightmares.

To get away from them, I dashed to the window, thrusting it open. Before I could clamber out the wind grasped me. I was dragged from my room as a lovelorn maid will snatch up flowers to pluck at their petals.

I flew over the village as free as the harvest spirit. The full moon glided beside me, throwing a gentle light upon the land.

No matter where I searched, I could not find the wheat fields. Someone had stolen them away.

I floated before the church, which thrummed with light and cheer. Outside, I peered within at the villagers toasting the good harvest with tankards frothing with cider. Couples danced together as someone played the fiddle. Jacob stood in the crowd, clapping along with a smile on his handsome face.

I jangled at the door and scratched at the windows, but I could not get inside. I was alone, with no love or friend. My home was gone.

Fury tore at me. I wished failure for the village who had forgotten me. Let their crops wither and their animals no longer heed them. Let this be their final harvest.

I awoke with a cry, scrabbling in the darkness. Dolls fell to the floor as I stumbled to the curtains. I ripped them away and the soft touch of sunlight warmed my cold, frightened face.

I leaned against the window, basking in the warmth as I tried to chase off my night terrors. It had only been a dream woven by my worrying. It was not real.

****

My cousin and I were making a cake for the harvest festival. I didn't know what type it was, as I was only half listening when Mary had told me.

I got my hands into the bowl, my fingers delving through the butter and rubbing it into the flour to give it a crumbly texture. I cringed and laughed at the squishy sensation, and the nightmare faded from me.

This was what life should be, baking cakes, milking the cows and wandering the fields hand in hand with a sweetheart, not trembling at a spirit that might not exist!

However, I had a faint stir of an idea of what cake we were making, as I tumbled in raisins, sultanas and sugar. If I was right, then it wasn't good news.

Once we had stirred in the cider vinegar, bicarbonate and milk, the mix went into the oven. Soon, the kitchen was consumed by the scent of baking. The smell made me breathe in as deeply as I could, already imagining the first bite of the light, fluffy pastry bursting with the sweet surprise of hidden fruits.

Old Coe John appeared at our window, his bulbous nose quivering in the grey forest of his beard.

"Vinegar cake!" he cried joyfully. "There wouldn't happen to be a slice going spare?"

"Perhaps, if you've a mind to be patient. I was hoping to make some harvest loaves too, but my hens are off lay. So, it'll just be vinegar cake," Mary complained.

"Ah, a shame that." He turned to me. "Best be ready to make the harvest spirit a good home, my dear, lest she becomes savage and all our hens forget how to lay!"

They laughed. I flushed fretfully, violently patting the flour from my arms.

Was the harvest spirit warning me? Could I bring bad luck to the entire village?

****

With worry pattering in my heart, I snuck into Mr Sykes' barn. As I shut the door, I was almost overwhelmed by the sharp, heady smell of animals.

I could not let strife still my fingers. However, a mound of straw began to pile up as I grumbled over every mistake I made.

How on earth did Mother make her dolly? She had made it seem effortless.

After another failed attempt, I sighed and threw down the half-made doll. My fingers were red and aching.

"What's the matter, Merry?" a voice suddenly asked.

I screeched and leapt up.

"Who's there? I'll box your ears if you've got ill will in mind!"

Laughter came from near the cows. I peered over to see Jacob laying there with Ness the sheepdog nestled into his side.

"What are you doing?" I asked, clambering over. I rubbed Ness' stomach and her tongue happily lolled.

"Hiding," he answered. "They're putting up the festival displays, but I think it's far too hot to be doing anything."

I shoved him lightly, calling him what his mother always did, "Lagarag!"

He smiled at me and I couldn't help but grin back. He had such an easy way about him.

"What were you up to? Hiding as well?"

"No! I'm making a corn dolly."

His eyebrows furrowed in confusion. "The harvest hasn't come yet."

"I'm practising. Mother was supposed to do it. She went to Ireland to stay with my brother, as he's ill. And as she's not going to be back until after the harvest, it's my job this year… I'm not very good at it."

"I can show you."

"Really?" I wanted to smile, but I was afraid he was teasing me.

"My sister makes them. I've watched her plenty of times."

We found some straw. When I made to start, Jacob stopped me.

"You're holding it too delicately. The harvest straw is strong. Grip it as you'd cling to a horse's neck while riding, else you'd slide off!"

My grip tightened and what I had worried about did not happen. The straw remained strong, and did not snap or crumble into nothing.

We began at the head and wove down until the straw had to fan out for the skirt. Jacob's hands were rough from hard labour, contrary to his shirking ways. His flesh was warm, as though I held my hands out to a cosy fire.

His eyes narrowed in concentration as he guided me. I forced myself to look down, in case I missed something. Then, we made the swirling arms and the doll's little vase.

We had done it! I smiled in disbelief that I now held a corn dolly fit for a harvest spirit.

I was so caught up in my joy that I leaned over and kissed Jacob on the cheek. When I pulled away, he pressed his fingers to where my lips had been.

Jacob tried to stammer something. I tilted my head in confusion. He rushed away. I laid back down and cuddled Ness, laughing.

****

On the night before the harvest, I slept deeply. No nightmares crept into my room. I clutched the doll Jacob had helped me make.

When my cousin rapped on my door, calling that the sun so I should be as well, I went to my window.

Left on the sill was a little horseshoe woven in straw, with a string of copper-roses. I picked it up, smiling softly. Jacob's horseshoe was made of seven straws, the show off!

With a start, I realised what it might be. The countryman's favour was a very special gift. Men gave it to their sweethearts as a declaration. Could I hope to believe that this was what Jacob meant?

All of us went down to the wheat fields. The muggy day made sweat prickle on our faces.

The men led the way, their scythes powerful and steady as they strode through the field, while the women followed to collect the wheat and tie it into bundles.

Old John, the sneaky fox, had dubbed himself the Lord of the Harvest. He dallied by the roadside, trying to glean a few coins from anyone passing so that the men, and most importantly him, could whet their whistles in the pub later.

I trailed behind one of the harvesters, distracted. I wasn't able to catch a glimpse of Jacob. He was lost in the golden sea.

Alongside the hiss of slicing metal, the snap of straw underfoot and the grunt of hard work, there was the click and mutter of insects. Midges nudged at me and I waved them off.

My stomach was tight with anticipation, with two different threads knotting up inside. There was the bubbling, roiling weave of excitement and then dull, dragging unease.

I told myself to unravel my worry. I would be able to make the doll again.

Birds swept overhead, like darts of night, as they checked on our progress. We were like ships cleaving through the sea. The wheat waves reared up at us, but we slashed them away.

From dawn to dusk we worked, only pausing for fourses when the sun's bite grew too harsh. Still, I did not see Jacob. Was he avoiding me?

The last sheaf of wheat was cut. They handed it to me. I sat down in the husk remains of the field and set to work.

I got a little fumble fisted at the beginning, but I thought of Jacob and his hands and my plaiting grew more certain.

Villagers crowded around. I pretended they weren't there.

The corn dolly was about the size of my forearm. Braids of golden corn fell down her head. She was a little squat, and one arm was shorter than the other, but she held when we placed her upon a pole.

The villagers peered up at her. I squirmed. It wasn't that awful, was it?

"Do you remember when the girl's mother made her first one?" one of the older women said.

A man chuckled. "The head fell off and hit the squire in the face!"

They all congratulated me on a fine corn dolly and that they were sure an even better one would be made next year. I stammered out a thank you.

With great cheer and song, the procession made their way to church, where the corn dolly would be housed until the next harvest. Children danced around the merry crowd, fingers dark and sticky with brame-berries.

I was amongst them. My feet were light with relief. All this worrying for nothing! I couldn't wait to ask Mother about her first dolly, and what the squire had done.

Someone caught my hand, pulling me away from the others.

I looked up at Jacob. "There you are!"

We had stopped. The procession continued, the music trailing into a murmur as we were left behind.

I could wait no longer. It was harvest, a day to reap what had been sown and nurtured over time. I would pluck the ripe fruit of my heart and hope its taste was not bitter.

I jiffled with the countryman's favour in my buttonhole, drawing his eye.

"Someone left me this." I glanced at Jacob under heavy lashes, trying to hide my mirth as he flushed.

"You're wearing a favour when you don't know who sent it?" he blustered. "It could be anyone!"

"I have my suspicions," I said, biting down on my smile. "It's probably Tom the blacksmith, as he helps shoe the horses."

Frustration curled his lips into a scowl. "He's got fat, stubby fingers. He'd barely manage with two, let alone seven straws."

I continued, "Or Henry or Sam. No, wait, I know. It's Old John!"

His eyes widened as it slowly dawned on him that I was teasing. With a roar of mock anger, he caught me up into his arms and spun me.

I clung on, laughing as the dusky sky and clouds swirled into a whirlpool. I begged him to stop when the dizziness grew too much.

My fingers curled into his hair, something I had long wanted to do, and I kissed him.

****

A year later, the harvest was the same as it had always been. The wheat was plenty and the weather fair.

Although my mother came home, she no longer made the corn dolly. When we reached the final sheaf of wheat, the villagers looked to me. My dolls were never perfect, but they didn't mind.

Jacob continued to come help with the harvest. And, when our wedding came along, I wore his countryman's favour pinned to my dress.

The Silver Darlings

1870

Since I was a girl, I'd followed the silver darlings. When I first heard the name, I thought they were birds. On the train journey from Scotland to Great Yarmouth, I watched the sea gallop past and searched for flapping wings sparkling like coins.

Mother had laughed. "In the water, Gellie, that is where they are."

"But won't they drown?" I asked.

"They're fish – herrings."

I had been twelve back then, with questions flooding from my mouth. Sometimes my mother would shut her eyes sadly, deeply breathing in salt air and smoke.

"Did you know," she told me, "whenever I smell this and hear the gulls cry, my heart beats too quickly?"

I did not understand. Mother had yet to tell me her story.

It had been so exciting. Normally I stayed behind with an aunt while my mother and father were gone for months. Desperately, I had wanted to follow.

Now my little one, only three, would be feeling the same. When I thought of her small, hopeful face, an ache throbbed in my chest. But this was where the work was.

Every woman in my family gutted fish. Our lives were spent following the migration of herring. In autumn, when the drifters set sail, we left our homes to gut and pack on the South Quay, watching our husbands and fathers return with heaving nets.

I finished wrapping the cloots around my fingers. Already the bandages were soaked through with strong, bitter brine.

Fish spilled from the swills, water splashing, fish tails flicking as they fell. The wind moaned and sighed against the dull sky backdrop, the air dense with threatened rain. Along the rows of women standing before the trough came distant snatches of folksong.

We reached in and grasped herring. Strands of hair pulled from my bun to flay my cheeks. I licked a sheen of salt off my lips.

With my gutting knife, I sliced the fish from throat to tail and heaved out the gills and innards. They squelched, squirting juices coating my oilskin apron that creaked stiffly each time I bent down.

I'd done this for so long I could do it with barely a thought. The girl next to me could gut thirty fish in the span of a minute.

I was twenty-nine this year, and it was my first time alone. Mother could no longer withstand the harsh rigours of the work. Now she mended nets by her hearthside. Perhaps she preferred it that way, as she no longer had to face painful memories.

She had told me the truth when I came of age, thinking I was strong enough.

My mother had been a young woman when she started coming here. A Norfolk fisherman stole her heart.

They planned to run off and marry, only for my grandfather to find out and drag her back home. He did not want her tying herself to someone so far away, a man they did not really know.

And yet it could not be forgotten, as I soon arrived.

She looked for my father each autumn, but he could not be found. A horrid thought, but it was as if he had sunk into the water and vanished. In the end, she married a childhood friend.

I loved my half-brothers, and my step-father treated us all the same, yet guiltily I'd felt there was something missing...

I knew the sound of my mother's singing, but when I tried to picture my father there was only an empty, wind-like whistle. Was there any part of me that was his? It was the wondering that frustrated me.

All I had was a name, George Seals, and a shell bracelet he had given my mother. I wore it for good luck. Time had left its cracks upon the delicate pleated creamy back.

My curiosity turned into demanding questions: Why had he not searched for my mother? *No doubt*, I thought bitterly, *he had a different family at every port.*

Then I married and had my own child. As I peered down at Holly, saw her blearily blink, fists waving, and realised how dependent she was on me, that was when I stopped looking. There were more important things. Sometimes I thought back with disappointment, like a slight cut that was barely healed.

Yet still I must follow the silver darlings.

****

No matter how much lard I applied to my hands, they still stung. I'd been gutting for hours, yet I had reached that point where sleep could do nothing.

My knitting needles and wool were stowed into the pocket of my apron. I pulled them out, and knitted while I walked along the jetty.

Seagulls swooped above, bodies black like ink prints from the glare of the sun. Spread out upon the beach were the baskets bearing the warps of herring, rows upon rows stacked atop one another, as though the sea had fallen away and left the fish behind.

Men in bowler hats stood upon boxes, voices booming like gulls as they auctioned off the fresh catch. Wives and mothers crowded around like heron intent upon stabbing their beaks for a stray fish to fall – any that escaped were left as a free supper.

"Alice!" a man laughingly shouted.

He called again, starting to become annoyed. I turned my head slightly, wondering, but the voice was too young.

Footsteps pounded, rattling the wooden planks. Before I could react, a pair of great huge hands caught me by the waist and flung me up!

"Alice, you're daydreaming again. Honestly, you'd end up walking off the pier!"

He made to chuck my chin, then stilled as I faced him. His mouth hung open slightly, thick eyebrows scrunched in confusion.

The stranger was nothing more than a boy, younger than my husband. A Norfolk man from his accent, with the same damp, salty scent that Cooper had. Face slightly furred with a wisp of beard pale as a winter sun.

"You're not..."

"I'd be greatly pleased if you unhanded me," I snapped, prodding his side with my knitting needle. He started and edged back. "Who are you?"

"Tommy Evans... But you're the spit of my Alice! You could be her mother –"

I sucked at my cheek. "I doubt I would be old enough to be that!"

"I'm sorry –"

Before he could say anything else, a woman called furiously, "Tom!"

A girl stood there, one hand upon her hip. Tucked under her arm was a pole, the speet used to hang herring for smoking. She had to be seventeen at most.

My breath caught in my throat. Now, I could understand Mr Evans' confusion.

This girl, Alice, could be the spit of me, if her face and throat weren't covered in pale freckles. Her eyes were the same green as mine, though had darkened from her narrowing of them. Hair the colour and consistency of knotted rope. We even shared the slight dimple in our chins.

I remembered all the times I stared at myself in the mirror when I'd been her age, wondering whose face stared back. I knew those features too well. A shudder went through me. How could this be?

My grandfather had told tales about doppelgängers: people who looked the same as you, and seeing them always foretold death. Watching him by the fireside, the shadows dripping from his wrinkled grooves, those stories had seemed so real.

Such tales were ridiculous. There had to be a more reasonable explanation.

We shared a face. I thought of my brothers, who all favoured Mother. I licked my lips, hopeful. It seemed just as impossible, her being my sister...

Alice grasped Evans' arm, shouting, "Did you forget you're marrying me next month? How could you do this in plain view of everyone!"

Evans tried to argue back. She did not want to hear. Her jealousy and fury had deafened her, and blinded her to me. To her, I was just a random woman.

People were noticeably staring. A flush of embarrassment settled around my throat and chest. I'd never caused much of a stir before, more used to being in a whole group of others, the Scottish fisher-girls, and part of the landscape.

"What's all this now?" a familiar voice called.

My husband, Cooper McAvoy, put his large comforting hand upon my shoulder. I leaned into the touch wearily and peered up at him.

Cooper towered over, but he was always willing to crane down his neck for a kiss. Sea life had whittled at his features, just as they did the cliffs. His dark eyes were scrunched up in humour, and they resembled two pearls about to be coaxed from the shadows of their shells, gleaming.

"Whatever the problem is," he said, "I'm sure we can get this sorted."

However, in the lull, Alice pulled away her fiancé. I shouted for her to return, but she ignored us.

Cooper kept on demanding to know what had happened. I didn't have the words to answer yet. I mollified him by promising to explain tomorrow.

What I loved about him was how he took everything in his stride. He walked me to my lodgings, then kissed me goodbye and returned to his ship.

My shared room overlooked the rows. These were thinly stretched houses packed in tight, the only way to get to them by going through the shoulder-breadth sized alleyways. I watched the people hurry through, some dragging troll-carts full of herring.

I was looking for that girl, wondering if I would ever see her again.

****

As promised, Cooper came to the gutting trough just as I started work.

Normally we weren't allowed to be distracted, but the packer was Cooper's aunt. She rolled her eyes at him when he winked at her.

"Now, I've been patient," he said cheerfully. "Most men who see another man swinging his wife about would want to know what was going on."

I flushed, spluttered, "It was nothing like that!" I saw that Aunt's gutting had noticeably slowed. "He thought I was someone else."

Quickly, I explained what had happened and what I suspected.

He rubbed the scar on his cheek, where a hook had caught him in a storm. Seeing his reaction would at least test what I might expect from Alice. Then I told myself not to be foolish. It was my father I should be looking for, not some random girl.

"You should go find that lass," he finally said. "She might have answers."

"Or none at all."

Was that why I was reluctant? This young woman was stirring my hopes again, but I did not want to feel the familiar sting of disappointment.

"You owe that boy some help as well. He's probably been apologising to her all night, if she's as stubborn as you were when we were courting. It's better than not doing anything."

"I..." But I did not finish the thought. Pain sliced across my palm. Instead of the fish, I'd cut myself. "Look what you've done, distracting me!"

He clucked his tongue in sympathy. "Best get yourself down to the dressing station."

Another woman took my place as I left the line. Cooper walked alongside. He was waiting for an answer.

"...I might go see her tonight." I couldn't help but mutter, "You're far more stubborn than me."

****

The woman who worked in the dressing station was a local who loved to gossip. In exchange for the name of the eldest of my younger brothers – who was handsome, often seen moodily surveying the tides, and quite unattached – she told me all she knew about Alice.

Alice Seals, soon to be Evans. She had recently arrived with her sweetheart, and now worked in the family smokehouse in the rows.

After my shift, when the sun had long since sunk into the sea and the moon sailed through the misty night, I went there. My hand wavered over the door. There was a candle lit upstairs, but all the other houses were dark. Someone's washing fluttered overhead so that the stars were obscured.

I knocked. Tiny footsteps padded up, then a boy's face peered in the crack of the open door.

"Who are you?"

"I'm sorry if I woke you up, but might I speak with Alice?"

"My cousin is in the smoky. I'll take you."

Alice was draped in the wispy smoke coming from the oak wood fire at her feet. Sweat peppered her face. She slowly slid the open mouths of herrings on the speet. Several rows hung overhead. Some had already turned dark and almost shrivelled, ready to be called bloaters.

I watched her, still trying to decide whether she could be my sister. The answer kept on changing.

She noticed me. Her lip curled, nose scrunching up.

"You again?"

"Did you believe your fiancé?" I began.

"I suppose I must, the amount he was begging." Her teeth ran over her lower lip. "So, we look the same, what about it?"

"My mother was once involved with a George Seals." I saw the slow lengthening of her back as she stiffened. "But her father took her away, and she gave birth to me."

"I – It can't be."

I lifted my hand, the shell bracelet dangling from my wrist.

"He gave this to my mother."

She felt her own wrist. "My mother had one like that."

"Could you tell me about your father?" I asked.

"He wasn't from Yarmouth, he lived around Happisburgh way. He met my mother here, though, and he took her to his village. It's where I grew up. I'm only here because my uncle perished in a wreck and my aunt couldn't cope with the children. I'll be back home once she's settled."

"...And are your parents waiting?"

There was something like a pebble stuck in my throat. It would not go when I swallowed.

"My mother died giving birth to me. Father was often away, so I was in the care of local women. But I always ran out of the house when I heard his singing coming up the hill..." She shoved another herring on the speet. "He was also on the ship with my uncle."

That pebble seemed to fracture, tiny shards scraping my throat. Suddenly, I could not breathe. The shadows in the smokehouse grew starker, the fishes glimmered, bulging eyes staring down at me.

I focused on Alice. Her shoulders had drawn in, head bent. I put my hand upon her arm.

"I'm sorry."

"I don't want your apologies – you're lying! My father wouldn't have kept this secret."

"He did not know about me."

"And I wish I didn't!" Her voice shook. "Leave. Now."

I left. I could breathe again, little puffs of mist snapping from my lips. I rubbed at my face with the corner of my shawl.

All this time, so close, and yet my father was dead. I would never know the sound of his singing or laughter, whether he smiled open or closed mouthed, if he was strict or indulgent. All those memories were locked away in another girl.

My eyes were wet, yet the tears had not fallen. It was a hollow sensation, rather like a bead rattling in a bottle. Not knowing the man made him feel more like a statue arising from the sea, distant and eroded. The truth was lost.

****

However, all my worries went when I heard the news.

The ships had sailed out. Those who returned had talked of storms, but the others out there would not come back until their holds heaved with herring.

Cooper's ship *Haven* had yet to dock. When work was over, I no longer wandered the jetty with my half-formed jumper. His voice was not there to waft over, teasing and flustering me.

I stood upon the pier. The inky waves gently lapped over one another beneath a sky sparsely pricked with needle point sized stars.

Always, I seemed to be cold. I had wrapped around me several of my shawls and the heaviness of them, damp from the wet air and flecks of sea water, settled upon my shoulders.

I did not turn at the sound of footsteps. Couples wandered the pier, too engrossed with one another to care what was upon the water. Moonlight fell and rose, resembling a slithering white snake.

"You're still here?"

Alice had her cream shawl wrapped around her head, and the man's coat she wore flapped about. She did not look at me, instead focused on the sea.

"My husband is out there," I stiffly told her.

We stood in silence. Somewhere distant the groan of an oak hull shifted where it was anchored in the dock.

Alice said, voice wavering, "Tommy's ship was due two days ago, but it still hasn't appeared."

Hours went by. We watched the stars fade and the moon drape itself in nets of mist. We did not speak, yet we knew the other remained.

Then, fluttering like a waving hand, was the swallowtail tied aft sail, the customary shape the Yarmouth ships had. Alice clung to the railing.

"It's him! Thank God he's back home."

"I'm glad." I smiled at her. "You'd best hurry, so you can scold and kiss him when he gets off."

Alice hopped back down, but she did not leave. Her cheeks were pinched red by the winds. The cold had got to me as well; my eyes were glistening.

"He'll be a while before he disembarks… I'll stay here."

"Do what you want." I checked myself, and said softly, "Thank you."

We turned back to the sea. After a few minutes, she took my hand. The gentle scrape of her woollen glove was comforting against my palm. I squeezed back.

When I finally saw *Haven* cresting, the dawn breaking behind the ship, Alice hugged me. Together, we ran to the docks to see Tom and Cooper wearily coming down the gangplanks.

We might or might not be sisters, yet it did not matter. She was there for me.

The Matchmaker

1817

"I've had enough of your interfering, Hazel! I'll marry who I like, rich or poor."

My bedroom door slammed as my step-sister left. Frustrated, I knocked the flung aside diary with my walking stick.

It had been for Emily's own good, even if my methods were more… underhanded than usual. Suspicious she was entangled with that sly snake Lord Blackstone, I'd rifled through her desk when she went to her riding lesson.

Of course, I'd hesitated before snatching the diary. I understood the sanctity of another woman's most private thoughts, as it was the only true thing we possessed. Desperation eroded my scruples.

Mother and her husband were away in London. They often were, leaving me to watch over Emily.

I remembered years ago, when we holidayed on the coast, Emily stamping over my footsteps in the sands while I hunted for seashells to show her. Now it seemed Emily raced ahead and I chased the kite-like flutter of her shadow, fearful she might blow away and never be found again.

She thought herself immune to what awaited women such as us, laughing if I mentioned the dreaded title of old maid. She was younger, prettier, and the one who received the most attention. She assumed I was jealous.

Perhaps I was. Hadn't I been the same as her, dreaming of some masked man asking to dance at a ball?

Such fancies had been exchanged for common sense. If a woman did not marry well, then poverty awaited.

Her father could not support us forever. Once he passed, his entailed assets would go to those who could inherit. I understood too well what happened next.

After my own father's death in a carriage accident, a distant male cousin arrived at the house and threw Mother and me out. He wouldn't even let me keep Father's pocket watch.

The threat of destitution meant women must dust the dark specks of grief from their hearts, trading them as easily as going to market. Emily and I were of age. Hunting for a husband was the only respectable employ for a lady.

I knew I would never marry. My dowry was meagre, I read too many books according to one man I quickly snubbed, and there was the complication of my leg. The carriage accident meant I had to rely on a walking stick.

If Emily was unwilling to go looking herself, then I would have to supply a suitable husband. Albeit, Duke Fallow was not my first choice. Step-father had suggested him and Mama urged me to obey. The man might care about hunting, port and sheep farming a bit too much, but he was easy on the eye.

Besides, he was a far sight better than Lord Blackstone. I'd caught him sniffing around after church, on the pretence of returning Emily's fallen gloves.

Lord Blackstone had slouched louchely as he peered down, lips twisted in a sardonic grin. He was handsome, I could not deny that.

Dark haired and browed, humorous green eyes, and a roguish scar running from the side of his temple to his chin, which he had received at Waterloo. And the way his features crinkled, he knew how he looked to impressionable young ladies.

That was the issue. He was a known gambler, wandered the marshlands well into the twilight hours – no doubt drunk – and had even come to blows with a group of farm labourers over a dairy girl.

Lord Blackstone had tried to ingratiate himself with me at first. I saw through him. He'd been bored and needed a distraction. Why else ask to dance at the harvest ball when all others avoided me?

Men such as him were not for marrying. He would claim what he liked and then abandon them. Trying to make him a suitable match would be the same as softening stone into clay.

He'd soon run off when I strode over. Emily had been tight lipped ever since, innocently remarking his questions centred upon me. I found that hardly likely!

Emily yearned for love, we all did, but there was nothing more attractive than a stable income.

I went to her room, rapping on the door. No answer. Normally she would pull me in to squabble, until we finally forgave one another.

"Emily?"

Dread pulsed in my throat. The door swung open, revealing a scene of disarray. Clothes were flung to the ground. I checked, but her mother's beloved book of prayers was missing.

I knew exactly what Emily had planned.

****

I hurried to the stables. Even though my leg ached, I heaved myself upon one of the horses.

I needed to find Emily before she left the village. I had to stop her from eloping. Only ruin awaited if she escaped with Blackstone.

The sun hovered like a bead in the thickened blue sky. I rode beyond the estate, past the stone dairy and the apple orchard gleaming red, hazy and swaying.

From the corner of my eye, a familiar steed flashed between the bushes. I urged my horse to stop before the rider.

"Where is she?" I demanded, walking stick clasped in hand.

Blackstone's horse reared, but he quickly grasped control. Instead of shock or anger, he laughed.

"What are you, a Valkyrie come to let loose her righteous rage?"

"Don't try to distract me. What have you done with my sister?"

His eyebrows lifted haughtily as he made a dismissive gesture.

"Why don't you put that down first?"

He remained calm, whereas my face burned and chest heaved. I lowered my stick.

"The girl is not with me," he answered. "I'm not disappointed to find you, though, even if it's not a happy meeting."

He might be lying, but arguing would get us nowhere. Sharply, I told him Emily was gone.

"No doubt escaping your interfering," he remarked. "Do not glower so! I believe I saw a pair of riders pass by an hour ago. I did not see the woman, but I recognised the man from your stables."

There was only one man it could be, for the others were mere boys. Julian! Emily's riding instructor. I should have realised.

This was even worse. Society would turn on her if they thought her willing to tie herself with someone below her station.

I gripped the reins, swallowing hard. I turned my horse towards the village outskirts.

"What are you doing?" Lord Blackstone called.

"Bringing my sister back."

"You can hardly – what about your leg?"

"I am not an invalid," I snapped. "And you are not my husband. Do not dare tell me what to do."

The stamp of another horse's hooves joined me.

"She'll hate you."

"She will, but I'm not about to leave her to her fate. She'll be ruined. Her father will abandon her. The gossips will tear her apart."

"And you cannot go unaccompanied." His horse drew level with mine. "I will guard you on your journey to… I suppose they'll go to Gretna Green?"

He was right. I would not be able to get far alone. So much could only be done with the guiding presence of a respectable father or husband!

If I was spotted riding off with Lord Blackstone, I too would have my reputation ruined. However, I would not abandon my step-sister.

****

We rode for Scotland. Rain sluiced the land, grasses plastered with burnt orange leaves, patchwork veins torn and suckered into one mass.

We stopped upon nightfall to rest the horses and eat. Quiet

countryside inns were the best places to hide in. There was too little family resemblance to pretend to be brother and sister; Lord Blackstone and I disguised ourselves as husband and wife.

It meant only one room was rented. He sat in a chair to smoke while I slept in the only bed. I found him dozing there upon sunrise, his scarred cheek supported by his hand.

Having company on the lonely roads felt comforting. He no longer warned me to turn back. Whatever I decided, he would assist.

"I know a soldier when they've got an order to complete," he told me. "Though I'm not surprised your sister ran off, if she realised you'd set Duke Fallow in pursuit of her!"

"There's nothing wrong with him," I argued.

I seemed to prefer arguing, rather than amicable discussions about the ton or weather. How else could you know a person's mind unless you sparked them into passion?

"He's a bore!" Daniel responded. "Idle, a gambler, only wants a pretty wife to show off. Never mind the slew of mistresses. Your sister would have been miserable."

"Slew of what?" I speared some ham sharply on my fork. "You're only comparing the Duke to your own ways."

"What's this? I have no entanglements."

"The young lady you had your nose broken over at the *George's Dragon*, sir."

"Oh, that! Why, I don't even know the girl's name." He laughed even harder while I bristled. "Some men too in their cups were harassing her. They did not take kindly to me telling them to leave her be. Is this the gossip that has so blackened my name? I yearn to not be a bachelor any longer, but the women fly off. I guess it's the scar."

And he stared into my eyes meaningfully. I flushed. Just as I hated people making assumptions about my leg, I had been just as biased.

"I suppose you hear all sorts about soldiers and their conquests," he went on. "I have spun many a sweet word for a lady, but since Waterloo I've had my priorities sorted. I'd prefer someone spirited."

He went to get more ale. I focused upon the golden glow of the firelight in the grate.

What were we doing here? I had a mission. Once I dragged Emily home, I would not have to associate with Daniel any longer.

Somehow, during this journey he had become Daniel rather than Lord Blackstone. It would feel quite strange upon my tongue to revert to his title again.

****

In England, a lady under the age of twenty-one could not marry without the permission of her guardian. On Scottish soil, you could be married wherever you liked and by anyone other than a priest.

Blacksmiths were often favoured, and so we rode down the village path to the smithy. There was no sign of the anvil priest.

Darkness fell, the thatch cottages slowly disappearing in the mists as their candles went out. Cattle were led to their beds. A lone sheepdog ran across a field, bark jarringly loud.

If we waited until morning, it might be too late. The anvil could be struck any moment, binding the couple forevermore.

What was I to do? I was meant to protect Emily.

An old woman sat against a stone wall amongst the curling heather. She sucked at her pipe, the lines upon her face fluttering, and weaved a basket upon her lap.

Somehow, she spoke with the pipe's tip clenched in the corner of her mouth, "If you're looking for the smithy, he's had a bit of business in the woods. Some girl wanting something a little fancier than beneath the village sign. If you hurry, you might be able to get yourselves tied before Jamie calls it a day and heads for the inn."

Soon enough the woodland paths become so narrow Daniel and I had to leave our horses behind. Night enveloped the trees, turning them into tall figures. Moonlight peered as shards between sharp twigs.

An owl screeched, triumphant as it caught its prey. It startled me and I whirled, staggering. I heard the whispery rush of a stream, not knowing where it lay. Stones stabbed into my boot, water clambering up my leg.

"Careful!" Daniel heaved me into his arms and strode through the stream. "You'll be griping about aches if you let the cold seep in."

Haltingly, I unlinked my arms from around his neck. "Thank you," I said stiffly, then sighed gently. "No, really, thank you. You did not have to come all this way, especially when I have been so rude to you."

His eyes shimmered with amusement, the brightest thing in this gloom.

"It has been quite an adventure, more interesting than the gambling dens."

He eased me back on to my feet, but I did not break free of his light embrace. Warmth radiated from him.

Rather than the smoky musk of his cologne, all I smelt was the bitter tinge of the frosty darkness. I did not want to brave the night just yet.

He inclined his head towards me. It seemed quite easy to push myself up to meet him. It was a gentle kiss, so small for something that could tear apart my good name.

Movement shifted over his shoulder. I broke away, squinting.

A lantern bobbed between the trees. In the flickering light, I saw a man leading a couple further in.

"We've found her," I heaved. "There's still a chance we can save her reputation."

"But what of her happiness?" Daniel murmured, eyes hooded and dark.

I pursed my mouth. The warmth of the kiss fluttered over my lips.

There was no time for my own wants. They had to be stopped. I ducked beneath Daniel's raised arm and used my stick to near propel me.

The small, abandoned chapel consisted of roughly hewn stones stacked atop one another to form a point. Tiny slits acted as holes on either side, the stars seeming to shine through. Moss coated the crumbling base while ivy and lichen crawled to the crown. Ageless and beautiful.

It was exactly what Emily would love. A tucked away spot where vows could be exchanged in secret. I myself once dreamed of such a place.

I forced the door open and strode inside –

"Stop this wedding at once!"

****

Emily looked radiant in her wedding dress. Rather than a hushed, anxious ceremony needing to be done quickly, sunlight stroked her face and painted rosiness and freckles. Julian held the wispy veil aside so he may kiss her again.

We weren't at Gretna Green; we were home. Emily had married the man she loved. No longer would I stand in her way.

When I had burst into the chapel, the couple remained clasping one another's hands as though staring down a feral dog. A muscle stood taut in Julian's cheek while Emily's eyes blazed with defiance.

"You're coming home. Now. No-one needs to know about this," I'd said.

"So I can be married to whomever my father, step-mother or even you deem suitable?" she seethed. "Someone I cannot stand to be with? I thought you were at least my friend, if not someone I could call a sister, Hazel."

My throat went tight. I felt like a villain in one of Emily's romances. Those stories were fiction – none of them touched upon harsh reality.

"I – I am." My voice faltered. "A lady cannot thrive on love confessions alone. Your father will not allow this. He'll throw you out the moment you return."

"I'm not going back, Hazel. Can't you understand I don't care about the size of my home or whether I am invited to the latest ball? I'll take the consequences."

I'd ridden with barely any rest, most likely sacrificed my own reputation. Had it all been for nothing?

The wet hem of my skirt had suckered itself to my ankles. A shiver rattled through me.

Would I ever find something to believe in so strongly and be willing to risk all? I did not want to waste my life waiting for things to slot into place or become bitter and alone.

So, I begged Emily to come home with me one more time. Not to go slinking back to her father, but to have the marriage she deserved. Not in shame but in clear view of the world.

There were two guests missing: my mother and step-father. Just as I feared, he had given permission, then cruelly cut all ties with his daughter, abandoning her to her fate. Mother had sided with him.

It was their loss, I decided. Emily did not care, so long as she had Julian. The rest of the village had come to clap and cheer.

Emily paused and tucked her bouquet under her arm. Julian stood before her, holding out his coat. There was a shuffle of movement, then her garter flew high in the air. Some of the farm boys crashed into one another as they leapt up.

A hand emerged beside me and caught the garter. Emily winked at me, then rushed over to Julian's parents. It was my first time seeing them: an old fisherman and a rather squat, ruby faced woman, both lined and sun-baked by the rigours of age and hard work. They looked like kindly people.

"Congratulations," a voice murmured against my ear.

"Lord Blackstone."

I'd seen him lurking at the back during the ceremony, but he had avoided getting involved. Now he stood much too close, grinning like a particularly hungry fox.

"It seems I need to ask for someone's hand –"

I snatched the garter and wrapped it around my wrist.

"No."

He started, began to splutter.

"I told you," I reminded him, "you are wholly unsuitable. You need to work harder to change my mind."

"And what occurred outside the chapel…?"

"Do not think that means you've won. There were no witnesses, so no threat to my honour. Besides, I'll be gone soon."

"Running away?"

"No, I'm going with them to the coast," I said. "I might not have much in savings, but I want to help support my sister. Mary Anning has been selling her discoveries on the beaches to men of science. I think it a worthwhile thing, contributing to our understanding of what once roamed."

"The sea air would do me some good," Daniel mused. "Very well, I accept your challenge."

I hid my smile behind my gloved fingers.

The Reluctant Passenger

1850

"You'll regret going there, Mercy. All that's in London is smog, noise, thieves and murderers!" My aunt's warning, all the way from Aldeby, was ringing in my ears as I stepped off the train.

I stood aside as the other passengers hurried out, like droves of bees rushing in formation. Someone barged into me from behind.

"Excuse me!" I called, but all they did was scowl.

Perhaps Auntie was right. Even Father had been uncertain.

Before I had left, he said, "It will all be very new to you, and you're young."

"I'm twenty-one!" I had said with a laugh.

"Youth. You all think you're invincible. A city is far different to our little village."

My grip tightened around the handle of my bag. I wouldn't let my family discourage me.

Although I was grateful they cared, I was a woman now. They still thought I was a little girl, running through wheat fields with canker roses in my pale hair.

However, as I walked out from underneath the station's arch, saw the crawling streets and looming buildings, my breath caught. It was, I would only admit to myself, somewhat daunting. Already, I missed the endless sweep of green flecked land, where the blue cloth of the river could be seen in the horizon.

But I was going to prove everyone back home wrong – I was prepared!

I had a map, my grandmother's journals from when she had worked here as a maid, and an umbrella and straw hat depending on the weather. I had even written up a schedule in my notebook, so I would arrive at Cousin Lucy's home at exactly the right time.

When I wrote to my brothers that night, I could happily tell them I had safely arrived and nothing untoward had happened. They never dared go to the city, but I had!

If I could brave London, then they could as well. We could set up a stall and bring our farm's produce to the city, just as our grandparents had done.

Earlier that day, the emerging sun had dimly lit my village. With it had been the morning's misty sigh: a slight shiver that had made me hold myself when I got out of bed.

On the train ride, as the cows watched us rush past with lazy stares, the sun's warmth had been chasing after. Grinning hopefully, I had put on my hat and loosened my shawl.

Now, here in London, I lifted my umbrella with a sigh. I paused. They weren't rain clouds. I touched my cheek and saw my fingers were dirty. The dark clouds galloping above were spat out by factories. I could barely see the sky.

Noises roared about me. Street sellers cried out their wares in jumbled shouts, horses reared and snorted in shock when child street sweepers darted across, wheels clattered, and feet stamped as late clerks hurried to work.

This city must never sleep. I'd compare it to a person's heart; full of life and constantly pounding. The strongest smells were the smoke and steam. I half expected them to merge into hands and clutch at people.

Houses looked like giants stacked atop one another, tightly pressed shoulder to shoulder. The streets between them were narrow, like marsh river streams.

My village only had twenty cottages, and everyone knew each other. I could imagine people within those apartments living their whole lives without meeting their neighbour. Such a thought unsettled me.

There were so many vehicles on the road. I had read about them, yet a simple pen and ink drawing did not compare to the overwhelming exhilaration of seeing one rattle past.

There were old hackney cabs with their enormous safety wheels, and private cabriolets with brightly liveried servants clinging to the back. Then there was the omnibus. Two horses pulled the jolting bus while the driver straddled his seat. Torn and faded on the sides were advertisements for cough drops and soap.

Passengers huddled on the roof. One woman had braved the top even with her crinoline. The poor thing was constantly pulling her skirts to hide her legs, as one of the decency boards had come away.

I watched in shock as the omnibus went on the pavement – forcing an oyster seller to dive out of the way – to be the first to pick up a gentleman with his arm raised. Buses were racing each other for fares.

"Bus from Euston to Ruby Queen Inn! Euston to Ruby!" cried a man, holding on to a leather strap connected to an omnibus. I caught his eye and he winked. "The skies are cloudy, miss. It's sure to be a wet one today. Why don't you climb in and keep your fine shoes dry? Plenty of room in here!"

"No, thank you, sir," I called back. "A bit of rain won't hurt me."

"Suit yourself, then."

And the omnibus rattled off.

As I continued on, a gust of wind rushed at me. My hat! I slapped my hand down and held on.

My eyes streamed as the smell of manure lunged at me. A city might be a place for great minds to meet, of opportunities and culture, but all I wanted was peace and fresh air. I wanted home.

An arm lassoed around my waist. I let out an almighty cry, but no-one on the street noticed or cared.

It was the bus conductor again. "So, you've changed your mind?"

"I haven't, sir. Put me down!"

"You raised your hand. You only do that when you want a bus."

He gave me no chance to argue. He opened the door, thrust me inside, and banged on the roof to tell the driver to go. I crashed into one of the other passengers.

For all intents and purposes, I had been kidnapped for the price of a fare!

"Stop this, please!" I shouted, hammering against the window.

I managed to get the door open, but the omnibus had set off. The street darted by. I'd probably be run down by a horse if I leapt out.

The omnibus jerked and thundered. My stomach lurched, and I had to cover my mouth as nausea squirmed. Back home, the fastest Father's horse would go was a happy canter. This thing might as well be tumbling down a cliff!

"Please, miss, could you move your foot?"

I looked behind me. The person I had fallen into was a half-sprawled young man, with his glasses askew and caught up in his red hair. My shoe was wedged against his stomach. I pulled it back.

"Sorry!"

He coughed, rubbing his side. Rather than the ire I'd been becoming used to seeing in the city, his flint-grey eyes were sharp with humour.

"It's fine."

There were seats for about twelve people, but I counted eighteen crammed in here. The young man's elbow kept on jabbing into my side. Everyone muttered apologies as we all tried to get comfortable, heads stooping from the low ceiling.

Straw squished beneath my shoes. A great many sodden boots had tramped over this, smearing mud and everything else they had picked up on their travels. Something small and black hopped amongst the straw. I scratched at my neck.

"I was just the same," a little old woman said opposite me, dabbing at her ruddy cheeks with her handkerchief. "One moment walking to market, the next some dirty hand grasping me from behind and throwing me in here! They compete to see how many they can snatch – willing or not! All young boys driving them now for fun."

There was a grumble in the sky, and then rain peppered the broken window panes. Everyone else groaned.

"They'll be charging extra for that!" a man with a scar on his cheek darkly remarked.

"This is going against my schedule," I couldn't help but hiss under my breath.

"Your what?"

It was the young man. I showed him my notebook.

"I had my entire day planned."

He laughed in disbelief. "It's just a set of directions! Where's the sightseeing? The landmarks? Surely you're going to see the palace?"

"I might. Another day. I'll have to note it down."

"Where's the fun in that?" He dipped his head. "I'm Harry Sedgewick. I'm guessing you're newly arrived?"

"Mercy Ashdown. I've only been here for five minutes –" Another jolt, which had my insides flipping. "– and already I want to go back to my village."

The omnibus swerved around the corner. My chest twisted as it tipped. I held my breath. Then the wheels crashed back down and a gasp whooshed out of me.

I hastily released Harry. In the fright, I'd clung to him. His warmth seemed to seep straight through my dress, heating up the bones of my corset.

Stop it, I told myself. *You didn't come here to have an attraction with a stranger.* Getting out of this death trap should be my main concern.

The air of the omnibus had thinned even more, and I knew it wasn't because my corset strings were too tight. Harry was so close I could smell the sharpness of his cologne. Admittedly, it was a lot better than the other things I smelt.

"My Fred," the old woman was saying, distracting me, "God bless him and his heart, would never have done such a thing. Might have overcharged by a shilling or two, but that was because he liked to get me and the children a fish supper –"

"But we will be let off?" I had to interrupt, or else I'd be even further away than I wanted by the time she had finished.

"You'll have to lean out and holler at them."

"Right. Hold on to me. I don't want to topple out!"

Before Harry could say no, I wrenched open the window and leaned out. His arm snapped around my waist.

"Be careful!" he cried. "You'll break your neck."

I clung to the window ledge and my hat. My whole body bounced and jerked. The driver harshly waved his whip, not at the horses but at the other drivers. All I saw, bobbing and streaked with rain, was the driver's white top hat and a rose clinging to his buttonhole.

"Excuse me!" No point in being polite anymore. "Oi!"

His head turned. A pair of ink drop eyes glared at me.

"This is my stop – let me off!"

He tugged on the reins. The omnibus near bucked, and I was thrown back into Harry's arms. A horse and cart full of fruit had to swerve past. I flushed as the shouts faded off.

The door was thrown open and I was dragged out, a puddle splashing as I stumbled. A gloved hand was thrust out for the fare while the conductor held my bag out of reach.

"I didn't even want a ride," I grumbled, but I paid. I did not want to be there any longer.

The omnibus was soon off again, hunting for more unwilling passengers.

I fumbled for my map, which I had shoved into my pocket. All that came out was a torn, sodden scrap. I was shivering, my skirt was soaked, and it was only luck that I still had my luggage.

I didn't need the map. Once I saw a familiar street sign, I could…

It took ten minutes of striding through the streets before I gave up. None of the signs made sense when I did find them. Most had the same names.

I was lost. What was I going to do? I covered my face to hide my shuddering lip. Less than a day in the city and I had been manhandled, robbed of my money and left wandering the streets.

It might be dark by the time I found Lucy's home. I'd read awful things about strange creatures wandering – something called Spring-Heeled Jack – never mind the all too human threat of pickpockets.

Oh, how misplaced my confidence was!

Lucy would tell them, of course, and my brothers would all have those infuriating, knowing smirks when I got home. Village people like us weren't cut out for city life.

"Miss Ashdown, you forgot this!"

Harry ran up to me, my umbrella in his hand. He held it over our heads, panting. I managed a grateful smile.

"Thank you." My smile widened. "You wouldn't want to help bring another lost thing to her home?"

Harry held out his arm and I took it. Surely, with a Londoner by my side, we'd get there in no time?

****

But living in London seemed to require no knowledge of the terrain.

"I'm certain it was this way," Harry murmured for a third time.

I suggested we try and walk alongside the Thames to get our bearings. Harry shook his head. At my confusion, he laughed and held his nose.

"When the weather gets warmer, you don't want to be downwind of there!"

We passed by Nelson's Column, and I had to crane my head to see the statue. Harry even took me through Borough Market and the beautiful Hyde Park, where there seemed to be something like a fair being set up. I was uncertain what route we were even taking.

We talked along the way. Harry told me about his uncle's business of steamers on the river and that they had originally come from a Suffolk village. It felt as if, in a day, I knew Harry better than any of the boys in my village.

"I found better things, though," he said, as we paused to look at the Wellington Arch. "The excitement and pace. A man can find his love in the day and have his heart broken by night time. When I step out of the door, I never know what will happen."

"So, you think villages are dull?"

"Life in the countryside does move, but it's different. London's like a steam engine hurtling through, while a village is a newly born calf working out how to walk."

"Oh, how wrong you are!"

I told him about the family farm. I was always rushing around cooking my brothers' meals, darning their clothes, tending the animals, doing almost everything. I had to cram so much into the day, as my mother lived with our youngest sister in Ireland, there was barely any time for myself. That was why I had come to London, to experience something other than the usual drudge.

"But the randomness of life here sounds like a nightmare," I joked. "I don't think I could cope."

"Sure you would. It's making good out of bad. You're doing well enough now."

"Well, I've got you."

"That's the point! You never know who you'll meet and whether you'll want to see them again."

There were street sellers down the road and there was one selling chips. My stomach pinched at me. I hadn't properly eaten since I left the village. I didn't have enough, because I had to pay that blasted fare.

Then I heard another grumble echoing my own. I looked to Harry. He smiled sheepishly.

"Hungry?" he said. "I've not got that much…"

"But we can share," I suggested.

We managed to scrape a few coins for one portion. As we walked along, our hands twined as we carried the warm, slightly damp paper. My eyes watered from the steam, the tips of my fingers reddening as I plucked a glistening, slightly crushed chip.

Considering we had been pressed hip to hip in the omnibus, it did not feel so scandalous to let our hands touch.

****

"It's getting dark," I murmured, clutching my shawl. Though the sky was still a haze, the smoke had darkened. "Are we ever going to find this place?"

A man went over to one of the streetlights, leaning a ladder against it so he could reach the gas lamp. We watched as, slowly, the lights tapered on, dimly illuminating the way.

Harry squeezed my hand. "I bet it's just around the corner."

"Bet what?"

It didn't take long for him to think. "That I'll see you again?"

I was starting to understand… I smiled.

"I promise."

And, sure enough, the apartment my cousin lived in was around the corner. I slapped his shoulder lightly with the fringe of my shawl.

"You knew all this time!"

"I didn't think it fair to let you go without showing you the fun side of the city. Didn't want you getting a bad impression on your first day here."

We hurried up the steps, where no doubt Lucy was anxiously waiting inside. Harry paused, still holding my hand.

"I'm sorry for tricking you." His mouth was quirked slightly to the side, giving him a hopeful look. "So, I guess our deal is off?"

I made him wait. He looked up at me, rain streaking his cheeks and glasses, hair sticking to his forehead.

"I never break a promise. When shall I expect you?"

"Sometime tomorrow. I won't say when." He laughed at my scowl. "It'll be a surprise! Just know that I'll come for certain."

I held out my umbrella. "Well, you will, won't you? You have to return this."

I watched him run through the rain, the umbrella bouncing in his grip, and waved when he looked back. Harry Sedgewick – It was a name I hoped to say more of.

I went inside, wringing out my hair and waving off my cousin's worried fluttering once she came down and saw me. A change of clothes, a steaming bowl of dumpling and herb stew, and I would be fine.

Tonight, I would write to my brothers an entirely different letter to what I had planned: On my first day, I had almost been kidnapped, met a handsome young man, become lost yet somehow managed to see the sights, and finally tried chips.

It wasn't a list of my woes, but excitement. Tomorrow, I would write to them again and I had no idea what would happen next.

I couldn't wait to find out.

The Fen-Nightingale

1879

I had been far and wide to draw a vast variety of birds. I was not one for colour, preferring to sketch hooked beaks in long, thick arches of ink or shadow downy breasts with flicks of pencil.

My travels had taken me to the Nile Valley to see the Egyptian goose with its brown and red markings, giving it a stitched together appearance that made it look like a child's toy. Then, when I saw amongst the archaeological sites paintings of the sacred ibis, I found the bird at the mudflats of Kenya.

I'd sketched birds from the furthest unknown corners of the world, yet I barely knew what flew in the skies of my mother's county. Although half of my blood was Norfolk, I knew nothing of this place. I knew not the foods they ate or their strange dialect. I did not even have a tinge of their drawling accent.

My father had taken me from England when I turned five to study birds with him. My sister was Mother's concern, while I was his only son and heir. I even had his name: Horace.

I turned twenty a few months ago. Father did not even write to wish me happy tidings. Such things never concerned him.

We parted ways when I was seventeen, after a disagreement over the mute swan. He had not responded to any of my communications since.

How had Mother coped with him? Or was it a case of out of sight, out of mind?

I could not remember a time when they were happy. Her simple country ways from being a vicar's daughter aggravated Father when once they delighted him.

The cart jolted and I clung to my bundle even tighter. Rain dripped from my hair, pattering over my spectacles.

I could have gone by train, I would have been drier, but I went cold all over if I even went near a station.

It had almost been four years, yet the train crash in '75 would never be forgotten. Sons, daughters, wives, husbands… a mother and sister, all lost.

My boat had been late, which meant I was not in time for the funeral. And, after all that, I did not even visit their graves. I reached as far as Wroxham, then went back to Southeast Asia in search of the large-tailed nightjar.

My mother and sister were still buried here, though. It was time I stopped being a coward. I was a man now, not a weeping child.

The river ran alongside the road, resembling slithering snakes. Reeds and rushes shuddered and bowed, whipped by the winds. Even though some were supposing the Broads were man-made, seeing them made me think differently. They were so long and deep, as if a mythical beast had scratched its claws across the land.

A dragonfly, bright and glimmering blue, had braved the wet. It fluttered by, hunting for shelter. Then a tongue lashed out and it was drawn into the dark cavern of a frog's mouth.

The frog settled back where it hid in the mud. I shuddered as thunder burst from the darkening clouds.

****

In the end, I had to find shelter. I stopped off at a small inn called the March Bird, which was close to the water's edge.

There were a few people within, the rain having chased them inside. Families sat together, enjoying their tea and someone else's fire, young men sat at the counter drinking and laughing, while a group of old men were close by the fireside. Their complaining of their aches, and that there would be more rain, storms and misery to come, seemed a continuous moan, as if they were the building's groaning foundations.

I went to stand by the fire, where some coats and shawls had been draped, and took off my drenched coat to dry. Out of the corner of my eye, I noticed one of the old men watching me.

He was a squat man with white bushy eyebrows, a beard like splattering sea foam and a thick tanned nose bursting out the same as a sand dune. His weather scratched cheek curved from what I assumed was a crooked smile hidden beneath his beard. My lips quirked faintly, but I hurried to an empty table.

The woman who served me was a few years older than myself. A mass of freckles arched on her cheeks in the same way as wings stretched out. Her plait, twisted into a bun, was a dark hue, but the loose, curling strands fluttering near her ear were softer, akin to feathers entangled in a nest. Her eyes were sharp and black, yet not as unnerving as how a bird eyed its prey, for they were almost engulfed by the light of her smile.

"What would you like, sir?"

"I, um..."

"My name's Jemima."

"Thank you, Jemima." I flushed when she grinned at me and fidgeted with my collar. "What would you suggest?"

"Well, seeing how I've got some still warm from earlier, I'd say dressmaker tripe."

She soon came with a plate. The tripe came in a little parcel, with a rich, dark gravy, boiled potatoes and peas. I cut into the tripe, and the filling of herbs and breadcrumbs broke free.

I took a hesitant bite, expecting it to be bitter, but it was somewhat sweet from the gravy. I fell upon the food. The heat from it seemed to ooze through me, chasing off the cold, making the heavy drenching I got from the rain seem a mere droplet tumbling from a leaf.

If I had gone to see Mother, lived with her, might she have made this for me? We could have sat around the table, me, Mother and my sister, and talked and laughed, passing the peas and hoarding the butter.

I near started when the chair next to me was pulled out. The old man I had noticed earlier sat down.

"You're new," he said. It did not sound like a question, more an accusation. "Are you here to stay?"

"I'm a traveller. I study birds."

I believe there was a distant great-uncle near here from Mother's side. I was reluctant to reveal it. Why? Was I afraid that he would turn around and say we shared a cousin? That these lands had a further claim to me?

He chuckled. "You'll have heard of the fen-nightingale, then? It's a beautiful creature. You always know it is there on account of its song. Quite a powerful, striking voice, too."

Pushing my plate aside, I pulled out my journal and found a fresh page. "Go on. What colour are its feathers?"

"Oh, normally quite dark, perhaps even a mossy hue. The eyes are very wide, as if they're gorping at you."

"A fen bird? There are only Broads around here. Does it fly over from the fens further inland, nearer Suffolk?"

"You could say that. Wherever there is marsh and water, there you will find it, but it scares easy."

I wanted to hear more about this elusive bird. When Jemima passed by, I ordered drinks for myself and the old man. He drained his in one go and quickly demanded another, and another.

"He isn't bothering you, sir?" Jemima asked after she returned for the fifth time.

"Oh no, he's telling me quite an interesting tale."

"Anything for some free drinks, eh, Granddad?" I could have sworn I heard her mutter to herself, but her back was turned to me as she went into the kitchen.

After a while, the old man stumbled upstairs to bed. When Jemima came to collect my empty plate, without a single trace of gravy, she laughed.

"You look like you enjoyed yourself." She tugged at one of her loose bracken curls and asked a little shyly, "You did like it?"

"Absolutely! I've never eaten so well in all my years."

"Would it be rude of me to ask you something?" She ploughed on, "I've not heard your accent before. Where are you from? I thought France at first, but it's not that."

"A little from here and there," I told her, fiddling with my pencil. "I've never been in one place for too long. My voice is a bit of a patchwork job."

"You travel? Where? You haven't been to Australia, have you? Is it true the bunyip beast is there?"

Before I could answer, there was a shout from the kitchen. Her father was calling for her to come help him, and she had to hurry back.

****

I decided to book a room at the inn. There was no need to go to the village immediately. It wasn't as if anyone was waiting for me. There was only an empty cottage and two cold graves.

I waited until night fell. With the people huddled up in bed, there was less chance of the birds being disturbed. The darkness meant peace and that was what I preferred.

Mindful of Jemima and her family, I was quiet as I could be as I slipped outside. I had borrowed a lantern earlier, but I kept the flame weak. Often in the past I went without such an aid, relying upon the pure, natural gaze of the moon. To do such a thing here would be foolish.

Clouds came to pull a misty curtain over the moon, like a crafty old man using the smoke of his pipe to confuse travellers. It was hard to tell land from water. A slightly soft, muddy bit of ground could slop down to pull you under the black, icy depths, and there awaited the unbreakable embrace of the weeds.

Somewhere in the distance came the familiar hoot of an owl. Others shuddered at such a noise, but it comforted me. Although, at its sudden shriek as it swooped for its prey, it startled me a little.

Thin droplets of rain still pattered against my cold cheek, yet the furious spit had lessened into a dull drizzle. Each shallow breath I took seemed peppered with frost.

I crouched by some rocks and bushes, quite near to the edge of the water. Mud squished beneath my boots and grass clung to the hem of my coat.

Being out here felt familiar. I had never sat by this stretch of Broad before but, as I stared at the bobbing scabs of moss, a picture formed. Elsewhere, when I was a boy, I had crouched near the edge and tried my hand at babbing, wrapping a baited line around my finger and dipping it in.

Mother had been there. Though I strained my mind so hard I feared it might set alight, she was a pale, translucent figure, more a smear of dark hair and a pale blue shawl just as night creeps over the day. My baby sister clung to her neck.

"You won't be catching any eels, Horace!" she called, soft, a whispering breeze that could be mistaken for a voice. "All that's here are polliwiggles – tadpoles!"

As quickly as the memory came it went, chased off by the chill alongside my warmth. Perhaps it was a dream I had years ago or something I made up. I hugged myself tighter.

This had been their home. It was the closest I had ever felt to them. Would more of these memories arise if I stayed?

Did I want to remember?

I watched and waited. Rain dribbled down my hat, making a constant slithering drumbeat echo in my skull. Once, when I saw a dark shadow glide across the water, I slowly raised my lantern, heart leaping in excitement, only to discover it to be an ordinary mallard.

I held my breath and listened, certain I might hear the faint, beautiful warble of the fen-nightingale. I heard and saw nothing to give me hope. All that punctuated the night air was the gurgling croak of frogs.

I returned to the March Bird just as the moon was fading. I was cold, wet, exhausted, exactly as I had been when I first arrived.

I could have left upon the morning, yet I promised myself one more night to find a trace of this bird. Just one more night.

****

"You've been here for a week, sir," Jemima said as she set down my breakfast, a plate of scrambled eggs and toasted Yarmouth herring, which she called toasters. "What are you looking for?"

"A bird," I told her, before setting upon my food.

"Which one? King Harry Redcap?"

"Who?"

"A goldfinch."

"No, it is the fen-nightingale."

She bit her lip. "Why don't I come out with you tonight? You'll be needing someone who knows what they look like."

Jemima was coming with me, whether I wanted her to or not.

****

Upon nightfall, Jemima and I crept outside.

"I hope no flittermouse…" She paused and chuckled. "I mean a bat doesn't fly at us."

The night almost went on just as any other night: the shadows tricked us into thinking creatures lurked, crows swooped overhead as if the night wept them, and every single other animal save for the fen-nightingale called out.

The only difference was the soft whisper of Jemima's voice. She talked of her father and mother, her aunt and cousins, all their joys and woes, as though I was her closest friend. Perhaps it was her way with everyone, even a stranger such as I.

Normally, I worked in silence. Others in my profession had been known to shush anyone nearby, and my father once threatened to glue my lips together with treacle. Birds were easily frightened.

Yet I did not mind Jemima's chatter. It comforted me.

Jemima took in a deep breath, and the next exhale held the faint trickle of laughter.

"Is this what you do when you travel?"

"I know it is a little unexciting," I murmured.

"I love it!" She covered her mouth, and spoke more quietly, "One day, I'm going to leave and discover every single one of the world's secrets. But, I wonder, why do you come here when you could be somewhere warm, not drowning in mud and rain?"

"My mother and sister are buried a few miles from here."

I pursed my lips. Why on earth had I told her that? She did not need to know, probably did not even want to know.

As she watched me, like a heron hidden amongst rushes, ready to snap its beak to pierce a slithering eel, it made my tongue loose.

Was there something within me, trapped in delicate eggshell and wanting to erupt and shake itself free?

"Have you been to see them?"

She made it sound as if they were at home, awaiting me. If only that were true.

I shook my head.

"Why not?"

"We were not close," I hesitantly admitted. "I am afraid that if I go there, I will feel nothing." I sighed. "No, that isn't right."

"Then what is it?"

"I will be numb, yet full of guilt. I should have written and visited them more, but I was too busy with my work."

"You were doing something you loved. They would have understood."

"What does it matter if, when you finally get home, the place is like another land and all who you love are gone?"

Her hand was on my shoulder. It was heavy and her warmth seeped through. I swallowed. My eyes felt wet, but it was only the sharp wind's nip causing them to weep. Nothing else.

"Promise me you will go visit their graves once you find the fen-nightingale," she said.

"I will."

She leaned over and softly kissed my cheek.

"Follow me."

Jemima led me by the hand further along the bank, towards one of the muddy slopes. I squeezed back. It felt right, as if we had always done this.

"You know nothing of our dialect, do you?" she said. "I suppose a fen-nightingale is our little joke. A trick to fool those not from the county. You won't be finding one of these in the sky."

We knelt by some rushes and she gently pulled them aside. There, squatting in the mud with river weeds clinging to its murky, spotted back, was a frog.

Its yellow eyes, like droplets of oozing butter, swivelled to glance at us. Startled, its frothy croak stopped mid-way. With a great leap, the frog flung itself into the water, splashing us.

"That, sir, is your fen-nightingale!"

An unnatural cry, mossy coat and a lover of all things muddy. I truly had been had.

Rather than a cry of frustration, a snort escaped from me. I wiped at the corners of my eyes, not caring that I was smearing goodness knew what on my cheeks.

These people and their strange words were a funny sort, but they were my people as well.

And now I had a promise to keep.

****

"Look, Horace," Jemima hissed, "an Indian peafowl!"

She handed me her field glasses. I could see a male and female picking about for food amongst the temple ruins. The male had such a stunning plumage. The bright, colourful tail feathers were spread out for its courtship ritual.

"Give it a few minutes, then we'll try getting closer," I said.

Our sketchbook was tucked underneath my arm. Alongside our recent sketches there were drawings of wood-sprites, duffy dows and barley birds: the Norfolk words for the woodpecker, baby dove and the true nightingale.

They were my words as well. I was starting to pick up the dialect, listening to Jemima, and there was a slight drawl in my voice.

Within my harsher, duller ink lines, colours burst. Jemima's watercolours were vibrant reds and yellows for birds in flight, and delicate pinks and blues for when they nested.

Incomplete when apart, but beautiful and whole when together.

Path to St Mary's ruins and Winterton lighthouse.

Group of House Sparrows and Western Gull.

Seal in the water and holly bush.

The Lantern Man

1863

Sensible women did not hunt ghosts in the dead of night, alone and on the marshes. Especially one such as the Lantern Man.

"Don't be insipid, Laura." The quiver of my voice brought no comfort. "Ghosts aren't coming to get you."

I needed to prove he wasn't real. There had to be an actual cause for my husband's accident. I would not accept spirits tried to do him in as the rest of the village wanted to!

Fallen reeds crunched under my boots. Every breath crawling into my mouth was sharp and brittle, as if frost-tinged cobwebs coated my tongue.

Something burst from the bushes. Cringing back, I pulled my lantern out from beneath my cloak.

Light flared in dark eyes. The owl screeched, wild and beautiful. Its wings stretched, pale and tawny feathers dripping with water.

Then I saw the dark shape wriggling futilely within its talons. Soon the poor mouse stilled. The owl swooped past and vanished over the ruins of the abbey.

Across the water, St Benet's seemed little more than rubble, a single stone gatehouse guarding the drainage mill. Not even the abbey itself remained, only impressions upon the grass, welling with shadows to hint at what might have been.

From where I stood, and from how the darkness hugged it, the ruins reminded me of a vile, enormous toad crouching. A shiver started at the back of my neck, jittering through me.

I came across the place the other marshmen had found Archie. The sedge lay crushed from where he'd washed up.

My throat burned as I imagined him in the water. The marshes could have claimed him completely, waterweed shackles dragging him somewhere I could not go –

I knew this place should not be trusted.

Steadying myself, I crouched. Straw and feather peppered sludge smeared over my gloves as I searched.

I should have come earlier, so I'd have the sun rather than the moon looking with me. Mother and I spent all day tending to Archie. I only dared light my lantern and creep out while she snored by the fire.

No-one knew who the Lantern Man had been when living. They never spoke of his face or gait, but the orbs of light that heralded him. They danced over the river, startling birds. Whistling drew him near. Once he heard you, nothing could shake him off.

Archie vanished two nights ago after going out to check his eel traps. When they found him, his eyes were wide and mouth pursed in a grimace. His smock had been badly burnt and his hair coated in glass.

Now, he lay abed and the doctor could not say whether he would wake.

Water splashed behind me. I snatched a nearby stone and lifted my lantern.

Instead of a creature's eyes, a person threw up their arm. I could just make out a blue neckerchief and curls of honey hued hair.

"Get it out of the way, Laura! You near blinded me."

"Joshua!" I swallowed back my relief. "What are you doing here?"

I turned back to the ground while my brother-in-law spluttered. My hand closed around something too bright to be part of the marshland.

"Me? You're the one ghost hunting. I promised Archie I'd keep an eye on you if anything happened to him. Family need to stick together. I don't want you getting in a state and hurting yourself and the baby."

I heaved myself up, steadying my heavily pregnant stomach. The boy darted over, helping even while I tried to shrug him off.

"Look at this."

I held a scrap of spotted cloth, part of the neckerchief Archie wore like all the marshmen hereabouts. The material was stained with blood.

"It must have come away when we moved him."

Something was within. I pulled it open. My teeth caught on my tongue.

A single bullet. This was proof Archie had not merely fallen into the water.

And a spirit would have no use for guns.

"Now do you believe me?" I demanded.

Joshua held my arm tighter as we made our way to the cottage.

"I never doubted you," he said. "You should have left it to me, though. He's my brother."

He's my husband, I wanted to snap, but arguing wouldn't help. This was something I had to do. Joshua would never understand.

My father vanished on the Broads when I was a girl. Spirited away my mother liked to pretend, as if none of it had been his fault. She'd been quick to silence gossips who swore they saw him in Cromer with a new wife and child.

I used to know all the safe paths of the marshland, listening out for fen-nightingales and collecting meadow thistle to lure butterflies. Then I found out how cruel the waters could be, that it took things and never gave them back. I detested the place.

Somehow, I ended up marrying a marshman. Archie had come to my door selling eels, and I'd bartered my heart instead.

He swore he'd show me the beauty of the marshes again. While I grimaced and held my skirts away from the muddy slopes, he quietly crept up to part rushes, showing me field mice, their tiny, fluffy bodies curled up in sleep.

It was impossible for me to believe Archie could so easily succumb to the waters. That was the fate for city dwellers, stumbling about and knowing nothing of how treacherous this place was.

The villagers had no faith. The whispers were starting again: they thought he had been sneaking away just as my father had done.

There had to been another reason. There must be.

I had just begun to love the marshes again. Would it be so cruel as to take someone else from me?

****

I could barely see past the herb garden because of how thick the mists were. Rain slithered down lavender. Feverfew bent back against the onslaught. White petals tore and crumpled.

After I slipped the stone hot water bottle into Archie's bed, I stood by the door and waited for Joshua. As darkness came, my unease grew.

Finding the bullet had set him off. He had gone to the pump, but had not returned.

Some of this was my fault. We'd been arguing.

"Are you going to confront Farmer Elias?" I'd demanded that morning.

"There's no proof he did this." Yet I had watched the muscles in his neck go taut. "The old cutthroat was in the pub the night Archie went missing."

"Then he told someone to do it. He's the only one who hates him."

Elias was the local smuggler. Never got his boots wet, though. He ordered wherrymen about, having them ferry his gin and tobacco to Norwich. Archie and I knew his type, getting others into trouble to save his own skin.

Elias had been after using Joshua as a stooge when his last boy was arrested and transported. My husband was having none of that.

Smuggled casks were being hidden on the Broads, so Archie sunk them all with his eel-spear as a warning for our family to be left alone. Elias had wanted revenge.

Now Joshua was gone. I had no clue where he might be. The marshes, possibly.

I remembered, on the day Archie was hurt, he had been reading a letter. I hadn't thought much of it at the time, only catching Joshua's name and mention of a signal noise.

Archie had gone pale then red with fury, soon storming out. Joshua swore he knew nothing of such a note, and I believed him.

I should have stopped Archie. He might not be close to death if I had. I couldn't let something happen to his brother as well.

I made my way to the local pub on the riverbank, the Broken Plough. The distant figure of the drainage mill loomed like a curved back. The ragged sails turned ever so slightly, as if they were capes of torn shadows. Emerging stars shone murky and watery.

Hollow moans spilled across the endless expanse of the Broads, most likely winds scuttling into the crevices of the ruins. I clasped my hands to stop their trembling.

Some said a giant serpent lived beneath the land. My father used to terrify me with the tale to stop me from following when he went walking there.

Hurrying inside, I stepped over the black shaggy dog draped over the doorstep. Charlie might know something. He was always out cutting reeds for thatching, ending each night with a drink or ten.

I bought a pitcher of ale and went to his usual table. He stood with the tails of his moleskin jacket held before the fire.

"Joshua is missing," I told him, as I refilled his cup. "Have you seen him?"

"I passed the boy not long ago, on one of the paths leading to the abbey. Listen, though, your Archie… I've been thinking."

I leaned forward. It was too loud in here, the men behind cursing and arguing over a game of Whist.

"It might be nothing," he went on, "but I remember a few nights ago Elias was here with some of his men. A couple of wherrymen from Catfield. Telling ghost stories, he was."

"About what?"

"Getting them het up and paranoid, so they wouldn't slack and get caught by customs. He was telling them about the Lantern Man, how he comes bobbing along with his light to carry off any man who whistles."

"But everyone knows the stories…"

The loud noises were now a rushing sensation in my ears. Sweat prickled on my neck.

"I heard one of them, Davey Seals, boasting he'd had the ghost whistling after him before. He saw him off by shooting his light. I don't know what use this is, but the wherryman is out there tonight, doing another run for Elias."

Something in my head tilted. The dread I'd been ignoring writhed in my throat.

Joshua was out there somewhere, alongside a man with a gun.

****

Somehow, I managed to run. The bridge I crossed flashed before me. Across the marshes only memory stopped me from plunging into the icy waters.

Hair streamed free from my bonnet. My heart hammered in the centre of my forehead. The marsh gasses were thick tendrils, stroking over my cheeks like insects. I wrenched up my scarf.

I saw another lantern, swinging jerkily over a crouched figure. The light washed out the features of his face.

I looked to the river, where a clump of bright feathers bobbed. It was a lure, it must be. Smugglers used them to mark out hidden brandy casks.

On the water a shape passed over: the white snout of a wherry. Its tarred sail stood stiff in the night, the lady shaped figurine atop the vane spinning as if she danced wildly.

In these mists, a lantern might be mistaken for a spirit.

I squinted, just making out the skipper. He gripped something in his hand, pointing towards my brother-in-law.

"Joshua!" I screeched, diving for him.

We crashed together, mud and marsh water cresting. The sound of a shot roared, smashing into one of the lanterns and spraying us with glass.

The wherry turned down another river path, vanishing in the gun smoke. I buried my face into Joshua's shoulder, unable to stop sobbing. If I hadn't come out in search for him!

"Quick," he said, his own voice shaky. "My mates can track that wherryman down before he gets away."

I thought the agonies of labour would hit me in an instant. Instead it was a strange sensation, like someone turning over in their sleep. My skirt became drenched from more than the rain.

Joshua choked in horror when he realised. “Not now! Can’t you hold your breath and wait until we’re home?”

“That isn’t how it works.” My breathing quickened, starting to panic. “I can’t go any further.”

He heaved my arm over his shoulder and helped me along. He turned, and I saw the lonely ruin I dreaded.

“Not the abbey –”

“There’s nowhere else we can use as shelter!”

Within, the elements boomed around us. Rain darted through the window’s slit, darkening the walls like claws scrabbling to get in.

Joshua set me down and wrapped his coat around me. Everything seemed to be moving, tilting like a rocking chair. Great groans and shrieks sounded as the mill shook.

All through it, Joshua held my hand and stammered encouragement. It shouldn’t have calmed me, yet the terror on his face did not frighten me either.

Everything had to be all right. There was nothing else that could be done.

Outside, thin trails of moonlight glistened on the river. Paths fringed with reeds were shadowy shards hunched together, like ruffled fur on a creature’s back. I thought I saw it slither away.

Our remaining lantern flickered, smears of candle wax coating the glass. Soon it would wink out and we’d be abandoned in the dark.

It was not the only light. I clutched at Joshua, unable to force out the words.

Tiny orbs floated past, weaving and flickering about like dragonflies. Gone was the drum of the rain or the seething of the winds.

I heard him. The jaunty trill of *Frog Went A-Courtin*, reedy but familiar. It sounded just like my father, signalling for me if I ever got lost.

And then all of it vanished, fragmented by a sharp wail. Emily was put into my arms, Joshua now laughing.

“I can’t believe it,” he muttered, wiping his hands on his jacket. “I’m certainly not having one of these things.”

"You'll change your mind," I promised.

She was small and warm, and I clung to her. The lights outside did not matter.

By the time we left, there was no-one out there besides a heron fishing. The mill's sails drifted across one of the ponds – the storm had torn them off completely.

****

A few days later, Joshua, Emily and I went to the Broken Plough. We'd had word Elias was there.

Farmer Elias sat alone. The fire gave him a flushed look, but the thick white eyebrows hanging over his eyes kept them shadowed. His hands pressed against the table, fingers slightly drumming. None of his men were here yet.

"We know you tried to have my husband killed," I announced.

His teeth gritted in such a way I couldn't tell if he smiled or snarled at us.

"What foolishness do you speak of? The ghost caught him, same as he does all who wander those marshes when they shouldn't. Leave me. I'll put this down to grief and befuddlement."

My throat lurched. There was no proof of what he had done. The wherryman had been the one to shoot, but we all knew who had tried luring Archie to his death.

Emily stirred. I tucked her into my shawl to shush her.

I could not let Elias get away with this. I didn't want my daughter growing up in a place where men such as him prospered.

I swallowed my anger and kept my voice steady. "We know he was shot at by a wherryman."

"Then you have your man."

"He told us the stories you fed him while drinking here."

I was beginning to shake, not certain if it was fear or anger. Whatever was on that note had been lost to the river. All I knew was the look on Archie's face as he had read it.

I knew it was a sin to lie, but I hoped it was a lesser one if it could catch this man.

"We also found the letter you sent." Seeing him start to pale urged me on. "You made Archie believe his brother was out smuggling, so he went in search for him. And, when my Archie whistled, thinking it the signal Joshua was meant to make, he didn't know one of your men was out there instead, terrified of the Lantern Man!"

"Then he should have kept out of my business!" Elias roared. He leapt from his seat, drink spilling across the table. "Give me that note!"

Emily wailed when I cried out in surprise. Joshua didn't let him touch me, though. He tackled Elias, the other men in the pub helping hold him down.

It was the smuggler's own tongue that had betrayed him.

****

Wanting to distract myself from my worries, I peeled the rushes on my lap and dipped them in fat to make into rushlights. Joshua threw himself out of his chair to pace, jiggling Emily in his arms.

The wherryman had been charged with smuggling and carrying a gun at night with ill intent. Elias managed to wriggle free. After all, the note no longer existed.

The rest of the village knew the truth, though. No longer was Elias welcome, and they chased him out when he tried to return. I heard he was picked up in Yarmouth for adulterating beer and sugar, so at least some of his misdeeds had caught up with him.

Archie had yet to wake. We still hoped, waiting by his bedside.

Emily fretted, sensing my anxiety. I hushed her, singing gently. Joshua joined in, but he always complained about his voice, instead whistling the tune.

There came a groan.

"Stop that whistling. I've warned you plenty of times." Archie's voice was no more than a whisper, drowned out by Joshua's shout of relief.

I flung myself half-over the bed, roughly kissing Archie's bearded cheek. Joshua was gabbling about what we had done.

"You're right," my husband wheezed. "I was fool enough to fall for Elias's tricks. I'm astounded you managed to work it all out. Now, then, who's this little mouse here?"

Joshua set his hand upon my shoulder. I grinned up at him.

"When family work together there's nothing to fear, not even the Lantern Man himself!" I answered, taking Emily into my arms so I could introduce her to her father.

Ghostly Footsteps

1890

When others asked me if I truly did see ghosts, I merely smiled. In my line of work, it was better to make them wonder.

The truth was I couldn't be certain myself.

At Briarwood Manor, a breath of wind might blow across the back of my neck. My hair would go as taut as an arching cat. The shadows thickened, darkness wrapping its fingers around candleflames.

The pounding of my heart steadily climbed to settle in my throat. Shivers fluttered over my shoulder, anticipating the touch of another's hand.

Soon I wouldn't have to worry and could flit into the night. The thought made my throat lurch.

I went on tiptoe, running my cloth along the books and trinkets on the library shelves. The candles I had lit flickered like the flash of a cat's eye slowly waking.

I paused by the edge of the rug, turning aside the bulging corner with my shoe. A coin had been placed beneath. I picked up the sovereign.

I'd been warned of this trick: the coin would most certainly be missed by the housekeeper. If it was left alone, I would lose my position for not cleaning properly. If it vanished, I would be charged with stealing.

"Good evening, Tessa."

My slight shudder wasn't from the cold. Heat fanned my cheeks.

There was another reason for my heightened senses and it wasn't always ghosts.

I looked to the window, where stood the figure of a man. One of the young masters.

Sunset's brittle fingers cradled wisps of his dark, curling hair and half of his face. A single green eye caught the light like glass, his full lips stretching into a grin.

Michael came and went as a trail of smoke did. I had yet to work out whether he did it on purpose. I swore I caught him laughing the first time he made me jump in fright.

I righted myself, but made no other move of acknowledgement. It was a game we played, which I had lost too many times.

Maids weren't meant to speak or even be noticed. We were hired as living ghosts.

I knew how impossible this was. Tessa did not exist. No-one must discover who I really was.

Michael almost fell back as I rounded on him and thrust out the coin.

"I found this beneath the rug, sir. Here, have it back."

Brazenly, I took his hand and pulled open his fingers. He was warm, the flesh notched and slightly tanned.

Doors slammed downstairs and a table scraped. Michael's smile vanished as I broke free.

"Finally," he murmured. "We might be able to clear things up now."

The medium had arrived.

****

Michael strode down to the drawing room. I followed behind, bearing a candle.

Paintings lined the walls of the corridors, the master's family regal and narrow eyed. Light passed over the glistening oils, cracked from age. I glanced a second time at one fan bearing lady, thinking she had smirked at me.

As we approached, already I heard raised voices. Michael sighed despairingly, rubbing between his furrowed eyebrows.

Within the room, most of the furniture had been pulled aside, leaving only a round table and chairs. Candles flickered in various states, obscuring the woman sitting there, making her face writhe. Wax spilled down the holders like bark peeling from pale trees.

Harold and Benjamin, the eldest and twins, had been the cause of all the banging. One of the chairs lay between them.

"Clumsy oaf," Harold snapped, patting furiously at his jacket where some of the melted wax had caught him. "Do you want to frighten the spirits away?"

"You're a belligerent fool. As if some ghoul is going to come floating over our heads!"

"I'd rather think Mama is at peace." This was James, who was already sitting and quickly emptying the brandy decanter. "Rather than rattling at the windows, desperate to be let in. It's all a bit *Wuthering Heights* for me."

"How about we all calm down?" Michael said, going over and righting the chair. "Mother would hate to see us arguing, especially if she is visiting tonight... You are certain she is here, Madame Granville?"

The medium arose, her face no longer distorted. I wavered in the doorway.

Madame Granville bulged in robes of speckled silver and black. Face powdered, white streaked hair wrenched into a bun and eyebrows plucked to make her widow's peak more pronounced. At the centre of her throat was a dark red jewel, which I knew was made of paste.

"I am hopeful, my child," she told him in a scraping, papery wheeze. She glanced at me, eyes narrowed in disapproving creases. "It is better this one does not remain. Only those who knew the deceased can be here."

I should have stayed away; the ghost wasn't due to come out yet.

I left, hurrying to my room where the veil and ectoplasm had been hidden. Waiting for the arrival of Madame Granville or, as I knew her, my aunt Mrs Spinks.

None of the other maids were here. Too afraid and hiding in the kitchens, while cook probably told them not to be so superstitious.

I was going to miss them, I always did, but I'd be working in another household by next week.

Quickly, I changed. I pulled the white robe over myself, the skirt so long it hid my scuffed shoes. The wispy veil flared around my head, making it seem as if I had no eyes.

Celebrities such as Mr Conan Doyle were greatly involved in the spiritualism movement. Those who wanted to emulate him sought out mediums.

My aunt was always willing to tell people what they wanted to hear. All for a small fee, of course.

Vagueness and lucky guesses were becoming more difficult to pass off as an actual message from the dead. People wanted more than knowing their loved ones were at peace. They wanted moving glasses, floating tables, and a ghostly apparition.

I used a small pot of rouge to redden my lips. Another pot's contents glistened and began to ooze as I unscrewed it. I dipped rags into the mixture, wrapping them around my hands. The pungent odour of soap mixed with rotting egg whites seemed to burrow in my mouth and choke me.

I was the eldest of five sisters. Our father ran out on us after Mother died in childbirth, abandoning us to his debts.

The only person I could turn to was my aunt. Playing at ghosts meant I could keep the roof over our heads and our plates full.

My aunt sent me to work in big houses she thought worthwhile targets. Maids were always leaving their posts due to indiscretions. I was her little bird, whispering the family's secrets.

I passed through the house unseen and crept back into the drawing room.

They had their heads bowed, hands held in a circle, while Mrs Spinks loudly beckoned for spirits to approach. More specifically, Mrs Adelaide.

Mrs Adelaide passed away last year, before I took this post. All I had to go on was what Michael had told me, when he was willing, and her portrait in the library.

She had seemed a kind woman. She reminded me of my own mother.

Mrs Adelaide was also far older than me. Aunt had an answer for the discrepancy.

"She is here! Your mother has pulled away the shackles of her mortal body and returns as the beautiful young woman she once was. Do not fear. So long as the circle remains unbroken, all will be well."

A snuffer was tucked in my hand. I snuffed the candles I passed, making it seem as if the flames were stolen in my grip.

The whites of the brothers' eyes shone back at me as they watched in shock. How could they not know? Their own need to believe tricked them.

Slowly, I unravelled the rags, letting them hang. Drops of the fake ectoplasm hit the floor, turning luminescent.

The cloth splattered on the table, writhing as I pulled it back. Harold whimpered, cringing. Benjamin made a soft sound of disgust. I dared not look at Michael.

I came behind Mrs Spinks, resting my hands upon her shoulders. More of the ectoplasm dribbled down her robes. She tilted her head, eyes rolling up as she puffed her chest.

"Ask your questions," my aunt commanded, and no longer did she whisper but boom furiously. "This woman shall be the vessel for my voice!"

It was Michael who leaned forward and spoke first.

"We need to know where you put the pocket watch, Mother, and all the other things you hid to stop Father pawning them. Harold is due to marry soon and needs proof he can support his wife."

"Are we certain James hasn't already bet the lot on horses?" Benjamin sniped.

"Do not argue, my children," Mrs Spinks interrupted. "My memories are... misted. I will bring my answer soon. Shut your eyes and pray for my return."

I slipped out in the darkness, hurrying through the corridors as I hitched my gown and pulled away my veil.

The ghost would not be returning. My aunt would make up a story, answer a few more questions, then her fee would be paid and she would leave.

It was never enough for her. If any valuables went missing from the houses we visited, it could always be blamed on spirits.

My few months working here meant I knew where the silver and gold were kept. My aunt would stall long enough for me to ferry them away.

I paused as I passed one of the windows, not quite recognising my reflection. Entangled in my disguise, only some of my face could be seen. Behind a gossamer cloud the full moon pulsed.

I had to forget Michael. My sisters needed me. A twisting sensation, like a key sharply turning, formed in my chest.

It hadn't felt so wrong at the start, when all Aunt and I did was offer sympathy and sweet words for the bereaved. I knew the truth now. All along we'd been frauds.

No matter how many séances I assisted, not once did I see my mother. It was impossible for me to believe in ghosts.

Outside in the gardens stood a tree, a cape of discoloured leaves engulfing the spindly arms. Shadows rippled amongst the forming purple berries, tiny sparrows snatching the glistening orbs and darting back into hiding. Spiderwebs bright with moonlight shuddered.

As I sighed, my breath misted across the glass. I wiped at it, but a pocket of fog stained the area just over my shoulder. I rubbed harder, tiny lumps of raised flesh crawling up my arm.

The shrill chitter of the birds warned of something. As they faded, it was replaced by my ragged breathing… and another person's footsteps.

Quick, furious taps of a woman's heels approached. I tensed, certain I felt a crinoline skirt brush against my hand.

Were a pair of eyes looking back at me in the window? They no longer seemed alive, instead dead as an oil painting.

The footsteps receded. I looked back and all I saw were pinprick dust motes floating.

Stories about ghosts always spoke of their past torments and turning that pain on others. The smile on Mrs Adelaide's portrait made me think otherwise.

If ghosts did roam, was it not because they had something that needed to be said? Perhaps my penance would be righting whatever wrong Mrs Adelaide felt.

I followed the sound. She took me to the small stairway only the servants used. My descent was halting and careful. The toes of my shoe teetered over the edge, the step only half the size of my foot.

In the shadows the stairway became endless, my only sense of balance my steadying hand on the wall, which seemed to be closing in. The footsteps stopped. Then came an impatient tap.

"I cannot," I whispered.

I dared not take another step. Even with a light these stairs could be treacherous. A misstep and the drop would be fatal.

My teeth gritted together. One London household invited Aunt to do a séance after one of their maids tripped and broke her neck on stairs such as these.

The ghost's footsteps started to move away.

"No, don't leave me!"

I had once skulked in charnel houses to scare my clients. Was a simple stairway going to unnerve me?

Still clinging to the wall, I risked edging my foot out. Empty air met me, until my heel knocked against the step.

Hesitatingly, I reached the next one. I was getting closer to escape.

The door stood open slightly, a sliver of light coming in. Now I was in the servants' quarters. Another door opened to an empty room no-one slept in.

It was small and barren, the bed draped in a dust sheet slightly twisted and misshaped. Rattling noises came from beneath. Dust billowed as I lifted the sheet and pried at the floorboards.

One came free. My hand dived into the cubby.

I scooped out necklaces, rings, coin purses, until my lap heaved with treasures. Mrs Adelaide had been quite the magpie.

I could take all of this now. Leave my aunt behind and start a new life with my sisters.

I paused as I was about to crawl out from under the bed. The pocket watch dangled from my fingers, swinging gently.

From behind me a floorboard creaked. Even though I was alone, I felt watched. Just the same as when Mother judged me for doing something dishonest.

In that moment I had a choice. I could cling to what I was or start anew.

For once, I was going to do what was right.

****

The ghost returned to the séance. Mrs Spinks paused mid-chant at the sudden presence looming behind, her knee still raised to tilt the table. She peered up, mouth pursed and dark eyes darting. However, she could not break from character.

"Welcome, spirit. What do you have left to say, before you depart?"

I went around the table. My skirt was held close to me, barely keeping hold of what I carried. Michael craned his neck to watch. My freezing cold hand pressed against his cheek and he let out a choked cry, shuddering. James shifted his chair away hurriedly.

Mrs Adelaide's hoard spilled over the table. My aunt gasped in disbelief. Furiously, she drew back her painted lips in a soundless snarl.

Harold broke the circle, picking up a necklace. "My Sarah must wear this on our wedding day. Oh, thank you, Mama!"

James had been about to slide towards him the coin purses when Michael gripped his arm.

"Thank you, spirit," Michael said, looking to me with his eyebrow lifted curiously. "I never thought I'd see my grandfather's watch again. Rest now."

All Mrs Spinks could do was dismiss me, breaking one of her smoke bombs beneath the table. Before they could discover me, I vanished in the smoke and rushed for my room. I undressed, scrubbing the ectoplasm from my arms and face in the water bowl.

My roommate arrived afterwards, whispering she had seen a ghost at the bottom of the stairs. I sat with her the rest of the night, until I managed to sway her into thinking it was only a shadow.

****

My aunt did not betray my secret. If she had done so, then she must reveal her own deception.

She left with her fee and a healthy tip from an overjoyed Harold. I knew how angry she would be at missing out on Mrs Adelaide's treasures.

She would also have to get another girl to be her ghost. I would remain here as a maid.

The work was long and boring, but at least it was honest. I could not distort my entire life with lies.

A few days later, I was cleaning in the library. A figure crept by the window.

"Morning, Tessa!" Michael said. I kept dusting. "Are you going to keep ignoring me?"

Turning to face him, I plucked at the end of my sleeve. It seemed easier to speak with ghosts rather than the living.

"Have you and your brothers settled your differences?" I asked.

"Some of it. The wedding will be going ahead soon."

"Good. Family need to stick together."

"I actually wanted to thank you," he said.

"What? Why?"

"Did you see the ghost Madame Granville summoned?"

"Ghosts do not exist," I told him, and made to go back to my work.

The library doorknob rattled, revolving in place. An open book ruffled its pages wildly.

Footsteps were coming, pounding furiously.

I gasped, not knowing what might happen. Michael lunged, his arms protectively embracing me.

The window burst open. Something grazed my forehead. I shut my eyes.

It was a gentle sensation, like the brush of a person's fingers. For some reason, gratitude flooded my chest.

Winds rushed not inside but out. Birds in the trees scattered, flying into the horizon. It felt as if more than just the wind had left.

Michael still held me. I knew I should push free, but my body would not obey.

The emerging day shone into the room, haloing a glow about our faces. He peered at me, concerned. His hand came to rest on my cheek.

"Are you well?" Mutely, I nodded. He grinned. "I don't think I've ever seen you directly in the light, Tessa. You've always kept to the shadows."

The warmth of his touch burned through my face. Seeing his eyes up close, and reading the kindness in them, made me believe.

For ghosts, real or imagined, it was better to reveal all. Thank you, Mrs Adelaide.

"Michael," I began as he leaned down. Hopefully he would still want to kiss me. "My real name is not Tessa, but Virtue."

The Marshland Monk

1860

"Hush," I hissed to Charlie. "I'm listening to Father's sermon."

"You've been avoiding me, Mary. I want an explanation."

"Not now."

I saw Father's lips move, but the sound could not reach us, stolen by the snarl of the storm. All around us wood and stone groaned, as if the church was grinding its teeth.

Charlie was being just as persistent as the wind. "What's the excuse this time?"

"Let's wait until summer," I said. "I want sunshine, not a gale whisking off my veil!"

"And when it's summer, you'll want a pretty winter wedding."

"Don't be so impatient."

How vast and wild the village seemed, after returning from smoky, packed London. It was like stepping into another world, one much older and darker, still caught in the bracken of the mysterious.

"Well, what else is stopping you? Did you meet someone when you were off studying, is that it?" Charlie roughly scratched at the scar on his chin, which he had got in an accident on his farm. "Or is it me? Am I beneath you now?"

"Of course not –"

"I knew I shouldn't have let you pester me into learning my letters. You think me the same as a boy from your ragged school. A fool."

I turned, about to have it out with him, the whole village could hear if they liked, when the church shuddered. The stained glass burst into shards as an oak tree crashed through. Rubble tumbled down. People shoved and shrieked as they tried to escape.

Then, as quick as a breath, it was over.

I heard Father shout for everyone not to panic. Gusts dashed inside, throwing dust into our faces. Coughing and choking, we staggered about, calling if everyone was all right.

Half of the church had been gouged out. Poor, beautiful, wrecked thing!

Mrs Grice and her daughters stood in a huddle, quivering. Father was examining his twisted spectacles. Charlie's hands were on my shoulders, rubbing them. I was trembling.

But I was also the first to start clearing away the rubble, once we had all calmed down. That was how I found it. Amongst the shattered stone and branches, part of the floor had fallen away. It did not lead into endless darkness, but to a set of stairs.

There was a tunnel beneath the church!

****

"There're ghosts here, Mary." Charlie combed cobwebs out of his pale hair, distaste curling his mouth.

I bit my lip, trying to keep the candle steady. It would be a long run back up in the dark.

"There's nothing here but spiders and rats," I said impatiently.

Shadows fluttered in the light. Charlie sucked in a breath.

I tensed, hissing, "What's that over your shoulder?"

He yelped and glanced back, but, of course, there was nothing there.

The stairs went in a ragged spiral and the steps were so narrow we had to go on tiptoe. Earlier, I had joked this must lead to the other side of the world. I was half afraid of being right.

Father had left the village, forbidding anyone from entering the tunnel, but my curiosity couldn't wait. There must be treasure and history to discover.

When I arrived, Charlie was already waiting. He knew me too well.

Somewhere in the distance came the maddening drip of water. Our steps echoed, as though our own shadows stalked us.

It was awfully cold. Any trace of the day's heat on our faces had been pinched away by the innate chill and damp of the stones.

The smell was overwhelming, but hard to describe, reminding me of peat and mud on rain drenched fields. It was like the earth was closing its hand around us. I swallowed at the thought.

Reaching out from behind me, I clasped Charlie's hand. Warmth seeped through, calming the jitter in my heart.

There, as dark and gaping as an animal's yawning mouth, was a room. Inside were books, tapestries and wooden carvings. I hesitated, afraid a simple touch would cause everything to crumble away. Then I saw glimmering trails of water like lightning cracks crawl over the wall.

Dismay had me snatching one of the tapestries. Absolutely sodden! Think how many stories had been lost to time.

Charlie bent over some pamphlets. His stone-grey eyes narrowed in that confused, inquisitive way I loved, as he tried to figure out the words he didn't know.

I'd admired him so much when he admitted he couldn't read. His mother needed him when he was younger, and he never went to school. I think it was harder asking for help than for my hand!

Yet he'd changed since then. Gave up our lessons. Pushed for us to be married quickly. Why did he have to bend things to suit himself? What was he afraid of?

I lifted another wasted tapestry to find a pot. The squat thing was a dark blue colour, with roses carved in whites and reds.

Rumbles trembled beneath my feet. A crash came overhead.

We rushed up the stairs, which crumbled with every step we took. I had to stop and Charlie almost knocked into me.

The stairs were gone. I caught up my skirts. Would I even manage the leap?

Suddenly, I was lifted. Charlie held me tight and I clung to him as he jumped over. My bonnet got knocked off and tumbled down.

Sunlight appeared, beckoning. We crawled free of the tunnel and over the church floor, gasping.

"Look at the state of you two!" Old Jeb sat on one of the surviving pews, wheezing with laughter. With a thin hand like stretched, stained paper, he wiped at a sunken eye. "Find anything of interest?"

All we managed to save was the pot. I held it out, and Jeb's laughter spluttered.

"That's the monk's urn, you foolish girl!"

"What?"

"When there was the reformation, the king's soldiers hunted a monk through the marshlands. He was never seen again but he swore, as he vanished amongst the rushes, he would return if his church was ever under threat again. Disturb his home and he shall arise."

Jeb reached for the urn, but I held on.

"When Father returns, he'll know what to do with this. He can bless it, if it really is a burial urn, and then we can see what's inside."

"You'd best leave that here," Jeb warned. "The monk will not let you get away with taking what's his."

"Perhaps Jeb is right," Charlie said. "Grandmother always said to be careful about the other world."

I felt a faint shiver go through me, but blamed it on the cold from the tunnel.

"They're only stories made to frighten children."

Jeb shook his head in dismay and hobbled out. I looked around. The entire church was in ruins from the fallen tree. Would a ghost return to rage against nature?

Charlie was patting cobwebs from his clothes. "I think I'll keep to the fields."

I near rolled my eyes. "Too old for excitement? I thought I was marrying someone my own age!"

"I know what I like, that's all." He paused. "So, the marriage *is* still on?"

"Once the church is fixed."

"That could be years! We don't even know if your father can get the money. You're stalling again."

"I'm not."

"I'd be happy marrying you in the woods or anywhere, so long as it's soon. Why don't you feel the same?"

Exasperated, he left as well. I wrapped my arms around myself.

I loved him. I did. It had always been him ever since we were children.

But I was afraid some of his suspicions were right. Could I be happy with just being a farmer's wife?

****

I left the cottage to sit in my wicker chair, sipping a cup of blackberry syrup. Before me were the marshes. The light of the setting sun made the rivers seem aflame.

A flock of blackbirds passed by. They glided so effortlessly, and they were so far, I could mistake them for leaves swept by the wind.

The birds flew over the church. I couldn't help but sigh. How were we going to repair it?

Faintly, I smelt smoke coming from the Fairman's, entwined with the familiar, spicy smell of apple dumplings. I shut my eyes.

It was silly, but I always came outside to catch this scent. Mother used to bake apple dumplings. After she passed I tried to make them, desperate to evoke those memories, but they never seemed to be right. All I had left were fragments.

Almost, just almost, I could picture my pigtails flying as I leapt about, running home to the shout of my name coming from the kitchen window. Her face would be there, smiling. She would wave, then turn to slap Father's hand away when he tried to steal a dumpling.

Mother's hair had been like wisps of fire, trailing slightly from the wind, as though she had unravelled some of the sunset –

I heard a splash. My eyes opened.

Mists roamed over the waters, curling around rushes. Distantly, there was the startled flutter of birds' wings.

"Who's there?"

I was not going to be frightened by a noise that could be explained by anything: a creature jumping into the water, someone taking a shortcut home, my own imagination.

The fantastical and frightening were stronger in my mind. Something had clambered out and was hunting for people to lure to its den.

My grip tightened around my cup. I stared hard at the darkening horizon.

I should go inside, but I wanted to stay, hoping a fox would stride out and glare at me, eyes gleaming with twilight. I wanted proof I was being foolish.

A figure shambled through the marshes. My breath stilled. Each throb of my heartbeat was slow and hard.

The man might be as pale as moonlight, but his eyes were pools of night. I did not recognise him, as it was as if he had no features. He wore a monk's robes and they hung off him like snow clinging to twigs.

Slowly, the monk swung an incense burner. I could smell it, yet it wasn't a scent I could describe. It was as old as stone and earth.

The spectre's head twisted to face me. He raised his hand. Even though he was far away, it was as if I could feel his fingers upon my shoulder.

My throat lurched. Sweat turned to ice even though my skin was feverish.

He was getting closer. A twig snapped and I ran into the cottage, slamming the door. I pressed my back to it, sinking to sit on my haunches.

I covered my head, expecting violent gusts, fingernails against the windows, shadows seeping through the cracks… Nothing came. The door creaked as I pulled it open.

The monk had vanished. Gentle breezes ruffled the rushes.

****

The monk came again the next night. As I lay in bed, whispers slipped through my window. I had no idea what the words were, but assumed he was chanting in Latin.

The night after that, something kept tapping against the glass. Knuckles knocking, asking to be let in.

I didn't want anyone to know, least of all Charlie. He would have at me for believing in ghosts, after all my teasing. I could already imagine him asking why someone with a level, book bred mind would be trembling over simple country folk stories.

If there was one thing I hated, it was looking a fool in front of him. I was the one who fixed the door when it broke, cooked, cleaned, did everything for Father because Mother was not there.

When Charlie got that ring on my finger, I wasn't about to change. I'd still be wanting to do everything, and I would do. People relied on me, and I had myself.

When I heard that whispering, I wished Charlie was sitting with me.

In the daytime, I tried to come up with rational explanations. Then, upon sunset, as the night chill drew in, my disbelief faded.

On the fourth night, when I was almost asleep, thinking he was not going to come, a bell rang. I grabbed my broom and stood at the door, yet I could not bring myself to swing it open.

When sunrise came, the bell went. I had gone days without proper sleep. I was exhausted and irritated, could barely get anything done. Each morning I kept on hoping I would see Father's horse and cart, but he had yet to return.

Charlie came round. Tiredly, I smiled, and it did not feel as wide as before.

Should I tell him? I pursed my lips. It felt like admitting defeat.

"I… I'm sorry, for the way I've been acting," he murmured, looking at anything other than me. "Every time you go away, I picture you liking life there more than here and leaving for good."

"I wouldn't do that."

He held my hand, his rough calluses gently rubbing against my palm.

"I promise I won't try to hold you back. We can drown the farm in books if you want. I want my name to be next to yours when we sign the marriage register, not just leave my mark!"

I pulled his hand so that he cupped my face. My dark curls twined around his fingers.

"I was afraid I wouldn't be the wife you were expecting. That you'd try to make me what I didn't want to be."

"We muddled together as friends well enough, though... didn't we?"

Yet we would be married soon. A marriage meant sharing burdens and helping each other, not arguing. The few years I remembered of Mother and Father being together, she would always be by Father's side. A friend as well as a wife.

What would be the point in marrying Charlie if I could not confide in him?

"Ever since I found that urn," I began, "strange things have been happening. Odd noises, shadows outside..."

"The night is full of strangeness," Charlie said.

"But I saw him – the monk!"

I told Charlie everything that had happened. He listened, yet from his face I could not tell what he was thinking. Then he leaned over and kissed me.

"You should have told me sooner," he said, stroking my hair.

"I thought I could deal with it myself."

"Do you think he'll come again tonight?"

"I guess so, until he gets the urn."

"But this time I'll be with you."

****

We set the urn on my doorstep. Charlie hid amongst the bushes, impossible to see with his long coat on and cap pulled down.

My hands clenched as I watched the sun sink into the marshes, unclasping its bonnet of day and revealing its hair, darkness shimmering with stars. Reeds were rustling, but not from any wind. They parted and the ghost stepped out.

He no longer staggered and groaned. I spied him as I peered from the corner of the window. He hitched up his robes and ran to the urn.

The moment he picked it up, Charlie jumped out. He got his arms around the ghost and it did not vanish. The hood fell down.

I couldn't believe it. I rushed outside.

"Jeb! Why did you do it?" I demanded.

How could he terrify me these past few nights? What was wrong with him?

Sweat beaded on Jeb's forehead. He looked anxiously at Charlie, who scowled down at him.

"I'm sorry, I only wanted the urn. I thought if I chased you out of the cottage, I could sneak in. Then the urn's disappearance would be blamed on the monk."

"But why would you want an urn?"

"It isn't ashes in there," Jeb answered.

I took the urn, went inside and came back with a knife. Jeb was telling the whole story to Charlie.

"When I was a boy, I snuck into the tunnel through a hole in the graveyard. There were two urns. I knocked one over, and there were coins inside!"

Carefully, I slid the knife into the groove.

"Then part of the tunnel began to cave in," Jeb continued, "and I barely managed to get out. I thought those riches were lost to me forever."

"If there is money," Charlie snapped, "it belongs to the church."

The lid came up. Dust flew out and I had to cover my eyes. Surely, if it was full of coins, it would rattle?

But, if it was full to the brim, there would not be any room at all to make a sound. I tipped the urn over slightly, and a trickle of gold coins fell out. They weakly glimmered in the moonlight.

There was only one thing we could do with this. We had to keep a centuries old promise.

****

I seemed to have little luck with the weather. On the day of my wedding, hail drummed upon the church roof. The stained glass faces of the angels shimmered from clinging snowflakes.

Not a single bit of snow fell inside, though. Using the monk's riches, we fixed the roof and round tower.

Jeb tipped his cap to me as I passed. Father stood at the altar, face ruddy with joy.

Charlie had not turned around yet, too busy fumbling with the silk flower in his buttonhole.

I leaned in close, and whispered in his ear, "There's someone behind you!"

He started, laughed, then clasped my hands.

"And you're not getting away this time!"

A storm roared about us. Winds heaved against the tower bell. We had to shout our vows over the ringing. The stones groaned and shuddered with each lashing gust.

It did not stop me, and we were wed. The church remained standing, as I knew it always would. Even if the story of the monk was not real, something out there watched over us.

I tilted my head, smiling. As Charlie kissed me, the storm began to hush and the bell rung a final time.

The Seashell Necklace

1827

The ships we had all been waiting for arrived just before the storm struck.

I sat by my window, cleaning my bodkin and knives. Lightning's damask was thrown over the dark sky then sharply whipped off.

Rain and sleet pelted. I stuck my head out to let it cascade down my face, trying to wash away my worries about tomorrow.

Most likely I was the only one awake, having spent the night pacing and telling myself not to be a coward. I'd never been one before, and I wasn't about to become one when there was nothing to truly fear.

If I was going to get the answer I wanted, I needed to step up and prove my worth.

My home was in the rows, narrow passageways of tightly packed houses. I had to hang myself half out my window so I could make out a strip of sea and the anchored ships.

Waves dark as ink, frothing with seafoam and snow, struck the sides. The ships tilted this way and that, as if they were toys that could be easily snatched away. Winds buffeted the sails so fiercely the impression of giant fists could almost be seen within them.

The lodging house opposite me was close enough to lean over and knock. My stomach jumbled like knotted rope, but I couldn't resist. I gently rapped on the window.

Morag appeared. There were still cloots wrapped around her fingers. A quilt covered her shoulders and her eyes were a bleary blue. Her copper-rose hair curled over her face like seaweed over stone.

"What's the matter with you, Eli?" she yawned.

"They're here," I whispered.

Her eyes widened and the grin I so loved stretched across her freckled cheeks.

"The Dutch traders!"

A snowflake fluttered on her eyelashes. Then she shivered and realised she was still in her nightdress. She flushed and I laughed.

Cold hit my face. It was my turn to splutter as I wiped snow off while Morag stuck out her tongue and shut her window. You would think we were still children the way we acted, not two people in their twenties and courting.

Excitement churned in my chest, quickening the rhythm of my heart. This had to be a sign. Some fisherman's luck that tomorrow would turn out successful.

The sky lit up again and the silver ring on my dresser gleamed.

****

Morag and I started out as friends. I was apprentice to a basket weaver and she came with her mother from Scotland for the herring season. Any time off we spent running across the sands, twilight burning our silhouettes.

When we were young, our families teasingly called us sweethearts. Morag often blushed and looked away while I stammered and denied it all. In some way I must have known, but had shut my eyes until it became too bright to ignore.

The night I realised had been at one of the Dutch fairs that appeared on Yarmouth beach each winter. I had held Morag's hand tight so as not to lose her in the crowd.

We stole each other's gingerbread, peered entranced at tiny wind up figurines and glimmering jewels bearing icons we did not know. A fairy tale market that came with the moon and departed with the sun.

I had watched Morag finger a bracelet and wanted to get it for her, even with my pitiful wage, just to see the joy on her face. That was when I knew and kissed her for the first time.

And now, as the Dutch traders set their stalls upon the beach again, I was going to let Morag know just how much she meant to me.

Guards strode past, their lanterns rattling in the wind. The glow danced over some local men playing their fiddles.

As Morag and I walked, people reared out then vanished back into the shadows. Fallen snow slowly oozing into slush bobbed upon dark waves, white seafoam so brittle it looked almost ready to snap like ice.

Chestnuts crackled as they were scooped out of the ash pit. The dark brown shells crunched in our fists. Even though the frigid winds lapped at my cheeks, the scalding heat of a chestnut against the roof of my mouth was enough to forget.

A bowl of shortbread spilled over. There were shouts as people ducked and covered their faces. Seagulls swarmed upon the food, cawing and bickering. Then they were gone, swiftly escaping in the night.

There sounded a heave of frustration and pain. An old man struggled with the weight of his stall against the sloping sands.

Morag didn't need to nudge me. I shoved up my sleeves and took the brunt of the stall, setting it back into place.

"Thank you, my son," he wheezed in a thick accent, dabbing his greying bracken beard with a spotted handkerchief. "It's been foul weather all the way across here, but it cheers my granddaughter Alyssa. She likes watching the birds flap about."

A little girl rushed over with small chests full of mythological carvings. The old man thanked us again, and we moved on after buying a wooden gnomish korrigan.

Another stall caught Morag's attention. Cakes and jewellery were side by side. She picked up a pearl necklace with a silver clam shell the size of my palm. I sucked at my cheek when I noticed the price.

"It's what a bride would wear," Morag murmured, breath misting.

My breathing stilled, but I laughed and said, "A queen, perhaps."

"It's just like before."

My smile was tight. All I felt was a sheen of sweat on the back of my neck, the stone-like pound of my heartbeat and the icy yet far too delicate impression of the ring in my pocket.

This would be my only chance. By the end of this fair Morag would return to Scotland and not come again until the next herring season, by which time her brothers would have been in her ear, dissuading her from me.

"Well, if it isn't Morag and her little basket weaver."

And it was as if the very thought had summoned them here.

My jaw ached as my teeth ground together. I straightened my back, tilted my head, and was reminded of all the times I'd raise myself higher when I was a lad.

There was little difference in height between myself and Jamie now. However, when he smirked, eyes flicking down to look at me, I was that boy again.

All of them were there. Morag's elder brothers.

They were always causing a ruckus in the pub. Flirting with a new girl every season. Whereas I settled myself in corners, quiet and at peace, twisting osier into whatever I fancied.

Jamie had a rug under his arm and a bloater on a stick. The rest glared at me as they heaved tables and dressers, Christmas presents for their mother, back to their drifter.

"You leave us be, Jamie," Morag snapped. "Don't you ruin tonight for me!"

"Can't your friend speak for himself?" Jamie jeered. "Or does he still stutter?"

"I have better things to be doing," I near growled.

His blue knitted hat was thrust down low, so all that could be seen was his wind burnt face and narrowed, gleaming eyes.

"I wouldn't get too close, Eli. You're just a fancy. Didn't you know there's someone back home waiting for her?"

Morag's gasp was ragged.

And then the worst of my doubts came for me. When Morag was here, she could be whoever she wanted. For all I knew she did have a husband back home.

Jamie's hands shot out. My back smashed into a stall and there were shouts all around.

I scrabbled up, lunging for him. I gripped his jersey. Our faces pressed together, and he was still laughing at me. I'd show him they couldn't scare me off.

Morag's arms wrapped around my waist. Calmly, she said, "Don't believe him, Eli. He's only bitter because he's fell out with his wife."

I let go of Jamie. This wasn't how I wanted Morag to see me.

I was about to say sorry to her, when there was a cry of rage. A woman snatched at Morag's shawl, pulling her back.

"Thief!" It was the owner from the last stall. "I saw you looking at it with your greedy eyes. I want my necklace back!"

"Let her go!" I forced my way between them, shielding Morag. "We've done nothing."

"I know what you were doing, causing a distraction so your girl could pocket what she wanted!"

I knew I'd knocked into the stall, I would have paid for anything damaged, but I hadn't expected this much of a mess. Most of the jewellery had been swept to the sands. A silltårta cake was gouged in the centre.

The seashell necklace could not be found amongst the destruction.

Already, arguments were hissed amongst the growing crowd, Dutch, Scottish and Norfolk. One moment of doubt, and distrust raged through us like fire.

A guard approached. We were to be searched.

Morag held out her arms, head jutting up defiantly. "Go on, then. You won't find anything."

And they didn't. I held open my coat, but realised too late just as the ring was pulled from an inner pocket.

"It's mine," I said. "Bought and paid."

I glanced at Morag. Her eyes were wide, colour flooding her face –

Quickly, I stuffed the ring away, not daring to see the rest of her reaction. Instead, I caught Jamie's. Thunderous fury darkened the sharp shadows of his face.

Yet there was no time to think on that; the woman would not believe us. She thought we had already ferried the necklace away.

Alyssa rushed over, tugging at the woman's skirt. "Witte Wieven!" she cried, gesturing to the sky. "Witte Wieven flew down and took it for her own!"

She was shrugged off. "Don't be foolish, child. It wasn't one of the white women. Spirits don't go after jewels, only greedy young girls who should know better."

"Please," Morag begged, "I swear I'm not a thief!"

****

My hands stung from sea salt. A furl of seaweed had caught on my cuff button. Damp sand encrusted my knees.

They'd taken Morag to the Custom House for questioning, and I'd not seen her since. The Scottish gutter girls were packing up. If Morag was kept here any longer, she'd have no way of safely getting back home.

Her brothers spent that night questioning everyone. I even saw a few forced searches.

Two days had passed and still the necklace had yet to be found.

Mine was a foolish hope, but might the necklace have fallen and been lost in the sands with the others? I'd been hunting, unable to rest, not when I pictured Morag pacing in a small, dark room.

The music did not return. Most of the stalls had packed up and so in the dull, almost milky daylight the fair looked sparse. I picked my way through dropped skewers and shards of domino clump sweets. The magic and excitement had eroded.

The tide might have carried it off by now for all I knew!

I took a breath, covered my face. I'd learnt patience when taking the spite out of my willow for basket weaving. I'd not leave until I had that accursed necklace.

The rest of Morag's family had been combing the beach as well. They needed to return to their ships, until only Jamie, myself and Alyssa remained.

I felt a scrabbly sensation on my back. Jamie was still glaring at me. All it took was a glance to get him to speak.

"None of this would have happened if she hadn't been swanning off with you. You're no good for her!"

I threw back, "Perhaps you shouldn't compare me to how you treat your own wife!"

I bit my tongue, but too late. Jamie dropped a piece of driftwood and bared his teeth.

Just faintly, I heard Alyssa shouting. I wasn't about to fight him with a child watching.

"If we can't work together for Morag's sake, then there's no hope for us," I said. "Let's hold our tongues, all right?"

He scowled, but turned back to dredging through the seaweed. At least we wouldn't get hauled in for brawling.

Then I heard him softly say, "We've got another sister we don't see, as her man works in Ireland. I get letters from Julie, once or twice. He's no good to her. She's too far for me to reach her and I feel helpless when I see the worry on my mother's face."

"...I'm sorry."

All I had here was my aunt, some cousins and the memory of my parents, lost in the last typhus outbreak. Not many would miss me, and yet I would miss Yarmouth if I were to leave. I had my ties, small as they were, and they were part of what had made me into the man I was now.

The gutter girls only came here for a few months, then the fish swam off and they were gone as well. Sometimes I wondered if that was what enticed me. Did the distance between us make it like my grandfather's stories about selkies? I'd wanted Morag to remain by my side, but not like this.

Perhaps Morag's family were being sensible. As much as we called each other friends, we only had glimpses of our lives. I knew nothing outside of my hometown, whereas she was flitting to and from home.

If she was willing to marry me, would I be able to do the same? As I searched, I knew my answer.

"Witte Wieven has returned!" Alyssa was on her feet, jumping and waving at the sky. The weak, frosted daylight caught upon something shiny.

I shielded my eyes and saw with dread the silhouette of a seagull.

"It couldn't be."

I remembered the mess of the stall, the stabbed cake. Only one bird would be so daring and gluttonous. Mightn't the necklace have caught around the gull's neck as it stretched out to sample the herring?

Whatever had led to this, all that mattered was getting that necklace back.

****

The bird had landed amongst the dune grass. It twisted its head uncomfortably to peck at the necklace tangled on its chest. Red speckled feathers came free as the bird made a pitiful noise of distress.

Alyssa made to run to it, but I called for her to stop. Any sort of excitement and the gull would fly off in fright, then the necklace would be gone and the creature would still be caught up.

I had some cheese straws wrapped in my pocket. I threw one down.

The seagull's head jerked in interest. Half-bowed, it waddled over, the necklace swaying.

Jamie tensed, about to lunge. I grasped his arm.

"Not yet."

"I can't wait –"

"Learn some patience for once."

I gave Jamie the rest of the straws. He held them out to tempt the bird, cursing as the vicious yellow beak jabbed him.

I wanted to snatch the necklace as well, but forced myself to be ever so gentle as I unwound the pearls, careful not to hurt the bird. My breath was half-held, pretending I was only fixing a mistake with one of my baskets.

"We'll get you free in a moment." Jamie's voice rumbled.

Alyssa was wide-eyed, biting into her thumb.

Then the seagull flapped wildly in our faces and took off, turning into an inkblot in the distance. Hanging limply in my hand was the necklace, scuffed, caught with tufts of feathers and crusted with sand, but safe.

Jamie slapped my back, making me choke. "Now we can get Morag back where she belongs!"

My face ached from how wide I was grinning.

And yet, where did Morag belong?

****

The moment we returned the necklace, Morag was released. I remained on the beach, lightly kicking aside damp shingle.

Slowly, the Scottish drifters were leaving our shores. Jamie had gone ahead on his ship, after sharing a drink with me. He'd muttered something about still hating me, but I think we'd come to an understanding.

Sand crunched behind. Morag was huddled up in a shawl, hair funnelling about her face.

"There you are!"

She crouched next to me. We watched as seafoam bubbled and burst upon clumps of red seaweed.

"It seems nothing lasts forever," I said. "It all melts away like the snow."

Had I made the right choice? Definitely. No matter what happened, at least I had the courage to follow what I wanted.

Morag rested her cheek against mine. "I think all women should have the chance to see the wedding ring beforehand," she told me, grinning as my throat went tight. "A proposal is always so sudden, and I've never been able to make a choice straightaway."

Our heads turned and we kissed. She tasted of the clotted cream fudge my aunt gave all her roomers the day they left. Home.

We were speaking at the same time:

"My tools are on your brother's boat, and my aunt has agreed to let out my house –"

"Your aunt has agreed to keep me on. Once we're wed, I can move in with you –"

She covered her mouth to stifle her laugh while I groaned in disbelief.

"So, what do we do?"

****

I came up with Morag to Scotland. There, I weaved cran baskets and cubbies with brambles and heather along with my osier.

I was unsettled at first, it seemed another land entirely at times. Morag was there to guide me through most of my blunders.

Then the herring set off, the ships sailed, and the Scottish gutter girls travelled south, just as the Dutch set off for the fair. And I followed.

So long as we were by each other's sides, Morag and I were the same as the silver darlings. Our home was theirs.

The Rushlight

1870

"Look at how many berries are growing there, Ruth," my mother said, shivering as she cradled her stomach.

I peered intently at the holly, in search of anything that might worry her. The dark, curling leaves tempted me to reach out and stroke them, yet I knew their sharp fangs would prick my fingers.

Scattered about in great clumps were glistening red berries. One of them had burst, the liquid pattering down.

"There are too many," Mother went on. "I saw this before when I was a girl. It means a harsh winter is coming. A bone rattler."

"Is that true?" a small voice piped up.

We both looked down at my sister Emily. She coughed and wiped her nose on the back of her glove.

I had been born in the winter and grown hardy from it. Emily was a summer child. Just like the flowers she loved to pick, she curled up in the cold. Her face seemed to carry little of the sun's warmth, no matter how long she played in it.

I squeezed her hand. "It's an old wives' tale. The only thing those berries mean is that the birds are going to have plenty to eat this year. Now, let's see about getting us fed. I promised something nice for our supper, didn't I?"

However, talk of the unknown seemed to be rife in the village. We were in the *Swan Inn* with stew and green parsley dumplings, when an old man burst in. It near made me drop my bowl, scalding my hand when some of it splashed.

He was making a wild dullor about a monster he had seen. The other villagers settled him down by the fire with an ale.

"What was it, Harry?" someone asked.

Harry bezzled down his drink in one go, and asked for another before he began, "I thought I'd take a walk through the marshes by the manor house, seeing how beautiful the moon and mists were."

"More like you were poaching!" the landlord laughed. "Did the new keeper chase you?"

"No, no, I was minding my own when I heard a sound in the darkness. Panting. I thought it was the wind at first. Something made me walk a little faster. The cold or because there seemed to be less stars in the sky, but then it leapt for me!"

Emily started. I placed my hand on her shoulder.

Harry continued, "It came out of the marsh water, pond scum showering down on me. It was the size of Thomas's plough horse and had black fur as wild and scratching as brambles. See, it cut me here."

There was a long scratch down the man's trouser leg, yet he could have snagged it on a bush or anything else but a ghostly hound.

"And its eyes, like two full moons glowing in its head! Well, I ran straight here. It's an omen, I tell you. The berries are thick and now Black Shuck roams. We'll all meet with some misfortune or other."

A few, who still held on to their superstitious ways, agreed. They whispered to one another anxiously.

The landlord scoffed. "It was probably some gypsy's dog. I think I saw a camp by Thurlow farm, hidden near the marshes."

"I reckon it's an escaped convict, whose broken free from Norwich prison," another suggested. "No-one decent would skulk about there. The womenfolk should be careful where they wander at night."

Emily tugged at my sleeve. "What's Black Shuck?"

"A silly ghost dog," I soothed. "He roams the Norfolk coast in search of his sea captain master who drowned."

"Do you think Mr Harry saw him?"

"No, of course not."

I remembered a night years ago when the sudden howl of a dog had awoken me. I had gone to my window, and what I had seen disappearing into the smoky roke had vaguely resembled what Harry described. I did not sleep for a week after that.

"Never you mind," I told her. "Get back to your supper."

Yet, when I swallowed a mouthful of my stew, it was cold and the dumplings hard. I had also been transfixed by the story.

I did not tell Emily the other tale about the dog. That all who it gazed upon were certain to die.

The sudden chill I felt was not from the stew.

****

The sparrows and robins had plucked the berries from the holly, yet nothing could halt the march of winter.

The marshes surrounding our village became freckled with frost and then completely iced over. The snow consumed all, including the quagmires and paths. The only way of telling what was unsafe ground was the sparse clutches of rushes that had clung on.

The days had become shorter. It was so frigid that the sun would burrow itself into the ground as soon as possible, abandoning the village to suffer the cold.

Our work in the fields dried up into nothing. What little money we had saved went on wood for the kitchen. The scant candles we had needed to be conserved.

****

I was in bed, dreaming of skating upon an ice lake with a handsome lad. Someone clambered under the covers and clung to my waist.

"Emily," I mumbled grumpily. I had been enjoying that dream. "What is it?"

"There was a rattling at my window," she whimpered, wide-eyed and shivering. "Ma said it was the wind, but I know it's Black Shuck!"

I carried her back to her bed to see just what had frightened her. Mother had been right. The wind rattled and scratched at Emily's shutters. There was nothing I could do to stop it, only try to calm her down.

"Silly goose. Why would Shuck want to get you?" I asked her as I tucked her in.

"Jamie at Sunday school said that Shuck likes to eat girls. That he creeps in when she's asleep and without a light."

I sighed. That blasted boy. I would like to stand at his window and hammer on it, growling all the while to make him think a ghost was after him.

"He's more likely to go after Jamie than you. I'm sure Shuck much prefers the taste of naughty children." I stroked her hair, murmuring, "Don't worry. I'll make you something to chase off the shadows."

****

With a bit of fat, a rush could be soaked and used as a candle. It was the cheapest way of bringing light to the dark winter months.

However, most of the rushes grew on the marshes owned by the manor people. I would have to trespass.

Most of the villagers would take a few rushes, as it wasn't as bad as poaching. We all looked the other way. My grandfather had been known to come home each night with rushes sprouting from his pockets.

This was my first time, and I was a little frightened. What if the gamekeeper tried to shoot me, thinking I was a poacher or burglar?

I crept out when night came and the family were asleep. I should be abed, yet Emily had not slept for several nights. Her nightmares of fiery eyed dogs had left her with reddened eyes and shadows so thick that it looked like smuts had been rubbed on her face.

Mother had enough to worry about with the new baby. I had to look after my little sister.

There were no birds calling in the dark. They had been sensible and flown elsewhere. The only noises alongside the unnerving quiet was the rise and fall of the wind, like the aggrieved muttering of an upset child, and the weary groan of trees stripped of their leaves.

It did nothing to make me feel better! If only I could hear the rustle of a fox creeping past or the call of a jilly-hooter, rather than this deathly stillness. It seemed the perfect time for spirits to leap from the water, out hunting for lost travellers.

In a few brief seconds, I forgot what smell was. The cold hooked into me, chasing off the lingering scent of burnt oak wood I had left back home. All that remained was a bitter sting, which made my eyes water. Mist spiralled from my lips, only to be snatched by the wind.

I would not be out here in this hunch-weather for long, I promised myself. Across the snow was the shadows of the trees. I dared not walk over them. They reminded me too much of grasping fingers.

I had taken my father's sickle. I grasped a handful of rushes and cut them free. There were only a few, but it would be enough. I scuffed off the snow on their drooping heads.

There was a sharp yank on my coat. I cried out in terror.

"It's only me, Ruth," Emily hissed.

Relief made me relax, but I couldn't stop myself from snapping, "What are you doing here? You'll freeze your bones into icicles!"

"I was worried about you."

"We shouldn't stay out here. Let's get home."

The air had been prickly with frost. It was the sky holding its breath, ready to shout out a storm. I thought I had enough time, but it opened its mouth. The snowflakes turned into a sharp, stinging scratch.

I clutched Emily's hand as we hurried. She tried to speak, yet I could not hear. The gale stole our voices.

I covered my eyes with my arm. The land before me was engulfed. I could not see.

My skirt caught on something and I fell. Emily's hand slipped free. I fumbled for her, but there was nothing.

I scrambled through the darkness, with the only thing guiding me the ticklish scrape of the rushes against my legs. I held out my hands, desperately feeling for the fronds.

"Emily!" I shrieked. "Emily!"

I thought I saw the wisp of her cloak. The bright red cleaved through the white.

I ran, still shouting. My foot dipped.

A howl roared out into the night. I stopped, glancing over my shoulder.

There, as if he was mightier than the blistering winds, strode a black dog. I might not have seen him had he not had a pair of glowing eyes, like bowls of shattered stars. The fur seemed wavy and dancing, just as river weeds swirl in water.

Rumbling, I could feel it vibrate all over my shivering flesh, the creature growled lowly. His eyes narrowed.

My breath grew fast and frantic. A pain shot through me as my heart hammered. Was he going to charge?

The sensation of an icy hand scratching my foot gripped me. Although I did not want to look away, I glanced down.

My shoe was half submerged in marsh water. Green flecked ice floated, bumping against it. I slowly pulled myself free. Had I gone a step further, I would have fallen in and drowned.

My gaze returned to Shuck. He turned around and walked away. It was madness, yet this spectre, dog, whatever he might be, was my only guide. I followed, but kept my distance.

Wherever the dog tread was safe ground. We made our way through the marsh maze and reached the outskirts.

I did not know how long I had been wandering, only that the cold had bitten me deeply. My tread slowed and my vision swam. The dog became a smear of shadows to me.

I thought of poor Emily. Mother would never forgive me, and neither would I.

The wind's shout quietened into a hiss. Snow still hit my face, but it had weakened into a wet slap of sleet.

The dog began to bark wildly. He leapt about to get my attention. A change had oddly come about him. Rather than wisps of shadow, he had become solid and real. His eyes no longer throbbed with light.

I forced myself onwards. I needed to get help.

However, what I entered was not the village but one of the old cattle barns that were on the manor grounds. Brittle, long old straw crunched as I collapsed.

The rough scrape of an animal's tongue swiped all over my face. I tried to bat it away.

"Get off of her, Badger!" a man shouted.

Strong arms wrapped around me and I was gently lifted. My head nestled into the warm, comforting nook of someone's neck.

I shut my eyes and slept.

****

When I woke up, a man was peering into my face. I had never seen him before.

He was about my age, with a wild swarm of black curls. Never mind a crow's nest, the bird was perched directly upon his head. His beard was much the same, with a thick bush that was peppered from the snow outside. But his eyes were soft and kind. The colour was a mix, like pebbles sluiced with seawater.

He held a cup to my lips and I sipped. Heat crawled through me as the sweetness of the cocoa nudged me awake. Panic returned as I remembered.

"My sister is out there. I have to..."

I stopped. The stranger had shifted so that I could see Emily sitting by a small fire.

"I found her wandering near the marshes before you stumbled in here," he told me.

She was clutching a splay of playing cards. "Mr Oak has been teaching me Old Maid," she said, smiling.

"Oh, Emily!" I wrapped my arms around her. "I thought I had lost you!"

A dog was nestled against Emily. He was as big as her, with dark fur and bright eyes glistening from the fire light. There was a patch of white fur over his snout.

I stroked him. Had he not found me, I would have been at the mercy of the storm.

"Good boy!" I whispered. It hadn't been Black Shuck after all. There was no need to worry about curses.

"It's a good job you heard him," Mr Oak said. "Badger was standing at the door, barking for all the world to hear. I thought it was just the wind he was angry at."

I stopped, and the dog grumbled in annoyance at having his fussing interrupted. If Badger had not gone far from the barn, what had led me through the marshes?

I could not sit there and stew in my fretting. Girls were always full of questions that weren't the most tactful. I didn't want Emily to anger Mr Oak so much that he threw us out into the cold!

Emily, remembering what had been said at the inn, asked him, "Are you a convict, sir?"

"Emily!" Although that had also worried me.

He laughed, and it sounded like rocks rolling down a hill. "No, I'm not. I'm the keeper. I got caught in the storm while making my rounds."

Mr Oak went to the door, opening it only slightly to peer out. When he came back, his beard was as white as an old man's.

Emily covered her mouth. Even I had to bite my lip as he dusted himself off.

"No luck of the wind going down for a while," he said. "We'll have to wait it out, if you don't mind the company?"

"Of course not," I said, flushing.

Mr Oak seemed a nice sort of fellow, though a little unkempt, with a certain rugged handsomeness to him. There were worse people I could imagine being trapped with.

We sat around the fire, drinking cocoa and playing cards, until the storm died down and a cobweb-morning arrived.

****

I never told anyone about what I saw on the marshes. They would have thought I had been cursed with bad luck.

Also, I felt a fool. I had gone out, risked both mine and Emily's lives, and I had dropped every single rush. It had all been for nothing.

Well, perhaps one good thing came from it. The day after we

returned home, a present was left for us from Mr Oak. It was a bundle of rushes.

When we lit them, they had a strong, comforting glow, which chased off any monsters lurking in the shadows of Emily's room. Our adventure in the storm was our secret.

Now, many years later, I sat in my bed. There was a rushlight nearby so that I could sit up and darn the dress Jemima had ripped again.

As much as I loved my daughter, she tore about the fields a lot more than her brother had done. I could barely catch up with her, especially with another one on the way.

The light was tall and steady, like a man's shadow aflame. Rushlights always cheered me up, thinking of the past.

The door opened and my husband entered. I tilted my head, hinting for a kiss, and smiled when he obliged.

"I saw something strange out on the marshes," Joseph murmured into my ear as he got in next to me.

I paused. Surely not?

"What was it?"

"A shadow bounding across the water. It reminded me of dear old Badge." The blue in his eyes deepened, overtaking the grey as he thought of his faithful hound.

I licked my lips. After all these years, I told him what I had really seen that night. That two dogs had helped me escape the storm. Amazingly, he believed me.

"I've heard tales of Shuck protecting women alone at night. He'll guide them back to the path if they get lost," Joseph said. "And it sounds like he led you to me."

He blew out the rushlight and we settled down. Just as my eyes shut, in the short breath before sleep, I thought I heard a noise outside. Perhaps it was a howl or merely the wind, yet this time it no longer frightened me.

Did you enjoy this collection of short stories?

If so, please leave a review and spread the word to your friends and family.
Reviews are a great way of showing appreciation to a writer as well as letting them know if a certain theme or location is popular.

Thanks for reading!

Bramble

Glossary

Locations

Aldeby: A Norfolk village near the Suffolk border. Its name is Old Norse for old fortification/settlement. The village used to have a railway station, which was opened in 1859. In *The Reluctant Passenger*, poor Mercy had to travel further afield and get several trains even before her misfortunes in London!

Borough Market: Location of the oldest food market in London. There was originally a market there in the 12th century. The buildings first appeared there in the 1850s.

Catfield: Norfolk village near Ludham. The name's origin is unknown, but is believed to come from rumours that a big black cat – a panther – was believed to roam here, which has also contributed to Black Shuck sightings.

Cromer: A town in North Norfolk which became a popular seaside resort in the 19th century. It is well known for its Cromer crabs and was dubbed Poppy Lands by Victorian theatre critic Clement Scott for its abundance of poppies. Surrounded by coastal cliffs full of prehistoric fossils.

Great Yarmouth: A town on the east coast which was famous for its booming herring trade. During the herring season in the autumn, Scottish gutters and fishermen used to come down and the Dutch would sail over. Nowadays, the town is known for its amusement holidays after the railway arrived in 1844. The area was featured in Charles Dickens' *David Copperfield*.

The **Yarmouth rows** were alleyways with houses packed so closely together you could walk between them and be able to touch each side at the same time. Only 80 remain from the original 145.

The **South Quay** features medieval town defences, Tolhouse gaol, a friary ruins, and the Time and Tide museum, which was originally a fish curing works with smoke houses. There is also the **Yarmouth Custom House**, which was built in 1720 by a merchant and used by the government in 1802.

Gretna Green: A village close to the Scottish/English border. Marriage laws during Regency times were not as strict in Scotland compared to England, and so young couples eloped there. They were married off by anyone willing to witness their handfasting, often the local smithy who would shoe the horses. These men became known as anvil priests for they would strike their hammer to finalise the union.

Happisburgh: A coastal village in North Norfolk that is currently in the news for extreme erosion problems. It has the oldest lighthouse in East Anglia. Haunted by a smuggler's ghost who was thrown down a well.

Hemsby: A coastal village just under eight miles from Yarmouth. Historically known for its countryside and fishing trades, now it is a holiday resort. Believed to originally be a Viking village because of the 'by' in its name, meaning settlement in Old Norse. It also has a medieval tithe barn, which is Norfolk's oldest timber building, as well as sanctuary markers dotted around the village.

Hyde Park: Royal park which was made public in the 17th century. The fair mentioned in *The Reluctant Passenger* is the Great Exhibition of 1851, which was being built during the events of the story.

Norfolk's Round Tower Churches: An unusual piece of church architecture found around East Anglia. There are 131 in Norfolk and were built during the 11th and 14th centuries.

Norwich: The capital of Norfolk. It was the second most important city after London due to its trading links via the rivers Wensum and Yare. Several medieval buildings remain, including the Tudor rich cobble lane at Elm Hill and the ruins of the city's wall defences. The city's most known landmarks are the cathedral and the castle upon the hill, which is now a museum. It is also known for its plethora of pubs and churches and was believed to have a church for every week of the year, and a pub for every day!

Norwich Yards: Whenever the yards are mentioned in Norwich they are in reference to house clusters around the city – about 650. Behind older buildings or pubs, through a thin passageway, were courtyards surrounded by homes where several families were housed. Due to how tightly packed in they were, these areas were in squalid conditions with a single toilet and water pump shared between multiple households.

Palace Yard shell garden: At St James Palace Yard, off Barrack Street, Robert Frewer created a garden made of seashells as a local attraction in the late 19th century. Unfortunately, it was washed away in the 1912 floods.

A side note: The sweet shop and the fish shop written about in *Carried by the Wind* did exist in Norwich – they were run by my ancestors and were later combined into a fish and chip shop. The shells would have most likely come from the Burrages who were running it at the time.

Sheringham: Coastal town just under five miles from Cromer. Known for its crab and whelk trade in the 19th and 20th centuries when the trains arrived in 1887. The railway line is now known as the Poppy Line and runs from Sheringham to Holt.

St. Benet's Abbey: A lonely, isolated medieval monastery near the river Bure. Most of what remains are only a few impressions on the ground, the surviving ruins an old gatehouse and mill – whose sails did blow off in 1863! Nowadays, the Bishop of Norwich still comes once a year to preach in August, as the abbey is still considered sacred ground. There is also the ghost of a traitorous monk who can be heard screaming at night from the gate.

Wellington Arch: The original arch to Buckingham Palace. It featured a statue of Wellington in the 1850s to commemorate his victory over Napoleon, but now has the Goddess of Victory riding a chariot drawn by four horses.

Winterton-On-Sea: A small coastal village around eight miles from Great Yarmouth. It is known for its picturesque cottages and the unspoilt natural beauty of its dunes and beach. Unfortunately, the beach is under threat from erosion. Further inland are the ruins of the medieval church St Mary's. There is also the Holy Trinity & All Saints Church, which has the third tallest tower in the county, with people being able to see as far as Happisburgh.

Wroxham: Village in the Norfolk Broads and considered the capital of the Broads. Was, and still is, popular for boating holidays.

Food

Blackberry syrup: A Suffolk drink made with blackberry juices, white wine vinegar, sugar and honey. It was used as a cordial and stirred into hot water – great for a cold night!

Bloaters: Cold smoked herring popular in 19th and 20th century Great Yarmouth. Intense, gamey flavour from having its guts kept in.

Calf's foot jelly: Fed to sick patients to build up their strength. Sweetened with lemon and cinnamon. Pale and see through.

Domino clump sweets: Domino tile (dominosteine), which were several layers of Lebkuchen, jelly and marzipan with a dark chocolate icing.

Dressmaker's tripe: Ox tripe with onions and breadcrumbs stuffed inside and sewn up, hence the name dressmaker.

Fair buttons: Also known as Tombland Fair Buttons as it was the speciality of this area of Norwich when the Easter fair arrived. Biscuit shaped cakes which were flavoured with ginger or lemon.

Harvest Loaves: Given to the people working in the fields. Loaves filled with currents or sultanas.

Hokey pokey: Ice-cream sold by street vendors from a pushcart, most who were of Italian descent. They would cry out *Oche poco!* (oh, how little!) regarding the price, and hokey pokey is a degradation of this phrase.

Honey cakes: No specific recipe was referenced for this, but I had fairy cakes in mind that had been soaked in and glazed with honey.

Norfolk dumplings: The word dumpling originates from the county back in the 17th century. Dough balls cooked to be light enough to float to the surface of a stew. A cheap and easy way to fill up in the past. Also used as an insult against Norfolk people.

Penny licks: Ice-cream served in a small serving glass, which were licked, handed back to the ice-cream seller, given a cursory wipe and then reused. Often the source of a cholera outbreak and was banned in 1898.

Raisin roly poly: Suffolk recipe. Looks like a stuffed swiss roll. Uses suet and raisins rather than jam.

Silltårta: Swedish herring cake with cream cheese and boiled eggs.

Vinegar Cake: Eggless cake made with cider vinegar, raisins and sultanas. Very light.

Yarmouth straws: Made with shortcrust pastry, cheese and shredded bloaters. Looks like a cheese straw but the pastry is twisted around the filling with some of it poking out.

Boating and Fishing Terms

Beatster: Occupation of someone who mended Yarmouth Herring fishing nets.

Cloots: Protective cotton strips that were wrapped around the fingers of gutters.

Cran baskets: Quarter cran baskets, which were used to carry and weigh the herring – they had to be a specific size or else a fisherman could be cheated out of the true value of his catch.

Gaff line: Rope which keeps the gaff (sail support) in control while lowering and raising a wherry's sail.

Gutter girls: Scottish herring girls and women who would come to Yarmouth during the herring season to gut and pack the fish. They would room with locals and could be seen wandering the quays and jetties while knitting.

Jenny Morgan: The wherry's vane. Named after a character in the Welsh folk song *The Maid of Llangollen*.

Quant: Pole used to move a wherry in low winds. Had a turned cap on top to brace the shoulder against. About 24 feet long.

Silver Darlings: Another name for herrings to signify how important they were to the economy. Also called silver of the sea. They rise to the surface at night, giving the sea a silvery sheen.

Speet: A long pole to hang the fish from in a smokehouse.

Swills: Yarmouth specific basket made of willow and hazel to carry herring in.

Troll-carts: Carts specially designed to move through the compact Yarmouth rows while transporting herring.

Warp of herrings: Four herrings, two in each hand.

Wherry: A boat that was used to travel the thin, complicated waterways of the Broads to transport wood, ice and reeds. They are now a rare sight. The most well-known example is the Albion from the Norfolk Wherry Trust.

Folklore and Folksongs

Black Shuck: He is Norfolk's most known – and most sighted – folk legend. His appearance and demeanour vary but the main characteristic is that he is a monstrous black dog. Some call him a protective spirit who guides lone women home while most know him as a fearsome beast who can kill people with a glance. East Anglia's coast is his favoured haunt. His claw marks are even said to be on the doors of Blythburgh church.

Bogles: Name for a ghost or goblin known for tricking people. They become especially mischievous at wintertime. Mainly said to roam Scotland and Northumbria, but have also appeared in various retellings of the Green Mist story – a folktale which appears in fenland areas, particularly Lincolnshire.

Bunyip beast: Australian mythology. An evil spirit who wanders swamps and looks like a stringy seal in appearance.

Corn dolly: Also called Corn Mother. The harvest spirit was believed to live in the fields. Creating the dolly gave her a home when the wheat was cut. The dolly was then housed in the home of the local community leader, then ploughed and returned to the soil in the new season.

Countryman's Favour: Plaited straw given to a sweetheart. If the recipient wore it over their heart it was an acceptance of their feelings.

Doppelgängers: Meaning double-walker. Two people who are unrelated but look exactly alike, but one of them is an omen for bad luck.

Frog went a-courtin: Folksong about a frog asking a mouse to marry him and the guests arriving for the wedding. The Scots version is *The Frog came to the Myl dur*. Several versions exist, with larger, predatory animals coming to swallow the couple up – the final verse tells the listener to sing the ending themselves.

Garter Toss: Marriage folklore believed to come from the Dark Ages. Wedding guests chased the bride and groom to try and rip off the garter. Now, the bride would remove it herself and toss it rather than be mobbed. Catching it promised marriage for a lucky bachelor.

Green Mists: Once upon a time, a young girl too sick to reach next spring wished she could live as long as a cowslip and see the green mists coming off the fenland. The bogles must have heard, for she grew strong and was playing outside again. But when a boy picks a cowslip to give to her she shrivels up, suffering the same fate as that picked flower!

Korrigan: Breton folktale creature. A small gnome who danced around fountains. The name also refers to female sirens who haunt wells.

Lantern Man: A ghost upon the marshes who lures travellers to a watery grave with his lights. Whistling attracts his attention.

Ludham serpent: This beast would appear from its burrow in the village to sunbathe near the local pub. However, when frightened villagers filled up its burrow, the dragon flew off to the abbey and was never seen again.

Selkie: Seal folk. Creatures that shed their skin and become human. Most stories involve humans kidnapping selkies by stealing their seal skins. Stories have appeared in Scotland and Iceland.

Spring-Heeled Jack: Urban legend. A supernatural creature that resembled a tall, thin gentleman with claws and flames for his eyes and tongue. Appeared in London, Midlands and Scotland. Would attack people and then leap away.

St. Christopher's Medal: Patron saint of travellers.

The Pretty Ploughboy: Folksong about a ploughboy being pressganged by his lover's parents and she must find him and pay for his freedom.

Up jumped the herring, queen of the sea!: Lyric from the sea shanty *Windy Old Weather*. A Happisburgh song about fishermen trawling for fish in the light of the village's lighthouse.

Will-o'-wisp: Ethereal lights that appear over marshland and will trick travellers away from the safe path. Also called Jack o' lantern, hinky punks and friar's lantern. Now believed to be the combustion of marsh gasses.

Witte Wieven: The spirit of a wise woman. The Dutch legend originates some time in the 7th century. Wise women who had died would remain on this earth, either assisting or complicating matters for those in trouble. They were depicted as wearing white, roaming gravesites and emerging from the mists.

Dialect

a-diddling: What's wrong with you? "What's a-diddling you?"

Afeared: Afraid.

Babbing: Fishing with a line tied to your finger, often used for eels and crabs.

Barley Bird: Nightingale.

Brame-berry: Blackberries.

Buffle-headed: (Suffolk) Confused.

Copper Rose: Poppies in the fields.

Crow time: When the crows go to their nests and night descends.

Cushies: Sweets.

Deeks: Streams.

Duddle (Suffolk): Cuddle up nice and warm with blankets.

Duffy dows: Baby doves

Fen-Nightingale: Frog.

Flittermouse: Bat.

Fourses: Four o'clock rest and snack while working in the fields.

Haller: Shout.

Jibby (Suffolk): Not a very complimentary remark about a young woman too big for her boots!

King Harry Redcap: Goldfinch

Lagarag: Lazy.

March Bird: Another word for frog.

Old Coe John: Coe was used for men who had funny ways about them.

Polliwiggles: Tadpoles.

Staithe: Place where ships unload their cargo.

Wood-sprites: Woodpecker.

Misc.

Apiary: A bee yard where hives are kept.

Assizes: Courts that were held periodically around England and Wales twice a year at Lent and Trinity.

Bodkin: Needle that resembles a metal spike. Used for making willow baskets.

Callisthenics: Exercise for young Victorian ladies which included movement and balancing of the body akin to gentle warm up exercises nowadays. Sometimes canes and ribbons were used as exercise equipment.

Carboy: These were large glass containers which were filled with bright, eye-catching liquids and placed in pharmacy windows to attract customers.

Charnel House: Vaults for human bones.

Cubbie: Small basket made of heather from Orkney.

Decency Board: Boards put up on the top of an omnibus so women could sit there without fear of someone below seeing their legs. Often plastered in advertisements.

Dutch fair: Depicted in George Vincent's painting *Dutch Fair on Yarmouth Beach, Norfolk (1821).* A herring fair that came to Yarmouth each winter. It was where Dutch, Norfolk and Scottish people could trade for fish, sweets and Christmas presents. The first one was back in the 12th century, with a hiatus during the Napoleonic wars, and the last one was in the 1830s.

Everlasting Pills: These were small metal pills made of antimony that were used as a purgative – they were then pulled out after passing, hopefully washed, and then reused. They were very popular in the 19th century.

Floriography: A hobby during Victorian times for lords and ladies. Conversing via the language of flowers where different coloured blooms could mean a budding courtship or a passive aggressive way of showing disdain.

Geneva: Very strong gin flavoured with juniper. Came from the Netherlands. Also called Hollands or Dutch gin.

Land guard: Band of customs men who rode on horseback. Patrolled the coast.

Making your mark: If a person could not read or write, they could draw an X in place of their signature on a document such as a census, birth, baptism or marriage record.

Marshman: Men who lived upon the marshes. Their work involved catching eels, cutting reeds for thatching, breaking up the icy rivers at wintertime and maintaining the drainage mills dotted around the

Broads. The best example of a marshman's home is Toad Hole Cottage at Howe Hill, Ludham.

Nelson's Column: In Trafalgar Square. Dedicated to Admiral Horatio Nelson – a Norfolk born man and considered one of history's greatest naval commanders.

Old Maid: Victorian card game where one card is removed from the pack. Players then have to match each set of cards to avoid being left with the single, unmatched card.

Omnibus: Horse drawn bus. Often cramped, dirty and driven by boy racers.

Pharmacopeia: Book with the latest information about drugs and medical practices, although at the time Victorians relied heavily on cocaine, laudanum and opiates for a simple cold.

Revenue cutter: Government vessel used to patrol the seas.

Rushlight: A cheap replacement for a candle, where the dried pith of the rush is dipped in fat.

Skep: Handmade beehive baskets made of woven straw. Were used up until the mid-19th century. Often, as the honeycomb was woven in with the straw, keepers destroyed the skep and the bees to get to the honey.

Spencer Jacket: Short, long sleeved jacket worn by men and women. Named after the second Earl Spencer, who had cut off his coattails to start a new fashion.

The Ton: High society during Regency times. French for *le bon ton*, meaning good manners.

Tinker: Tinsmith who travelled around mending household items, pots, pans etc and sharpened knives.

Tub men: Men who were used by smugglers to heave the heavy contraband by carrying casks tied to their chests and backs. By old age their spines were normally severely curved due to the rigours of their night time work.

Whist: Trick taking card game popular in the 18th and 19th century. Four players, two against two.

Printed in Great Britain
by Amazon

85287794R00169